SNOW BURN

A TOM ROLLINS THRILLER

PAUL HEATLEY

INKUBATOR
BOOKS

Published by Inkubator Books
www.inkubatorbooks.com

ISBN (eBook): 978-1-7398132-9-1
ISBN (Paperback): 978-1-7398132-8-4

For Aidan

1

The hunter hides himself in a bush, lying flat on the snow and trying to make himself comfortable.

Down the pass, through the scope of his Mossberg Patriot, he spotted a Sitka deer. It's coming his way. It wasn't a clear shot, not at first. Too many trees, too many bushes. The deer kept stopping, disappearing behind branches, rummaging.

The hunter waits for it to get closer. It is cold up the Chugach Mountains, but he barely feels it. This isn't his first time, isn't even his fiftieth, and it certainly won't be his last. He's Alaskan, born and bred, raised in the nearby town of White Spruce Hill. He's never been anywhere else. Never hunted anywhere else, for that matter. Today, however, has not been the best day. No sign of any bucks. He was on his way back down the mountain, to his truck, when he finally spotted the doe. It's small. He's going to have to settle for it. It's better than nothing.

He hears its gentle footfalls in the snow as it gets closer. The hunter lets out a breath, nice and slow, and rests the stock of the rifle against his cheek. His movements are small and concise, so as not to make any noise. Nothing abrupt. Nothing that will startle the deer, that will send her running. She comes into view. She's close. So close he barely needs to bother with the scope, but he uses it anyway. Sights her up, aims at the side of her head, between her left eye and her ear. The hunter readies his finger on the trigger. His breathing is calm and level. He begins to exhale, and prepares to place pressure on the trigger.

"You might not wanna do that, buddy."

The hunter gives a start, almost chokes on his own breath. The voice comes from beside him, to his right. He did not hear anyone approach. He looks up, an eyebrow raised. A man is beside him, crouched low, watching the doe. From his profile, the hunter sees he has a sharp nose and blue eyes. His cheeks and jaw are covered in a beard that needs a trim. He's wearing a wool hat pulled down over his ears, with jeans and a heavy, faux-fur-lined jacket over a thick sweater. He has a neon orange vest pulled over the jacket, much like the hunter's own, to avoid being shot. The hunter looks back at his feet, sees he is wearing snow boots, and again wonders how he did not hear his approach. He checks, and can barely see his prints in the snow.

The hunter spots three dead rabbits hanging from the man's hip, then sees the Winchester M70 slung over his shoulder. "This is my kill," the hunter hisses, staying quiet so as not to alarm the deer. If it bolts, if he loses it, he's going to be pissed off.

The man looks down at him, raises an eyebrow. "She's been foraging," the man says. "Don't you see all the food in her mouth? She isn't eating it. She's taking it back to her fawns. It's for them." The man is silent for a moment, watching the hunter. The hunter feels uncomfortable under his gaze. "Do you really want to orphan those children?"

"Man, fuck you," the hunter says. "Mind your business."

He turns his attention back to the scope, to the doe, before she can disappear from view.

The man puts his hand over the end of the scope, blocking the view. The hunter rears back, showing his teeth. "What is your fucking *problem*?"

"I've told you my problem," the man says. "Now, I've asked you nicely. I've appealed to your better nature. If I have to ask you again, I'm not going to be so polite."

The hunter bristles, feeling his temper rise. He doesn't know who this asshole is, this wannabe savior of the mountain animals, and he doesn't care, either. He starts getting to his knees, reaching down to his side where he keeps his bowie knife. "And I'm through entertaining your bullshit –"

The man sees what he's doing, where his hand is going. While the hunter is rising, the man grabs the barrel of the Mossberg and raises it fast, slams it into the center of the hunter's face. The hunter is dazed, tasting his own blood as it runs from his nose down the back of his throat. The man grabs him by the back of his skull to stop him from falling, then punches him in the side of the head to keep him compliant. He lays the hunter down in the snow.

The hunter blinks up at the sky through the branches, feeling sick. He manages to turn his head. He sees the man still crouching, watching the doe disappear into the bushes. The man watches until it is out of sight, completely gone from view, submerged within the branches, then he turns to the hunter. He looks down at the hunter, who is still trying to pull himself back together, to shake the fuzz from his head. The man watches him for a while, seeming to silently deliberate.

Finally, the man reaches to his hip, pulls one of the rabbits loose. He places it next to the hunter's Mossberg. "A gift," the man says. "For doing the right thing, with such minimal persuasion." The man stands and steps out of the trees.

The hunter struggles to push himself up. The man had looked decidedly average – average height, average build (though he'd been wearing heavy clothes, which disguised his body size, admittedly) – and the hunter had never expected him to be able to hit so hard. He manages to drag himself up to his feet with the aid of the nearest tree, then stumbles out into the opening, pushing aside the branches as he goes. It's the noisiest he's been all day, but it doesn't matter now. The doe is gone. Taken from him, left to run free.

And so is the man. There's no sign of him. The hunter looks left and right. He tries to follow the footprints, but they disappear abruptly, and the hunter can only assume he has stepped into the trees and gone off through the woods.

The hunter heads back for his rifle, wiping the blood from his top lip and nostrils as he goes. He spits a wad of it onto the snow, then looks back over his shoulder. Still no sign of the man. He retrieves his Mossberg.

After a moment's thought, he picks up the rabbit, too.

2

T om Rollins has called Alaska his home for the last six months. More specifically, he's called a small cabin in the Chugach Mountains home.

After his brief altercation with the hunter out in the woods, he returns to the cabin. The hunter will not be able to track him. Tom is careful. He makes sure to cover his tracks. The spot where they were in the woods is an hour away from where Tom is now.

The cabin is secluded, closed in on either side and around the back by tall pine trees. Without thorough directions, no one knows how to find the cabin. Few know it is here. Tom likes it this way. He likes the peace. His truck is parked down the side of the cabin, and there is a road, which only he uses, that takes him down off the mountain.

The cabin is made of wood and, he has been told, has been here for more than thirty years. There is a stone chimney at the side, from which wisps of smoke from the remnants of the burning wood in the fireplace inside rise into the sky.

Tom, despite the cold and the two dead rabbits on his hip,

does not go straight in. Instead, he checks the area around the cabin first. Looks in the snow for footprints that do not belong to him. He goes into the trees on either side and checks in there, too. He looks his traps over – the bear traps and the snares. He's dug a bear pit at the back of the cabin, outside his bedroom window, but it remains empty. They're all empty, and there are no footprints.

Old habits die hard, especially for a man with Tom Rollins's past. He's had enemies. Most of them are dead, but there are still a few out there. There may even be some he's unaware of. Friends of enemies that he doesn't know about. It's always worth being prepared. His military background comes to the fore. His time with CIA black ops. It keeps him alert, even in a place like this. It keeps him paranoid. It keeps him alive.

He goes inside the cabin. The logs in the fireplace are down to cinders and ash, almost burned out completely. The floors are bare wood, the varnish on them worn down and in need of a new coat. There is a rug in front of the fireplace, with a sofa directly opposite and two chairs, one on each side. The kitchen is to Tom's left, all inside one big open-plan room. The bedroom is at the back of the cabin, with the bathroom opposite. The oven is powered by gas, the canisters bought in the nearest town, and the electric is powered by a gas generator.

Tom puts his rifle down by the door, shrugs off his coat and hangs it up, then takes the dead rabbits into the kitchen. The rifle is not the only gun here. There are others dotted around the cabin, all of them within easy reach. He skins and guts the rabbits in the sink. Then, while they're cooking, he goes down into the basement. The entrance is in the center of the kitchen. A trapdoor, with a bullring handle.

When he first came here, the basement was in need of a good dusting. Spiderwebs clung thickly to every corner and every wall. The shelves, where he stores his dry foods, were an inch deep with dust. It's spotless now. Tom made some further alterations, too. There is a wire pinned to a wall that wasn't here before. It runs up through the floorboards, to where explosives are strategically placed throughout the cabin. When Tom leaves, he'll disconnect them, take them with him, but in the meantime – well. Old habits die hard.

His bag is down here, too. Kept packed in case he needs to move fast. It contains spare clothes, weapons, and his burner phones, which he takes down into town with him at least once every couple of weeks, gives them a chance to get a signal and see if anyone has tried to get in touch. There is no cell reception at the cabin. So far, there have been no missed calls or messages.

He keeps the picture of Alejandra in his bag, too. Wherever he goes, he always makes sure to store her in the safest place. These days, there are some bloodstains around the outside of the picture. The blood is his. The Santa Muerte pendant she gifted him, long before she died, is kept with her picture.

From the shelves he takes a jar of yellow foot mushrooms, and another two containing lowbush cranberries, and thimbleberries. He picked these before the snows came, and has stored them since, dipping into them every so often. There are cans of beans, green beans, and chickpeas on the shelves, too, items he has picked up in town when he has ventured down. His trips have been rarer since the snows came.

Back upstairs, he fries the mushrooms and eats them with the rabbit. He sits out on the porch while he does, watching the sky. Looking at the snow. There's little else to see, but he doesn't mind. He likes it. He's called this place home for the last six months, and he hasn't tired of it yet. He enjoys the peace. The altercation with the hunter earlier is the closest he's come to action since he was down in Arizona.

Since he was stabbed. The wounds have healed, but they've left a big scar low down on his torso. Another added to the collection. He finishes the rabbit and mushrooms and has the berries.

He's kept himself busy. He's stayed in shape. Works out every day, as well as his regular walks atop the mountains. Checking his traps, foraging for what he can. On occasion, he sees people down in town. Well, a *person*.

He washes up, then throws his jacket back on, without the high-viz vest over the top of it this time. He goes to his truck and drives down off the mountain, drives to town.

He's careful on his descent. Takes his time. After that, it's a couple of hours to White Spruce Hill. It's getting dark by the time he arrives.

Tom passes the town's namesake as he drives through. Said hill, with the white spruce growing out of it, is smack bang in the center of the small town square.

There's not much to the town. Rows of small houses, and mobile homes. A post office that is open every day, but only between the hours of nine and eleven a.m. A bar that never seems to close, often frequented by the two mechanics who work in the garage down the road, passing time while they wait for another car to work on. The roads and the pavements here are often cleared of snow. It gets bunched up in the gutters, dirty and melting, shoveled by retirees looking to pass the time. It doesn't make the streets look any better, though. It makes them look wet and miserable. The snow, at least, hides what is beneath. Makes everything look postcard pretty.

White Spruce Hill is not a big place. Tom drives to the other end of it, to the local store, in a couple of minutes. He parks outside and goes in. It's quiet. The owner, Emma Raven, is behind the counter, along with a younger lady who looks high school age and likely works here in the evenings to save money for the baby that is growing in her ever-expanding belly.

"Tom," Emma says, smiling as he walks toward her. "What a rare and pleasant surprise." She winks at him. Emma is Tlingit. She's never known her tribe. When her parents died in a car crash, she was still too young to have asked. She was adopted by a white couple who either didn't know, or were willfully ignorant of her heritage. What they *did* give her, however, was an inheritance in the form of this store, which has been here almost as long as White Spruce Hill itself. "What can we do for you today? Have you come to peruse our selection of non-perishables?"

Tom picks up a couple of cans of beans from a nearby shelf. "Can never have too many," he says. "Especially with the weather being what it is."

"Uh-huh. Speaking of, I was thinking I might come up again, spend a weekend sometime soon."

"Well, it *is* your cabin."

Emma grins. "I'd be coming more for the company."

Tom winks. "You know I'll be there. I need some more gas canisters, though."

"You know where we keep them," Emma says, but she comes around the counter and joins him on the way to the far wall where they're stored. "You heard there's a blizzard coming in?"

"I heard," Tom says. "Due tomorrow night, right?"

"Can feel it coming in already. Can feel it in the air."

"Can see it in the clouds," Tom says, thinking of how they've been lingering on the horizon for a couple of days now, filled with threat.

"That too. It's been real dark lately."

Tom picks up a couple of canisters of gas.

"Whenever it comes," Emma says, "you be careful."

"I'm always careful." They head back toward the counter,

taking their time. "When do you finish?" Emma's store is the only one in town. It stays open late.

"Gwen's here now," Emma says. "She knows what she's doing. I can leave anytime I want." She checks her watch. "Now feels good. You in a rush to get back on up the mountain?"

"Not particularly. Do you have plans?"

"I was thinking about heading to the bar. You care to join me?"

"I'd hate to think of you drinking all by yourself."

She smirks. "I'll *still* be drinking by myself."

Tom swings the gas canisters onto the counter, next to the beans. Gwen smiles at him, then starts ringing up his items. "I told you," Tom says to Emma. "I don't drink much."

"Not alcoholic, anyway," Emma says. "You can sure put away a glass of water."

Tom and Emma first met in the bar. They got to talking. Emma asked him why he bothered coming in if he wasn't planning on getting drunk. Tom looked around, the room dark and dingy and silent save for the jukebox, and said he came for the 'ambience.' Emma laughed. Tom admitted bars were usually a good place to find a cheap meal and, in some cases, to make connections. Emma turned out to be a good connection to make. She rented him the cabin on the spot.

Emma carries the beans while Tom takes out the canisters. They put the items in the bed of Tom's truck, then continue on down the road to the bar on foot, trudging through the slush on the sidewalks. They head inside.

3

There's a band playing in the bar. They started up a half hour after Tom and Emma sat down. They're playing country music. They're loud, and not very good, but the people in the bar are trying to enjoy themselves. Women wearing too few clothes for the weather outside are dancing in front of the stage, aggressively shaking their hips, and men with beers in hand try their best to get close to them.

It's hot in the bar, though. It feels like it's holding half the population of White Spruce Hill tonight. Tom has ice in his water. He wipes the condensation from the side of his glass and runs it back over his head, through his hair. Emma takes a drink of her beer and pulls at the collar of her sweater.

"Jesus Christ," she says, laughing. She pulls the sweater up over her head, drops it onto the seat beside her. Beneath her sweater, she is wearing a black vest, though even with her arms and shoulders bare, she doesn't look any cooler and has to waft herself with her hand. They have a booth, at the back of the bar and as far away from the stage as they can get. "Are you enjoying the music?" she says.

"I've heard worse," Tom says. He takes a drink. "I mean, I've heard *better*, too."

Emma laughs. She looks toward the stage and bobs her head along with the music. The lead guitarist attempts a solo. He keeps missing notes, but the crowd doesn't seem to notice. Emma does. She turns back to Tom, laughing. Tom raises his eyebrows. "Are they local?" he says.

"They're on *tour*," Emma says.

"What're they called?"

Emma laughs harder. "I have no idea!"

The song ends. People whoop and cheer. They applaud. The singer tells everyone they're going to take a short break, but they'll be back real soon. The silence doesn't last long. Someone is quick to slot money into the jukebox and start the music back up. No one wants to stop dancing, not yet.

Emma drains her beer. "Do you want another water?" she says.

Tom's glass is still half full. "I'll make do."

Emma nods, then heads up to the bar. Tom watches her go. He looks around the room. His back is to the wall, covered. He has a view of the entrance. Soon after they entered, he spotted the hunter from earlier sitting alone at the bar, nursing a beer. He's kept his back to the room the whole while, putting away drink after drink. He's not here for the music, or to ogle the dancing women in their denim cut-offs, their heavy winter coats shrugged off while indoors. He's here to get drunk.

Tom sees Emma return. She stops and talks to someone on the way. A woman. They glance toward the booth, to Tom. They laugh about something, then Emma gets back to the table.

"Friend of yours?" Tom says.

"An acquaintance," Emma says. She looks at him coquettishly. "She was asking about you."

"A new face in town is always going to raise some curiosity."

"She wasn't asking those kinds of questions. Don't worry, I told her you're spoken for. Unless, of course, you're interested? I could always give you her number. I'd offer to pass yours along, but it wouldn't do her much good while you're up the mountain."

Tom sees the girl on the dance floor. Sees how she dances. He turns back to Emma. "She's not my type."

Emma grins. She looks across the room, tapping a finger on the side of her new glass. "The incoming blizzard's got me thinking," she says when she finally turns back to him. "It's got me remembering, like when I was a child and one blew in so bad we couldn't find the cabin. We had to wait for spring to come for everything to thaw out enough we could find the chimney."

"Sounds bad," Tom says.

"It *was* bad. Especially up in the mountains. Not *as* bad down here in town, but I still missed a couple weeks of school."

"You turned out well enough."

"My mom insisted on home-schooling me. She'd take me to the store with her, because save for Christmas the store *never* closes, and she'd make me do math while we were there, making me do additions and subtractions on items we sold. She'd grab five or six or however many random things, tell me what they cost, and get me to work out their total. Then she'd start taking things away, and I had to work out the subtractions. *Anyway* – I don't mention this to take a trip down memory lane. I mention it to let you know that things can get dangerous up in those mountains, especially when it snows. I won't think any less of you if you wanna stay at my place until it's over. Just to be safe. You're more than welcome."

"It's a tempting offer," Tom says. "And don't take this the wrong way, but I like it at the cabin. I've survived all the other blizzards and storms that've blown through. I think I'm gonna take my chance with this one."

Emma doesn't look offended. "Suit yourself," she says. "You change your mind, the offer's still there. You know where I'll be. Speaking *of* – what're your plans for tonight? It's getting late."

Tom finishes his water. "It's looking like the band is getting ready to come back onstage, so I'm starting to think I might head off."

"You're in a rush to get back to the cabin?"

"I wouldn't call it a rush."

"Good. Then you can be a gentleman and drive me home."

"I'm always eager to be a gentleman, but what about your truck? You're gonna leave it at the store?"

"It'll still be there in the morning." She smiles, and Tom returns it. It's clear – he's going to spend the night with Emma. They both know it. It won't be the first time. He's stayed over plenty. First night they met, he stayed over.

Tom registers movement out the corner of his eye, at the bar, where the hunter was. He's standing now, getting ready to leave. Unsteady on his feet after a night of putting down drink after drink. He stops to take a look around the room, at the gathered people. He sees the band getting back up onstage, instruments in hand, and he seems surprised to see them, as if they haven't been playing right behind him.

The hunter starts heading for the door, but then he stops. He sees Tom. Does a double take. Frowns and narrows his eyes, squinting to make Tom out, to be sure if he's who he thinks he is. Resolved that it is indeed the man who put him on his ass earlier in the day, the hunter takes a deep breath and starts toward the booth.

Emma sees that Tom is watching something, and she turns. The hunter is getting closer. Tom is not concerned. He's drunk. If he's looking for trouble, looking to continue what he was going to start earlier when he reached for his bowie knife, Tom can handle him. He can do it quick, and quiet, and in a noisy room like this, he can do it without attracting any attention.

"Lee?" Emma says to the hunter as he reaches their booth.

The hunter ignores her. "I wanna talk to you," he says, bleary eyes only for Tom.

"So talk," Tom says, ready to move, to react, one eye watching the knife still hanging at the hunter's waist.

The hunter – Lee – slides into the booth next to Tom. He sits close. He stinks of alcohol. The whites of his eyes are bloodshot, and look a little like he's been crying. "I've been..." he says, then has to gather himself. "I've been...*thinking*... about what you said. Earlier. When we saw the doe."

Emma looks over the top of Lee's head to catch Tom's attention, raises a puzzled eyebrow.

Lee continues. "I'm...I'm glad you spotted that she had babies," he says. "I...I almost made Bambi!" A choked sound escapes his throat. "I was almost the bad guy from Bambi! I don't wanna be the bad guy from Bambi..."

He lowers his face, presses his index finger and his thumb into his eyes, rubs them. Shakes his head and squeezes the bridge of his nose. He looks back up, at Tom, while taking a deep breath through his nose. Tom thinks he's about to say something else, but he doesn't. Instead, he holds out a hand. He wants to shake. Tom obliges. Lee nods, satisfied. He stands, almost loses his balance, spreads out his arms to remain upright. He looks at Emma as if seeing her for the first time, gives her a drunken smile and a wave, then heads toward the exit.

Tom and Emma watch him go, Emma twisting out of the

booth to look back. She turns to Tom when he's left. "So, Lee's a friend of yours?" she says.

"One of the few," Tom says.

4

R oger Noakes lives in a quiet suburb on the outskirts of Valdez, Alaska. It's a pleasant place where the neighbors are friendly, but not *too* friendly, and the children are all safe to play in the street together. He works for an accounting firm in Valdez itself, a forty-minute drive from his home. Roger is well paid, well dressed, and in good health. He has a beautiful family, whom he can currently hear downstairs, having breakfast, while he's in the bedroom getting ready for the day ahead. To an outside observer, Roger is a happy man who has everything he could possibly want.

Were an outside observer granted a look inside his home this morning, however, they would be perturbed by what they find.

Roger has been trying to button up his shirt for the last ten minutes, distracted by an SUV he sees parked across the road and three doors down. An SUV that he is sure was parked there last night, too, as he got into bed. An SUV he has never seen before, either on this street or anywhere else.

An outside observer would be alarmed by his level of paranoia. An outside observer would wonder what kind of secret life – hidden from the rest of the street, from his family, from the world – Roger Noakes is living that could cause such paranoia.

Roger stands at the window and stares at the SUV, like he expects something to change. Like the license plate will suddenly become familiar, or someone will step outside and he'll recognize them and know why they're here, that it turns out his neighbor has got a new car, that's all. There are people inside; he's sure of it. Every so often, he sees the way the vehicle rocks, caused by someone's uncomfortable movements within – stretching their legs, their arms, shifting their positions after a night spent sitting in one place.

"Roger!"

Roger gives a start. It's Lily's voice, calling up the stairs. He has to clear his throat to respond. "Yes?"

"Are you coming down for breakfast?"

"Yeah, just give me a minute." He keeps one eye turned to the window, to the SUV.

"You're going to be late if you're not careful," Lily says.

Roger takes a sharp breath. "*Okay*," he says. "I'll be right down."

He sets his jaw and forces himself to turn away from the window and to get his shirt buttoned up properly. Reminds himself to keep taking deep breaths, in through his nose and out through his mouth, and to stay *calm*.

Staying calm is as difficult as staying away from the window.

Eventually, Roger manages to tear himself out of the bedroom. His tie is on, and his suit jacket, but when he gets to the bottom of the stairs, Lily starts fussing over his tie. "Did you do this with your eyes closed?" she says.

Roger thinks of the window, and the SUV, and how he may as well have had his eyes closed.

Roger and Lily have been married seven years, and been together nine. They went to high school together, though their relationship did not begin there. They were friends, with the occasional flirtation. They started dating after college. Roger had studied accounting, of course, and Lily had done American literature, with the idea that eventually she'd like to get into teaching it herself. But, before she could begin applying for teaching courses, her romance with Roger began. She got pregnant fast, but suffered a miscarriage. Soon after, after the long nights spent crying and mourning, she got pregnant again.

Cue miscarriage number two.

The second miscarriage almost split what was left of Lily's heart in two. She battled through it, through the misery and the depression, and then Roger proposed to her. Sometimes, he thinks back on the proposal and wonders if he presented the offer of marriage almost as a consolation prize for the loss of two unborn children.

Regardless, Lily accepted. Soon after, she got pregnant a third time. Lily was terrified all through the long nine months, fearing she would lose another.

Instead, Elijah came to term. He sits behind them now, at the kitchen table, six years old and eating chocolate hoop cereal.

"I made you toast," Lily says. "I don't think you have time for anything else."

Roger nods, distracted, checks the time. He has enough to eat his breakfast, so long as he's fast about it. He sits beside Elijah, forces a smile at him, ruffles his hair, then picks up a triangle of toast by the corner. Lily sits opposite. She has a boiled egg.

Roger chews the cold toast and stares at the center of the table, distracted.

"Is everything all right?" Lily says, picking up on his mood.

"What?" Roger says, looking up, snapping.

Lily doesn't react. She's calm. She's always so calm. Roger is jealous. "You seem irritable, is all," she says.

Roger sees Elijah is looking up at him, too. He swallows down the toast congealing in his mouth, almost chokes on it. Lily sees. She pushes his mug of coffee toward him. Roger washes down the blockage, but the coffee is still a little hot, and it burns the roof of his mouth. "Ah, *shit!*" he says.

Elijah raises his eyebrows, purses his lips. His eyes flicker between his mother and father. "Bad word," he says, stifling a laugh.

"Yes," Lily says, arching an eyebrow. "It *is* a bad word." She looks at Roger with an expression like, *See what I mean?*

Roger takes a deep breath. "Sorry," he says, though his mouth is still burning, and he thinks a blister may be forming. He looks at Elijah, apologizes again, then turns back to Lily. "I just didn't sleep too well, is all," he says. "I guess I *am* a little irritable this morning."

"Well, try to perk yourself up before you get to work," Lily says. "Why didn't you sleep well?"

Roger snorts. "*Work*, probably. There's a lot going on at the moment."

"Oh? Is everything all right?"

He shrugs noncommittally. "It'll be fine," he says. "You know how these things are. They'll work themselves out." He doesn't confide in Lily. Doesn't tell her the truth of his concerns. Doesn't tell her anything about the suspicious SUV parked down the road. He can't.

He finishes the toast and drains the cooled coffee, then kisses the top of Elijah's head and gives Lily a quick embrace. "I'd best get going," he says.

Elijah shouts goodbye from the kitchen while Roger

heads to the door, slips into his shoes and grabs his car keys. Lily accompanies him. "I'll see you tonight," she says as he steps outside. "Try to tire yourself out today. Make it so you get a better night's sleep tonight." She smiles. She looks like she expects a goodbye kiss, maybe just a little one on the cheek, but Roger doesn't take her up on it. He's too distracted. He absently waves goodbye as he gets into his car, trying hard not to stare at the SUV.

As he reverses off their driveway, taking his time so as not to slip and slide on any black ice, Elijah comes racing to the open door and stands beside his mother, waving. Roger waves back, then drives. He leaves the street, watching his rearview mirror as he goes. He reaches the end of the street and turns right, and as he does, he notices the SUV start rolling.

It's out of view as he continues down the road, and he tries to persuade himself it's just a coincidence. It's not following him. It's going somewhere else, and it just so happened to pull out at the same time he did.

It reappears at the junction. It follows. It doesn't pull up right behind him. It keeps its distance. It's not in any kind of hurry.

Roger swallows hard and feels a click in his dry throat. His eyes flicker between the road and the mirror. It keeps well back, but he's convinced now that it's following him. He can't see who is inside, who is behind the wheel, who the passenger is. Roger feels himself getting antsy. He glances at the clock on his dashboard. It's still twenty minutes until work starts. Twenty minutes for him to reach the office.

He tries to lose the SUV. His detours will add to his journey, but right now he doesn't care. He just wants to shake his pursuers and feel like he can breathe again.

The SUV remains on his tail, maintaining a safe distance all the while. No matter which side street Roger takes, nor

how he loops back on himself, he can't lose them. Sweat drips
down Roger's neck. It soaks into his collar. He has to turn off
the car's heating, despite the cold that instantly seeps into the
vehicle from the outside. Roger doesn't feel it. He's breathing
hard, one eye constantly on the SUV behind him. He almost
misses the brake lights of the vehicle in front. He slams on his
own, blares his horn in frustration, pulls out and gets round
them.

Again, the SUV follows.

"*Fuck!*" Roger hits the steering wheel, clenches his jaw. He
bites down hard, until it hurts. Until the muscles in his face
and neck cramp.

The SUV persists. It maintains its distance, and its pace. It
never gets close enough for him to see who is inside.

Roger sees an intersection up ahead. There are three cars
ahead of him. They're slowing for the traffic lights hanging
above the road. The lights are turning red.

"Oh shit," Roger says to himself, barely able to believe
what he is about to do, already pulling out to get past the
three in front. "Oh shit, oh shit, oh *shit* –"

He slams his foot down *hard* and lurches through the
intersection. Cars coming from the right blast their horns as
they narrowly avoid him by mere inches. Roger gets to the
other side and realizes he's had his eyes closed as he sped
through. His hands are wrapped tightly around the steering
wheel, his knuckles bone white. He looks into the mirror. The
SUV has tried to follow, but it has been cut off.

Roger whoops, slams his hand against the roof of the
car, and begins to laugh with uncontrollable relief. He
slumps into his seat, though makes sure to continue putting
distance between himself and the SUV, now that he has the
chance.

But he can breathe again. His muscles all relax. Endor-
phins flood his system. Now, he just needs to get to work.

Once he's at work, in his office, behind his desk, he's safe. Nice and secure. No one can get him there.

The rest of the journey proceeds without incident. Roger makes sure to keep an eye on the mirror as he goes, watching out for the reappearance of the SUV. There's no sign of it. Finally, his building comes into view. The road ahead is clear. He will be secure once he's inside. The final remnants of the tension knotted in his stomach and balled in his shoulders will dissipate.

He pulls up to the Stop sign opposite his building. He looks to his left. It's clear. As he looks to his right, the SUV pulls across the road before him, blocking his way. It got ahead of him. It's been waiting for him.

Roger feels his face fall. Feels a hole open in his stomach.

The front and rear doors on the passenger side open, and two men get out. Roger recognizes one of them, the one from the front. It's Reagan. And where Reagan is, Teddy is sure to be, too. Driving the SUV, more than likely. The other man, however, is a stranger to Roger. Just another heavy. Roger knows who they work for, and this fills him with a deep dread.

Really, all along, he'd suspected who had sent the men. Had he been able to see Teddy and Reagan in his mirror, he wouldn't have been surprised to find they were the ones following him.

Roger goes to put his car in reverse in a last-ditch effort to escape, but the stranger notices. He pulls his jacket to the side, opens it enough to show Roger that he's carrying a gun. Roger lets his hands drop. He knows he wouldn't get far before a bullet buried itself in his chest.

Reagan is coming to his window, motioning for him to wind it down. Roger does. Reagan leans inside. "Good morning, Mr. Noakes," he says, grinning. "It would be such a lovely one if it weren't for all these gray fuckin' clouds, huh?"

Roger doesn't respond. The stranger stands in front of the car, hands on his hips to draw his jacket back, keep his weapon on show.

"Come with us," Reagan says, reaching down and pulling open the door.

Roger hesitates, chewing his bottom lip.

"We ain't got all day," Reagan says. "Fuckin' move it, huh?"

Roger takes a deep breath, and gets out of the car.

"Leave the keys," Reagan says, taking Roger by the arm, digging his fingers into the crook of his elbow. He starts dragging him along, leading him toward the SUV. Roger sees the stranger climb inside his car. He turns it around, then drives away in it. Roger's throat tightens. His chest feels empty. His knees almost buckle beneath him. Reagan keeps him upright, then shoves him into the back of the SUV. He climbs in beside him.

Sure enough, Teddy is in the front, hands on the wheel. He's grinning back at Roger over his shoulder. "Hey," he says. "Good to see ya, Roger. Why don't we all go for a little ride together, huh?"

Roger stares straight ahead as the SUV starts moving. He's numb. Frozen in his seat. Neither of the men try to talk to him. After a while, his car long gone and his workplace far behind him, Roger closes his eyes.

5

Tom wakes. Emma is still sleeping beside him, her face buried in her pillow and turned the other way. The blanket has ridden down her bare back in the night, and Tom can see the way her skin is goose-pimpling in the cold. Gently, he pulls the blanket back up, covers her with it.

Tom slides out of the bed and gathers up his clothes from the floor. He gets dressed, being careful so as not to disturb Emma. She wakes as he's pulling his shirt on. She rolls onto her back and looks up at him. "You weren't planning on sneaking out, were you, Tom?" she says with a smile.

"How could I sneak away?" Tom says. "You know where I'd go. And *that* place is yours, too." He looks at the time. "I don't usually sleep in so late."

Emma stretches, her arms above her head and her back arching. "Must be the company," she says.

"I was going to make you breakfast," Tom says. "A late breakfast. More of a brunch."

"Don't bother," Emma says, lying flat again. "I should get up and get dressed, too. I need to get to the store. There's always a rush on when people know there's a blizzard coming. I don't wanna leave my staff shorthanded."

"How noble," Tom says. He's dressed now. His jacket and his boots are at the door.

"Lead by example," Emma says. She sits up and rubs her eyes, then reaches for her watch on the bedside table, checks the time. "Shit," she says, "we *have* slept in. Blizzard's due in a few hours." She gets out the bed, heads to her bathroom and starts the shower running to warm the water. She comes back to Tom, still undressed. He's outside her room now.

"I'd best get back up to the cabin," he says.

"I left my truck at the store," she says. "Are you okay to drop me off?"

"Sure."

Emma places her hands upon his chest, then a kiss upon his lips. "Any other day I'd just walk, but this is a blizzard day," she says. "I'll be quick," she adds, then goes back to the bathroom. Tom watches her go, admiring her body and not trying to hide it. There's nothing to hide. Emma pauses at the door, turns back like she knows he'll be watching, and she winks. The door closes, and then Tom hears her stepping under the water, the sound of it splashing off her body.

He knows she'll be fast. A quick wash, and then along to the store.

Tom goes to the front door, and by the time he's slipped on his boots and finished lacing them up, he can hear Emma heading back to her room to dress. He pulls on his jacket and steps outside, into the morning cold, to wait. He goes to his truck and starts it up, running the engine to warm both it and the inside of the cab.

Soon after, Emma emerges from the house, dressed, her wet hair concealed under a hat. She gets into the passenger seat, and Tom sets off.

"You be careful heading back up there," Emma says. "And

you remember what I said last night – you start getting wary of the snow, you're more than welcome to come back down here to me. You know I'll keep you warm." She squeezes his thigh.

"I'll be fine," Tom says, "but you know I'll keep the offer in mind."

"Only if it's safe," she says. "I don't want you rolling your truck and getting stuck up there."

"I don't do anything unless it's safe," Tom says, pulling to a stop in front of the store and flashing her a grin.

Already, the store looks busier than Tom has ever seen it. People are hurrying to and from it, the ones leaving laden with overflowing grocery bags.

"It's begun," Emma says, getting out of the truck. "When the blizzard's blown over, let me know you're all right, okay?"

Tom nods.

Emma smiles, then closes the door and heads inside, nodding at and saying hello to people she passes on her way.

Tom turns his truck and points it back toward the mountains. To the cabin. His current home. He sees the ominous dark clouds on the horizon blowing in, replacing the already gray ones hanging low overhead. He'll make it back to the cabin before the snow starts falling. Might even make it there with enough time to check the traps before he has to lock himself away for the night. He already has enough firewood chopped, and plenty of dried food to eat, but he doesn't like leaving the traps unattended for too long. If something's caught, that's good meat left to go to waste, buried under all the snow. Once that's done, he'll get himself settled, and he'll wait for the blizzard to pass. He doesn't have anything to worry about.

6

The clouds are so dark, and they hang so low on the mountain, that it almost feels like night. Flakes of snow are beginning to fall languidly to the ground, a mild precursor of what is soon to come.

Tom trudges through the snow, heading to his traps. He has parked the truck, checked around the cabin for any signs of approach, from man or bear – of which there were none – then grabbed his rifle and headed out. The rifle is a Winchester M70, loaded with .338 Winchester Magnum cartridges. He doesn't carry it to pick off rabbits, or deer. The .338s would blow a rabbit apart in a cloud of red mist and ragged fur. He has it for bigger animals, which pose a bigger risk of doing him harm: bears, or moose.

The first rabbit snare is still in place, nothing caught. Tom moves on. He's deep in the woods now, far from the cabin. He has time enough to check another two traps, and then he will have to head back. If he leaves it any longer, it's going to be too dangerous to be outdoors.

There is a rabbit, dead, in the second snare. He kneels down to unhook it, then pulls the trap down and sets it back into place. As he straightens, reaching for the rabbit, he hears something. He pauses, stays very still, and listens.

He can hear an engine roaring loudly as it battles up the mountain through the snow.

Tom listens further to be sure the vehicle is coming *up*hill, and not descending. It's coming up, getting louder. He frowns. There are no other cabins around here, and from the direction they're coming, they certainly aren't looking for his. There are no other signs of civilization for miles around, and certainly nothing worth venturing into a blizzard for.

Tom straightens, peering through the trees, trying to see them. Still too far away. They must be lost. There's no other reason for them to be driving around up here, especially not at such a potentially lethal time.

He sets off toward them through the trees. He's going to have to warn them before the blizzard can set in, before they get themselves trapped.

7

The clouds are threatening. Snow is already beginning to fall, and Roger thinks he can remember hearing something about a blizzard coming. He used to pay a lot more attention to the weather, but he's been so distracted lately. Right now, it seems like the least of his concerns.

He's still in the back of the SUV, with Reagan. Neither he nor Teddy have said a word to him since they picked him up back in Valdez. It has been a long, uncomfortable journey.

Roger has tried to talk to them. He's asked them what's going on, what the problem is. He's told them he's sure they're making a mistake. He's even tried dropping the name of their boss, but nothing has moved them to words. He's asked what he's supposed to have done wrong.

Teddy begins to slow the SUV. Roger knows where they are. The Chugach Mountains. He's heard stories about these mountains. He knows what can happen to people up here, where there's no one else around, and no one to help. He's heard about the executions, and the bodies that are never found.

He begins to tremble and sweat. He can't stop himself. Reagan notices. He looks at Roger and grins. "Try not to piss yourself," he says.

"You know we ain't gonna like it if you piss in the vehicle," Teddy says, hearing what Reagan has said. "We're the ones gotta clean it out."

Roger opens his mouth, tries to engage them, now that they are finally speaking. But his teeth are chattering, and he's not able to form a sentence.

Reagan laughs at him. "Are we there yet?" he says to Teddy.

"I think this'll do," Teddy says. He stops the SUV, kills the engine.

Roger looks out the window. They're in the middle of nowhere. Nothing but snow, and some nearby woodland. He wonders if he'd be able to make a run for the trees. He knows he wouldn't. He's not fast enough. He's never been a runner, and he's never been particularly athletic. But, even if he got lucky and he *did* somehow make it to the trees, what then? They'd just come after him, but if he was somehow able to hide himself and shake them, he wouldn't be able to get back down off the mountain before he froze to death.

"Out," Reagan says. He's pulled his handgun, and he nudges Roger in the ribs with it, hard enough to give him a bruise.

Roger gets out of the SUV to find Teddy is waiting for him, with his own gun drawn. "Start walking," he says. He points him toward the trees.

Roger doesn't move. "Don't do this," he says. "*Please*. Whatever you think I might've done, it's a mistake, okay? I haven't done anything wrong. I've only ever done what I've been told to –"

"Shut up and *walk*," Reagan says, appearing behind him and sticking the gun into his lower back now.

Roger feels tears begin to run down his face. It's undignified, but he doesn't care. They're walking him toward his death – his execution. There's nothing dignified to be found in anything that's happening right now.

His knees begin to buckle as he gets closer to the trees. They get taller before him, looming over him. Roger goes down. He's crying, and he's trying to beg through his tears, but his sobs twist and snarl his words into an unintelligible mess.

"Jesus Christ, get *up*," Reagan says, exasperated.

"I can't," Roger says. It's true. All the strength has left his limbs.

"Fuck's sake," Teddy says, grabbing him under the arms and hauling him to his feet. Roger is not steady. He starts to go back down. Teddy grabs him by the front of his shirt, keeps him up. He's getting annoyed at Roger's sniveling, though. He slams him in the side of the face with the handle of his gun. Roger sees stars. The trees start moving – they're spinning around him. He falls, and Teddy lets him.

"Goddamnit, Teddy," Reagan says. "That ain't gonna help things, is it?"

"Well, he's pissing me off," Teddy says.

"He's pissing me off too, but you don't see me pistol-whipping him. You know why that is? Because I want him to still be able to talk, and, more importantly, I still want him to be able to *walk*."

"Fuck the walking," Teddy says. "We've come far enough. This'll do."

"You don't want him in the trees?"

"Ain't gonna make any difference. Snow's coming, and looking at those clouds, it's gonna be a lot of it. It'll bury him. No one'll find him. Not for a good long while, anyway."

Roger stays flat on his back, the snow melting through his clothes. It chills him, makes him shiver. He doesn't mind. He turns his head to the side, throbbing where Teddy struck him, and presses his face into the snow, cooling it. When he looks, he sees a bright red splash of blood among all the white. He's bleeding. He raises a tentative finger to his temple, feels where his skin has split, where the blood is coming from.

"All right, Roger," Reagan says, leaning over him. "We ain't going any further, but you need to stand up."

Roger nods, but makes no effort to move.

"It wasn't a request," Teddy says, stepping in and pulling him up again.

Roger is unsteady on his feet, but he manages to remain standing. He feels dizzy and sick. He sways. The trees are still circling him, but slower now than they were before. He feels the blood running down his face. It's hot. Some of it gets into his mouth.

"Look at me, Roger," Reagan says, standing in front of him. "Focus on me. That's right, that's right, pay attention. Listen to what I'm about to ask you. I got your attention?"

"Yes," Roger says. He realizes he isn't crying anymore, that sobs are not racking his chest and heaving his shoulders.

"Where's the money, Roger?" Reagan says.

Roger blinks. He doesn't understand.

Teddy is as pissed off with his vacant stare as he was with his sniveling. He steps up next to Reagan, waves his gun around. "Half a million dollars," he says. "He wants to know what you've done with it. You're the only one who has access to his money. You either give it back, or you die right here."

Roger blinks again. He continues to sway. He's trying to think, but the blow to his skull has scrambled his thoughts. Nothing makes sense. He sees the way the snow is falling, how it lies on Teddy's and Reagan's shoulders, and in their hair. He sees how they must be getting colder, as their hands are shaking, and Reagan is stomping his feet.

Roger opens his mouth, though he has no idea what he's about to say. He sees the look on Teddy's face, though, and he knows he's getting impatient and annoyed. Knows there's a risk he might hit him again, or worse. Roger doesn't want to get hit.

He doesn't get a chance to say anything. To his right, from the trees, comes a voice. "Gentlemen," it says.

They all turn. A man has emerged from the woods. He looks like a hunter. He's holding a rifle, and it's pointed at Teddy and Reagan.

"Gentlemen," he says again, "there's a blizzard coming."

8

Tom reached the scene not long before he made himself known. He isn't sure what exactly he's come across, but the logistics of the situation are quite clear. Two men, two stereotypical heavies, are holding another, bloodied, man at gunpoint in the middle of a snowy nowhere up a mountain. It doesn't take a genius to work out that they have bad intentions.

"What's your names?" Tom says.

"Reagan," says one of them, motioning to himself. He points to his silent comrade. "Teddy."

"All right then, Teddy and Reagan," Tom says. "Toss your guns over here."

The one called Reagan starts to oblige, but the bigger of the two, Teddy, stops him. He throws his gun to the side, not toward Tom as he has requested, and motions for Reagan to do the same. Reagan does. Tom can see their intention. Throwing their guns to the side is bait, to lure him in. Jump him from either side, try to get the rifle off him. If he doesn't shoot them right here and right now, they're going to follow, and they're going to do so armed.

Tom grits his teeth. He's not going to shoot them. While it's true it looked like they were about to kill this third man, there's nothing to guarantee it. He doesn't know who this third man is, either. Doesn't know what he's potentially done, why they've brought him up here. It's not enough for Tom to kill anyone over. He's involved himself more than he already should have in order to prevent one death. He's in no rush to replace it with two others.

"Suit yourself," Tom says. Teddy smirks. Tom signals to the third man, tells him to come to him. The third man is eager to oblige. He glances back at Teddy and Reagan, a mixture of fear and relief on his face as he comes, and almost trips over his own feet. Tom sees the wound on the side of his head. Sees how hard it is bleeding through the thin skin high up on his skull. "Go into the trees," Tom tells him. "Walk in my footprints. You understand?"

The man nods, then starts stepping into the woods, following Tom's light-footed route. He takes his time. Concentrates on each step, to do as he was told.

Tom keeps the rifle on Teddy and Reagan. He listens, and waits for the third man to get far enough away.

"You don't wanna get involved in this," Teddy says.

"It's too late for that," Tom says.

"It ain't," Reagan says. "Just give him up. He's nothing to you. Just give him back to us, and we can all walk away, pretend like we never saw you."

Tom presses a finger to his lips. The third man is in the trees. Tom starts stepping back, into the tracks that the other man has now deepened. He keeps his eyes and the rifle on Teddy and Reagan as he goes. Watches them until he slips back through the branches, then turns and goes in search of the other man.

There's not as much snow on the ground here, kept off by all the leaves and branches. The man has no trail to follow, but he's easily spotted up ahead, weaving between the trees. Tom slings the rifle over his shoulder and hurries to him. The man cries out as he grabs him by the arm, guiding him, but he calms when he sees it is his rescuer.

"Stay quiet," Tom says. "And stay close to me."

The man does as told, though it's clear he's struggling after the blow to the head. Some of the blood is getting into his eyes. He keeps wiping it away.

Teddy and Reagan are shouting behind them. They've come into the trees. More than likely, they retrieved their weapons before they did so.

"Come on," Tom says, keeping his voice low. "You're going to have to move faster."

"I'm...trying..." the man says. He sounds like he's about to faint.

Teddy and Reagan are not attempting to be quiet in their pursuit. They come crashing through foliage. Tom has managed to put a few thick trunks and bushes between them, to obscure their sight lines, but it's becoming increasingly clear that he is going to have to do something to throw them off. Something physical. There isn't enough space here in the trees to keep hiding.

Tom and the man are coming to the end of the woodland, to the pass that will eventually lead them back to the cabin. The man drops to a knee. He starts breathing hard, like he might be about to throw up, and Tom wonders how hard he was hit. He didn't see it happen. It's possible the man could have a concussion. He's exhibiting all the symptoms.

Tom can't keep him moving. Even if he hauls him back up to his feet, he's just going to slow them down. Tom looks around, still listening to the sound of Teddy and Reagan getting closer. He spots a long-fallen tree, and directs the man toward it. The man is getting slower and slower, can barely move now. Tom has to bodily carry him, slinging one arm

over his shoulders and hugging the man around the waist.
They reach the fallen tree, so old it is hollow, has become a
burrow, and Tom lowers him to the ground, being careful
with his head. He rolls him inside it, all the way to the back
where he's out of view. Tom takes the rifle from his shoulder
and puts that inside the burrow, too. The man doesn't register
it. His eyes are fluttering. He keeps dabbing at the wound on
his head, as if he keeps discovering it for the first time.

Tom stays low, leaves the tree, heads toward Teddy and
Reagan, though giving them a wide berth. He moves faster
without the rifle. He conceals himself behind trees, peering
out behind them. He catches glimpses of them barreling
through.

"We've gotta split up," Teddy says, breathing hard. "We've
gotta find them!"

"Split up?" Reagan says. "I don't think that's a good idea,
man."

"We've *gotta*!" Teddy says. "We don't find them – we don't
find *him* – and it's gonna be our ass! We can't fuck this up,
man. You know he already thinks we're fuckin' deadweight."

Tom moves from the tree to a nearby bush. Even under
the canopy of leaves and branches, he can tell the snow is
getting heavier. The blizzard coming in, now. Before long, it's
really going to come down. Even the floor of the woodland is
going to be covered.

He hears Reagan agree to separate, and they split. Reagan
is closest. He's coming his way. Teddy runs off in the other
direction, shouting something. Tom lies in wait, getting down
low, onto his belly, and watching Reagan's approach through
the branches. Reagan is taking his time. His gun is raised,
clasped in two hands. His eyes are constantly roaming, scan-
ning, searching. Tom can hear how he's breathing, though.
It's ragged. He's scared. He's out of his comfort zone, and he
doesn't like it.

He passes by the bush. Close enough to reach out and touch, and Tom does exactly this. He grabs him around the bottom of his right leg and pulls it out from beneath him. Reagan goes down, face-first. He hits the ground with a grunt. Tom is on him in a flash. He presses his knee into his lower back, then twists his right arm to subdue him. He takes the gun from him. It's a Glock. Tom ejects the magazine, and takes the round from the chamber.

"Stay there," he says. "Kiss the dirt, or I'll slit your throat."

Reagan whimpers.

"Stay right there until you hear otherwise."

Reagan's body moves a little, and Tom thinks he's trying to nod.

Tom leaves him in the dirt, taking the Glock with him. He throws the magazine and the extra round to the side, but keeps the gun itself in his hand. He follows the sound of Teddy, being careful as he goes. Is sure to be quiet as he can as he glides from tree to tree, finally getting him in view. Once he has him, he doesn't take his eyes off him.

Teddy is standing, looking lost. It's clear he's getting desperate. He doesn't know which way to go, where to look next. Likely can't fathom how they've disappeared so abruptly. He kicks a tree and curses loudly.

Tom gets close. He presses his back up against a wide spruce, then picks up a branch and snaps it to get Teddy's attention. Tom hears how he spins.

"Reagan," he says, "that you?"

Tom waits.

"If it's you, you better speak up, man!"

Tom is silent.

"Damn it!" Teddy fires into the bushes. One of his bullets nicks the tree Tom is hiding behind. Splinters fly from it. Tom turns his face away from them.

"I ain't fucking around here!" Teddy says. "Come the fuck

out right now, or I'll shoot this whole fuckin' place up! I got the bullets – don't think I don't!"

Tom throws the empty gun to his left, into some bushes. Teddy wheels on the sound, starts shooting at it. Tom slips to his right, around the tree. He closes the ground between himself and Teddy at speed, Teddy deafened to his approach by the sound of his own gunshots. He has no idea Tom is coming, or anywhere near, until Tom punches him in the side, in the ribs. The blow twists his body. Tom continues to move on him. He grabs his arm and slams his wrist down across his knee. Teddy's hand goes loose around the gun – another Glock. Tom slips it from his loose grip and turns it on him, strikes him across the bridge of the nose with it. It's not a hard enough blow to break the bone, but it splits the skin. Blood pours. Teddy stumbles back. Tom points the gun at him. Teddy raises his hands in surrender. He swallows.

"Next time," Tom says, "I'll shoot back. Now, I asked you nicely before, this time I'm telling you. Get the fuck off my mountain."

Teddy walks backward, hands still raised, staring at the gun, staring at Tom.

"Reagan," Tom calls, "you can get up now. Get on out of here."

Tom hears Reagan scramble to his feet. Hears him start to run. Teddy hears it too, and he's prompted to turn and start running to catch up to his buddy.

Tom ejects the magazine from Teddy's Glock, too, then throws the whole thing into the bushes. He hurries back to where he has left the third man. He's still in the tree. He's unconscious. Tom will need to wake him soon, but he leaves him alone for the moment. Goes through his pockets first, spotting the bulge of his wallet. He checks the man's ID. Roger Noakes, thirty-two years old. Tom would have guessed him for older, with his thinning hair and paunch. He sees his address and commits it to memory, in case he needs to contact someone after this is through. He's noticed that Roger is wearing a wedding ring. Tom may have to get in touch with his wife.

He slips the wallet back into Roger's pocket, then shakes him awake. The wind is howling, and the snow is soon going to fall hard. Tom squeezes into the tree next to him. "Open your eyes, Roger. That's good. Now, sit up. Don't worry about banging your head, there's enough space."

Roger manages to get himself up. Tom raises a finger in front of his face, slowly moves it from side to side, gets Roger to follow its movements. He moves it in and out, checking the dilation of his pupils.

"How do you feel?" he says.

"Not great," Roger says, "but not as bad as before."

"Dizzy?"

Roger swallows. "A bit."

"What about sick? Do you feel like you might be sick?"

"A little, but again, it's not as bad as before."

Tom nods. "That's good. Your eyes are good, too. I don't think you have a concussion, but it's still an ugly wound."

Roger is very pale. The blood around the wound itself is starting to scab over. "It's snowing," he says.

"I know," Tom says. "It's only going to get heavier. Who were those men, Roger?"

"I..." Roger frowns. "I don't know."

"You're sure about that?"

"Uh...no. Not really."

Tom puts his vagueness down to the head injury. Give him some time to rest and recover, and it'll likely all come back to him. Chances are he knows just who Teddy and Reagan are, and exactly what they want.

Tom wants to ask more questions, but he knows the answers can wait. They have more pressing matters at hand, namely their survival. They're in the blizzard now. The wind is whipping around them, and this is just the beginning. It will only get stronger. If Tom were alone, he'd continue on to the cabin. Roger will slow them down, though. It's not worth the risk.

"We're going to have to wait the snow out here," he says. "Make yourself comfortable. We need to try to stay warm through the night."

Roger is wide-eyed. He doesn't know what to make of this, and it's likely he's still too dazed to fully comprehend.

Tom leaves him, and watches outside the tree. Sees how the snow is already covering the ground. He waits for it to build.

"Um," Roger says. "Should we...should we start a fire?"

Tom looks at him. "We're in a tree, Roger."

"Just a small one?"

"This tree is dead. It's dry. I don't want to run the risk of setting fire to the thing we're busy sheltering inside of."

"Okay," Roger says. "It was...it was just an idea."

Tom continues to wait for the snow to build. When there's enough of it, he starts dragging it toward the opening, building up a wall between themselves and the outside.

"What are you doing?" Roger says.

"The snow will act as insulation," Tom says.

"Like in an igloo, right?" Roger says.

"Right," Tom says. They're close together inside the dead tree. The heat from their bodies in such proximity should carry them through the night, too.

Tom finishes building the wall, padding it out. It's dark inside the tree, now. There's nothing else for them to do but wait for it to end. He glances at Roger. He's been quiet for a while now. He's pressed up against the bark, his arms wrapped around himself. He's sleeping.

9

I t's morning. Tom has not slept. He's kept track of the time, and made sure the wall of snow he created didn't collapse in on them. The wind was wild, and helped keep him awake. It battered against the side of their fallen shelter, feeling like it would tear the old wood to splinters. It's calmed, now. Outside is still. Every couple of hours, he's checked on Roger while he slept, making sure he hasn't slipped into a coma. Tom is confident now there is no concussion. A bad headache, sure, and a deep cut, but nothing more serious.

Tom creates a hole in the top of his snow wall, peers out. The blizzard has stopped. The sky has cleared. The sun is shining. He wakes Roger. "It's time to go."

Roger blinks hard and rubs the sleep from his eyes. "Is it over?"

Tom has a feeling it's only beginning.

He starts digging them out. The snow got deep. The dead tree is covered. "It's morning," he says. "Let's move. We'll go to my cabin, take things from there."

Roger doesn't make any effort to help. He pushes himself

up to his knees, wincing, pressing his hands to either side of his head. He massages his temples, eyes closed tight. "Jesus," he says. "I hope you've got some painkillers there."

Tom grunts. "I don't."

"Well, shit," Roger says.

Tom climbs out of the tree's burrow, reaches in and pulls Roger out after him. They start walking. Roger has his arms wrapped around himself. He's shivering. He's not dressed for the mountain. "How far is it?" he says.

"About a mile," Tom says.

"I don't know if I can make it that far."

"You're gonna have to," Tom says, glancing at him. "The other option is you stay here and freeze to death. Out here, when it's this cold, you wanna keep moving. That, and find shelter. Those are your options. Everything else is death."

Roger doesn't say anything to this. Tom can hear his teeth chattering.

The cabin eventually comes into view. The sight of it seems to thaw Roger. "Do you have a phone?" he says, his voice suddenly strong and firm, as if something has just occurred to him, and it's important.

"I have phones," Tom says, "but they're no good up here."

"Shit," Roger says. "I need to call my wife. I need to –" He swallows. "I need to make sure they're all right."

"Are they in danger?" Tom says. "The men who had you, will they go after your family?"

"I..." He trails off. He doesn't want to think about this possibility. "I need to be sure they're all right."

They reach the cabin. Tom unlocks the door. "Get inside," he says. "I'll be right in after you."

Roger does as he's told, fidgeting as he goes, no doubt thinking about his family. Tom circles around the cabin, looks for tracks. Checks his traps. All clear. The snow is deep. It lies heavy on his roof. If anyone came here last night, before the blizzard, their footprints will be well hidden by now. He knew this when he first started to check, but it's routine. It's always worth looking. Never know what a quick search might turn up.

He goes inside. Roger is in the kitchen, leaning on the counter with his face buried in his hands. "You have kids?" Tom says.

Roger lets his hands fall away from his face, takes a deep breath through his nose. "One," he says. "A boy. Elijah. He's six."

"What's your wife's name?"

"Lily."

"Where are they now?"

"I don't know," Roger says. "But they should be at home. Elijah would've been at school yesterday. Oh, Jesus..." He trails off, looking worried. "I don't know if Lily would've sent him today, when I didn't come home last night. She's got to be worried sick. You're sure there's no signal here?"

"I'm certain," Tom says. "Who were the men? Teddy and Reagan. What did they want?"

Roger hesitates. Tom sees him do it. His mind is racing. It's clear in his eyes. He's trying to come up with a story, or an excuse. "I...I don't know," he finally settles on. It's weak. He's hiding something. He's being cagey, but he knows more about what was happening than he's willing to let on. This morning, however, he doesn't have the excuse of a head injury to hide behind.

"I don't believe you," Tom says. "You know something, and you're going to tell me what it is."

"Why do you even care?" Roger says, deciding upon belligerence. "This hasn't got anything to do with you. Now look, I appreciate what you did, but I have to get off this mountain *right now*. I noticed a truck down the side." His eyes flicker to the counter, to where the keys are. "And I'd appreciate it a whole hell of a lot if you could give me a ride."

"I'll give you a ride," Tom says, "as soon as you cut the bullshit and tell me what's going on. Why were those men threatening to kill you?"

Roger throws up his arms. "I don't know! Mistaken identity?"

Tom stares at him, unimpressed.

Roger wilts under his glare. "Fine, fine, I didn't expect you to believe that," he says. "But the truth is, I honestly don't know what they think I've done. I don't, I swear! So, maybe, it *is* a case of mistaken identity after all?"

"They didn't say anything to you?"

"Not a word, until we got up here."

Again, Tom has his doubts. He watches Roger, and tries to understand why he would lie. "They were going to kill you," he says. "That's serious."

Roger snorts. "I'm very aware of how *serious* it was," he says. He spreads his arms wide. "But, shit, how many dead bodies do you think are already up here, buried under all this snow – some of them even in the dirt? You think I was gonna be the first?" He snorts again. "Hell, I sure as shit wasn't ever gonna be the last."

Tom's eyes narrow. Roger is giving himself away – why would he know such a thing? "Who brings them up here, Roger?" he says. "Who's putting all these bodies in the ground?"

Roger's mouth clamps shut. He realizes what he's said.

Tom takes a step closer to him and Roger flinches, but Tom stops, listening. He turns toward the door, frowning. He can hear something, outside, approaching his cabin.

A voice. He can hear a man's voice.

After a moment, Roger hears it too. "Oh, *shit*," he says.

Tom ignores him for now, moves toward the door to better hear. He stays away from the windows.

"Little pigs, little pigs, let me in," the voice is reciting. A man's voice. He's speaking English, but his accent is thick. *"Not by the hair on my chinny-chin-chin!* Well! Then I will *huff*, and I will *puff*, and I will *blow your house in!"*

"It's Fedorov," Roger says, his voice a croak. Tom looks at him. His face has blanched. He's sweating.

Tom goes back to the kitchen, grabs his Beretta from where he's kept it taped under the counter. "Stay here," he says to Roger. "Stay low, and stay away from the windows."

"What're you gonna do?" Roger says.

Tom tucks the Beretta down the back of his jeans, covers it with his shirt. "I'm gonna go talk to Mr. Wolf."

Roger crouches down behind the counter, tongue flickering out over his dry lips.

Tom opens the front door with care. He peers out, sees the rhyming man standing in the middle of the walkway about a hundred feet away. He wears a long coat, has his hands in the pockets. His shoulders are broad. He's smiling. Tom is guessing, from his accent and from the name Roger called him, that he is Russian. Tom supposes it shouldn't be too much of a surprise to find a Russian when, at their closest and not including the small islands between them in the Bering Strait, there are only fifty-five miles between Russia and Alaska. But he does find it curious to find one *here*, further inland, and under such circumstances. It would seem Roger is keeping more from him than it first appeared.

Tom and Fedorov meet eyes across the distance. "No, Mr. Wolf," Tom says, reciting the nursery rhyme back to him. "I will not let you in."

Fedorov throws his head back and laughs. "Very good, my friend, very good," he says, wiping a tear from his eye with the back of one finger. The hand is promptly returned to his coat pocket. "I believe you are having someone I am looking for. A Mr. Noakes. Perhaps you are knowing him as Roger, yes?"

Tom shrugs, noncommittal. "Maybe. Who's this Roger to you?"

Fedorov's smile never falters. "An acquaintance," he says. "We are serving the same master. I know he is inside your cabin, my friend. Hand him over to me and there will be no trouble. Surely, we can agree we do not want any trouble, yes?"

"What's he done?" Tom says.

Fedorov's smile shows his teeth. "He has been a very, very naughty boy, my friend."

Tom is growing tired of the vague answers.

"Now," Fedorov says, "you will be handing him over to me, please, yes? Otherwise, I am afraid, we will be forced to be taking your cabin, and Mr. Noakes, by force. It is such a pretty cabin, my friend. It looks like it belongs on a Christmas card, yes? I am not wishing to damage it."

We. Tom suspected Fedorov was not alone. This statement confirms it. He lets his eyes flicker to the left, then to the right. Into the trees. Searching them. He spots movement. There are men there, either side. They're wearing Disruptive Overwhite – snow camouflage. Tom has seen it in action. It works well, but not when the wearer is upright and peering out from behind a tree.

Fedorov chuckles. "Ah, you have seen them, yes? I am impressed, my friend."

Tom counts six. Three on either side, trying to get by him, to surround the cabin. Seven, including the Russian. Tom runs his tongue around the inside of his mouth, over his teeth. He looks at the Russian. "Fedorov, right?"

Fedorov grins darkly. "I knew he was in there. He has told you who I am, yes?"

Tom ignores the question. "I assume you've already spoken to the two men who brought Roger up here." It's a fair assumption. How else would Fedorov know which area to search? "Did they tell you what I told them?"

"Ah, don't worry about them," Fedorov says, waving a hand, "they are, how you say, *small time*. Clearly very disappointing. No, this time, I come with better men. Men I have trained myself."

"Did they tell you what I said?" Tom says again. "I don't like to repeat myself, Mr. Fedorov."

"Please, please, *just* Fedorov. They told me what you said, my friend. That next time – that *this* time – you will fire back."

"You should've listened."

Fedorov chuckles. "I am afraid this is your last chance, my friend."

Tom stands his ground. "And this is yours. Get off my mountain."

Fedorov's smile turns somber, as if he already regrets what he is about to do. He takes his right hand from his pocket, and raises it to shoulder height, elbow bent. A signal is coming. The signal to attack, Tom knows. He braces himself.

Fedorov flicks his wrist.

10

Tom doesn't wait. He reacts as soon as Fedorov gives the signal, pulling the Beretta free and firing upon the group in the trees to his left. They're the closest. He dives back inside the cabin as the group to his right open up with automatic fire. He hears their bullets pounding into the wood, tearing it to splinters, blasting through it. They whizz by overhead. Tom stays low as wood and glass fall to the ground around him.

Outside, over the explosive gunfire, Tom hears Fedorov barking orders. He's giving them in English, and Tom guesses that his men are American, much like Teddy and Reagan. Tom has a lot of questions about this situation, about what is going on, but they're going to have to wait. Right now, he has a firefight on his hands.

He crawls toward his rifle. The firing upon the cabin has calmed, only the occasional pot-shot being taken at a window when the men likely think they glimpse some movement, or else to keep Tom away while they get into position. He knows they'll be advancing in pincer formation, preparing to come at the cabin from every side.

Tom goes to where he left Roger sheltering in the kitchen, the rifle in his hands and the Beretta tucked back into his waistband.

Roger is gone.

Tom feels a breeze, blowing from the back of the cabin, where as yet there has been no gunfire. He looks, sees an open window there. He chances rising to a knee, looks at the counter. The keys to his truck are gone.

"Son of a bitch," he says, lowering himself back down, back to the counter.

Fedorov calls into the cabin. From the direction of his voice, he's near the front door, at the foot of the porch. "Lucky for you, my friend, you did not hit any of my men," he says. "Because of that, I am still open to negotiate. This is your final opportunity. Send out Noakes, or else we come in. You will not survive the next five minutes, my friend."

Tom knows this is a lie. Fedorov expects him to be dead in the next five minutes, regardless of the choice he makes. And, without Roger, there's no choice *to* make. He braces himself for the attack.

11

Roger hides in the truck, lying low across the driver and passenger seats. His breath is coming hard. He sticks a knuckle into his mouth, bites down on it. He doesn't think anyone will hear him, but it's freaking him out.

No one can see inside the truck. The windows are all covered with snow. They'll hear it, though. Soon as he starts it up, they'll come running. He's biding his time. Waiting for an opportunity to drive away without being apprehended. To drive away from this messy situation and get down off this freezing fucking mountain.

He grabbed the keys from the counter as soon as Tom stepped out onto the porch to confront Fedorov. Roger knew Fedorov would not have come alone, and knew he had to move fast. He pocketed the keys and booked it straight for the window. Crept out the back and down the side, to the truck. He waded through the deep snowdrifts. It came up to his shins, soaked him through his trousers. His feet are wet and cold.

He was careful getting inside the truck. Careful opening

the door. As he did so, the brief burst of shooting at the front of the cabin started. He didn't have to be so careful anymore. He yanked the door open and leapt inside, slammed it shut behind him.

He hasn't moved since, though the shooting has mostly stopped. The hand that isn't in his mouth is slung over his head. It's still holding the keys. He chances moving. Pushing himself into a seated position, though he stays low. His hand is shaking as he slots the key into the ignition. His breath mists in front of his face. When he slammed the door shut behind him, a little of the snow fell from the window. Not much, but enough that he's able to see the side mirror. He watches it now, waiting for his chance. By sight or by sound, he'll know when to take it.

12

_____

A man begins to scream, and Tom knows he has stepped into a bear trap. The sound comes from the left. Rifle in hand, Tom monkey-runs toward the sound. He stands by the window next to the fireplace, peers out. Sees the man on the ground. Blood from his leg has splashed up the side of his camo, making him easier to spot. Tom sees movement to the injured man's right. Another of the men, moving to him, to help him, or to shut him up.

Tom raises the rifle. He doesn't bother raising the window, or smashing the glass. He fires through it. The glass shatters. The shot hits the man in the center of the chest. He's thrown back by the impact as blood sprays out behind him.

Bullets strafe the left side of the cabin. Tom ducks low and rushes to the other side, to cut off the men on the right. As he passes between the sitting area and the kitchen, the front door is kicked in. Tom spins toward it as he goes, expecting to find Fedorov. It isn't the Russian. Another of his men, all in white. He drops instantly to a knee, raising his M16. Tom doesn't let him get it all the way up. He fires. The first shot catches the man in the shoulder, causes him to drop the automatic rifle. His arm is hanging, useless. Tom fires again, and the second shot takes him through the face. It throws him back onto the porch. The door closes after him, but not fully.

On the right side of the cabin, someone is crying out. They've come across another of the traps. By the sounds of his helpless cries, it's a snare rather than a bear trap. Tom can see him through the window above the sink. He's hanging upside down. Tom sights him with the rifle. As he does so, he hears the familiar sound of his truck roaring to life. *Roger.* Tom can't think about that right now. That's a problem for later, if the damn fool doesn't get himself killed before then.

Tom shoots the man hanging upside down in the snare as he hears his truck speeding away. Hears how it skids and slides in the snow. Hears how it's fired upon, and shouted after, but he doesn't think they stop it. Roger gets away.

Tom moves to the back of the cabin, to the window Roger left open in his escape. At least one prong of the pincer formation is sure to have made it to the rear. Tom needs to cut it off. He reaches the window in time to see one of the men from the right falling into his bear pit, crying out as he goes. Tom leaves him. He won't be able to get out.

The Russian is still outside, along with the man still screaming in the bear trap. There's another, too. Tom doesn't know if he's on the left or the right. The one who came through the front door has thrown off his tally.

Tom goes to the left, to the bear-trapped man. No one else has been lured by his cries.

Tom waits. He can't do anything rash. Needs to be patient.

The screaming man makes the only sounds Tom can hear, though even now his cries are reducing to whimpers and sobs. Tom listens. He gets low by the fireplace, watching the windows and the door. Roger and his truck are long gone, now. He wonders if the others have gone after him. Of course, there's a chance the men still outside want him to think that. They want him to step outside, unaware, whereupon they can put an easy bullet through his head.

Tom waits.

Finally, his patience is rewarded with the sound of movement. With feet crunching through snow. Stomping up the porch steps. Almost slipping, losing balance, and then crashing through the door at a run. The man, the last man in camo, is charging, firing wildly into the center of the room. He's hoping for the best, hoping to catch Tom unaware in his careless attack.

Tom stays where he is. The bullets are nowhere near him. He raises his rifle, aims. Thinks how, despite the Russian's boasts of having trained these men, they are still nothing more than low-level criminals – just like Teddy and Reagan. They aren't soldiers. They didn't have to die like this. Tom warned them. When it comes down to him or them, he's always going to choose himself.

He shoots the last man high in the chest, drops him. Only Fedorov remains.

The Russian promptly makes himself known. He comes from behind, striking Tom in the side of the head with a rock-like fist, then taking the rifle from him and throwing it across the room. It becomes clear – the man recklessly attacking through the front door was a distraction while Fedorov sneaked in through the back. "You will tell me where Roger has gone, yes?" he says.

The blow has dazed Tom, but he knows he needs to keep fighting. He pulls out the Beretta. Fedorov has anticipated this, and Tom wonders if he spotted the gun on his approach. He moves to the outside and clamps his hand around Tom's wrist, pushes it to the side as he fires. The bullet flies wide. Fedorov twists his arm and takes the gun from him. He drops it to the ground and kicks it away.

"This is all very impressive, my friend," he says. He's still grinning, just like outside. He keeps grinning as he punches Tom in the mouth, rocking his head back on his shoulders and busting his lip. Tom spits blood, raises his arms defensively. "The traps. Your proficiency with weapons. You have training, no? You are not some, how you Americans say, *average Joe.*"

Fedorov has the height and weight advantage. He has a greater reach. Tom lashes out with a kick, aiming it low, at the Russian's knees. Knows he needs to cut his legs out from under him. Fedorov turns his leg inward to avoid the worst of the blow, then bats Tom's foot away with a low sweep of his arm. Tom moves in fast while Fedorov's body is twisted, defensive but not defending, and he's able to land a couple of blows to Fedorov's face, head, and chest.

Fedorov laughs them off. "My friend," he says, striking Tom with a backfist that makes him take a few steps back. "Your little friend has abandoned you." He's referring to Roger. He advances while he talks. "You and I, we shall go find him together, yes? You know where he is going, yes?"

Tom doesn't answer. He throws a punch, but it's easily blocked, and Fedorov deals one of his own. It connects with Tom's nose. He feels it begin to swell. He can taste blood. A lot of blood.

"Had you not allowed for him to get away, I would have killed you already," Fedorov says, and Tom doesn't doubt this. He's overwhelmed by the Russian. He's running on zero sleep. But he knows that even fully rested and having not just fought off six other men, he would still be struggling to match Fedorov. "You are a – a *detour*, right now. A distraction. Nothing more. Just give it up, my friend. There is no need to get yourself hurt further. Come with me, and we shall find Roger together, yes?"

"I thought Russians called everyone comrade," Tom says.

Fedorov places a hand to his chest in mock indignation. "My friend, *please*. Do not be reducing me to such a stereotype." He lunges for Tom.

Tom ducks his arms, rolls through. He makes it to the kitchen, to the trapdoor. He thinks about what is down there. What is laced throughout the cabin. Emma's cabin. It's an extreme step, but it may be one he has to take. He may not survive, otherwise.

He throws open the trapdoor.

Fedorov laughs. "It is too late for hide-and-go-seek, my friend," he says. He kicks Tom in the chest, sends him toppling backward into the basement. "And you have given away your hiding place!" Fedorov tuts, shaking his head. "I am thinking you are not the best at this game, no?"

Tom hits the concrete ground hard, the air knocked out of him. Fedorov looms above, filling the trapdoor. Soon, he will descend. Tom can't stay lying there. He pushes himself up, ignoring every ache and pain that screams throughout his body. He reaches to the table, next to his bag, and he grabs the switch. He looks back up at Fedorov. Fedorov frowns, then sees what he has grabbed. His eyes go wide.

"It's not a hiding place," Tom says. "It's a bomb shelter."

He dives for the corner of the basement with all the energy he has left, and pulls the shelves from their place against the wall and angles the top of them against another wall to create a cover. The jars of fungi and fruits fall and shatter on the ground around him. He presses the switch.

Above, the bombs explode, and tear the cabin apart.

13

Fedorov makes it to the porch as the explosions erupt. He manages to clear the steps, but as he's running, the concussive force of the bombs catches him from behind, lifts him from his feet. He's thrown far.

He hits the ground. The left side of his face is burning. It feels like it's on fire, though it's not. It caught the worst of the blowback from the explosion, of the hot air that has propelled him away from the cabin.

The smell of burnt hair and flesh is in his nostrils. He scurries away, as far away from the explosion, the fires, as he can get before exhaustion overwhelms him, makes his limbs feel heavy, like leaden weights. He buries his face in the snow, cools it. He scoops it up by the handful and rubs it onto the back and front of his neck. He rolls in it, cools his body. He lies flat on his back, gulping in air. He presses snow to his lips and sucks on it. His vision is blurred. He's dazed. His ears are ringing. The left side of his face still feels as though it's burning. The burn is deep-seated. It feels like it's under his skin. He wonders what it looks like. He presses more snow to it. He rolls onto his side, tries to push himself back up to his feet. The strength still has not returned to his body. He collapses flat on his front.

He passes out.

14

Tom has to stay in the basement and wait for the fires overhead to calm, for it all to cool enough that he's able to go up. The temperatures around the cabin were already low. He imagines it should only take a couple of hours.

He used C-4 for the explosives. It was the easiest explosive to mold and conceal, and the least volatile to live with.

He's eaten what was left of the mushrooms and berries from the jars that did not shatter. He remains in the corner, under his makeshift shelter, cross-legged and waiting. He watches the trapdoor, should anyone else arrive, try to find him. He wouldn't expect them to be firefighters, or emergency services. The cabin is too far out of the way. No one will have heard it explode. No one will have seen it.

He has his bag, ready to leave. His burner phones. Spare set of clothes. Beretta and KA-BAR. Picture of Alejandra. Santa Muerte pendant. When the time comes, he slings it over his back and heads up top.

Most of the fires have calmed, now. They're small, dotted here and there. Wisps of smoke rise from blackened wood.

Tom checks the area. He counts up six dead men. The man in the bear trap got caught up in the explosion. The right side of his body is crisped. The man who fell in the bear pit is buried under snow and burned logs from the cabin.

There is no sign of Fedorov. He's not where the cabin used to be, and he's not around it, either. Tom finds some footprints down the way, but they disappear into the woods. They look unsteady. They drag. They were not able to keep to a straight line.

Tom looks down the mountain, toward town. It's a long way to go. He looks back at where his truck should still be parked. Where Roger stole it from. He shakes his head, silently cursing the man whose life he saved. He starts walking. There's nothing else for it. He heads for White Spruce Hill.

15

Roger speeds home, jostled side to side, up and down in the cab of the truck he is struggling to handle. He wipes sweat from his brow and runs his tongue over his dried and cracked lips. He doesn't know what happened back at the cabin. Halfway down the mountain, he thought he heard an explosion. He tried looking back, but it was too far. There was nothing to see.

He's almost home, now. Almost back to the outskirts of Valdez. He's been driving for hours. A couple of times, he's almost fallen asleep at the wheel. The events of yesterday and today are catching up to him. His adrenaline is draining away. He's feeling flat. He's battled to keep his eyes open. A number of times he's found himself suddenly on the other side of the road. Luckily, most of the time the roads have been empty.

This has not always been the case. He's snapped awake to the sound of blaring horns twice. He had to pull over at a gas station. He bought a coffee, black, and drank it down in one go. It tasted awful, like it had sat in the pot for a few days already, but it would do the job. He filled the truck's tank, too.

He hates driving it, but it's the only vehicle he has. Who knows where they took his car, or what they did with it.

He gets home without further incident. Screeches to a halt in front of his house. He leaps out of the truck and races toward the front door. It opens as he gets close. Lily stands within its frame, like she's been watching out, waiting for his return. "Oh my God, Roger," she says, looking at him, alarmed. "Where have you *been*? I was about to call the police!"

Roger hurries her inside the house, closes the door after himself, locks it, presses his back to it. Lily is able to get a good look at him when he stops moving, as he's trying to catch his breath. Her eyes are wide. She sees how his clothes are disheveled. She smells how he has not washed. She sees the wound on his head, the thick scab that seals it closed.

"What's *happened*?" she says. "Roger, I've been so worried! Where have you been?"

Roger places his shaking hands on her shoulders, squeezes her, tries to calm himself before he speaks. "Where's – where's Elijah?" he says.

"He's at school – Roger, you're frightening me. Speak to me, will you? Tell me what's going on?"

"Has anyone been by the house?" he says. "Has anyone come to the door, asking for me, looking for me?"

Lily is shaking her head, scared.

"Have you seen any vehicles on the street you didn't recognize? Anyone suspicious, anyone who looked like they might have been checking the house out?"

"No, no, I – I mean, I don't think so, not in the street, anyway... No one's come to the house. I know that for sure."

"What about..." Roger hesitates. "Has anyone...has anyone *Russian* been here? Have you heard any Russian accents? Outside, anywhere?"

She frowns. "Russian? No – *why*?"

Roger keeps his hands on her shoulders. He looks around, looks toward the living room, then the stairs. Listens to the upstairs. "Where's Elijah?"

Lily blinks. "Roger, I already told you – he's at school. How hard did you hit your head? We might need to take you to a doctor, or a hospital –"

"*No*," Roger says, wheeling on her, knowing he must look crazed, but unable to make himself look or sound any other way. "No, not a hospital, not a doctor. Nowhere public." He lets go of her shoulders now and leans back against the wall. His heart is hammering. He can't catch his breath. It feels like he's about to crash again. The disgusting coffee didn't do anything after all.

"Whose truck were you driving?" Lily says, looking toward the closed door, remembering the vehicle she saw him pull up in.

"Later," Roger says, waving a weak arm. "I need you to listen to me, Lily. I need you to listen to what we're going to do."

She comes to him, presses her hands to him, tries to comfort him, to prop him up. "You need to lie down," she says. "I need – Roger, I need you to tell me what's happened to you. I've been worried sick. Should I...should I call the police?"

"God, no, not the police," Roger says. He brushes off her hands. "Just *listen* to me, all right?"

Lily recoils, and Roger realizes his tone is harsher than he intended. He holds up his empty hands, palms out. "Just *listen, please*. I need you to go upstairs and pack some bags, as quick as you can, okay? And then we're going to the school, and we're going to get Elijah. We're going to have to take him out of school. We'll tell him we're going on a little trip, okay? A spontaneous, last-minute trip. No one needs to know where we're going. You don't even know – it's a surprise. I'm surprising you, surprising you both."

"Roger, what are you *talking* about?" Lily says. "You're not making any sense."

He takes a deep breath. He puts his hands on her shoulders again. Turns her body toward him. He squeezes, harder than he should, but he needs her to pay attention, to understand the severity of the situation. He looks into her eyes. "We need to go and get Elijah," he says, "and then we need to get out of here. We need to go somewhere secret, and we need to lie low. Do you understand?"

"No, I – no, not at all –"

"Lily!" He doesn't care when she recoils this time. "Lily, we're in *danger*. Why can't you get that through your head? We're in danger, all of us. I... I can't explain right now. There's no time. We need to just gather up some things, and we need to get out of here. Can you do that?" He raises his voice again when she doesn't answer, doesn't move. "*Can you do that?*"

She flinches. There are tears in her eyes. "Roger, I..."

He lets go of her, presses his back against the wall again. "I'll explain later," he says, closing his eyes and sliding down it until he's seated. "Just be quick. Go now. Be quick. I'll explain everything later..."

16

Yuri Ivanov wonders to himself if there is anything more boring than a meeting with his shareholders. They're tedious at the best of times, but now, when his mind is preoccupied with so many other things, it's fucking *endless*.

The offices of AI Construction Services are located in Valdez. Yuri founded the company more than ten years ago, when he first came to America. In a short amount of time, he has made it into one of the state's leading construction firms. While some of this is down to the reputation and expertise of the workers he employs, most of it is down to the contracts he is able to procure. He will go to any length in order to gain these contracts. The building and architectural craftsmanship of his employees does not figure into it. No, it takes a different kind of craftsmanship altogether. Techniques he is sure would horrify his shareholders gathered here in the boardroom, though he has no doubts some of them will already have their suspicions. They don't care, not really. None of them do. All they care about is money. So long as they continue to get rich, they leave him to it.

If anyone ever asks what the A in AI Construction Services stands for, Yuri tells them *Alaska*. It appeals to their sense of regional pride. Alaska, number one. In truth, it stands for Anderson. Anderson was the original face of the company, back when Yuri first arrived from Russia, and he did not have citizenship. He could not found the business in his own name. He needed someone else to do it for him, from whom he could buy it back at a later date.

Yuri never had to buy Anderson out, though. Joe Anderson disappeared without a trace shortly after Yuri became an American citizen, the process of which was sped along by the greasing of some highly influential palms. By then, Yuri was already the company's majority shareholder. He'd always been running things. Everyone involved in the business answered to him. Most of them had never even met Anderson, and those who had thought of him as just a foolish man who signed his name away for a promise of riches.

The table in the center of the boardroom is varnished birchwood, as is the paneling on the walls. It's an ostentatious display, certainly, but Yuri doesn't mind. He believes that if you show off your money, people will be more inclined to spend their own money with you. It's worked so far. He sits at the head of the table, head resting on his hand, barely listening. Someone at the front of the room, motioning to the illustration projected onto the board, is talking about projected earnings. The other men in the room seem pleased with what they're hearing. They nod along, murmuring excitedly between themselves.

They have no idea. They have no idea what is coming their way, of their *true* 'projected earnings.' Yuri grins to himself at this. They don't know what he's planning. He has far bigger fish to fry.

Of course, first he has to get through frying some much *smaller* fish.

There's a gentle knock at the door, distracting him. Distracting everyone. The man at the front of the room ceases his spiel about how much they'll have made by quarter's end. All heads turn toward the door, the knock. A couple of people glance at Yuri.

Yuri pushes himself upright. "Come in," he says.

His secretary sheepishly pokes her head around the door. She steps inside and hurries over to him. She's an older lady. She looks like she has been doing this job, or some variation of it, for the last forty years. That's why Yuri hired her. She looked like she knew what she was doing, and her résumé bore that impression out. She hasn't let him down so far, though interrupting his board meeting – as boring and redundant as it may be – is disappointing.

"There's a man to see you," the secretary says, eyes only on Yuri, too embarrassed to look around the rest of the room and see all the other men impatiently staring back at her. "He's in your office."

Yuri raises an eyebrow. "Is that all?" he says. "You know we are not to be disturbed in here. Whoever it is, he can wait."

"I know, sir, I'm so sorry," she says, looking distraught. "But he insisted...he... He said to tell you..." Her brows furrow, like she's struggling to remember something.

Yuri waits. "Well?"

"I'm sorry, I just, I don't want to get it wrong. He said...*vazhnyy*. I...I think that was it. I think that's right."

Vazhnyy. *Important*. It's Fedorov.

"I see," Yuri says. He sends the secretary away, then turns back to his shareholders. "My apologies, gentlemen, but something has come up, and I'm afraid it cannot wait. Please, continue without me. I will catch up on the minutes later."

The secretary is waiting for him outside the boardroom, bouncing from foot to foot. "Mr. Ivanov," she says, "I'm so, *so* sorry."

Yuri waves her off. "Do not worry about it," he says. They walk together back to his office. "You did the right thing."

"Sir, Mr. Ivanov, just so you know...the man..." She hesitates, wringing her hands together. "The man, he –" She starts raising her hands to her face.

"That's enough," Yuri says. "Don't concern yourself with him. He's a friend of mine." He motions to the seat behind her desk outside his office. "Now, back to work, yes?"

She swallows. "Yes, Mr. Ivanov. Of course, Mr. Ivanov."

Yuri smiles, then steps into his office. He closes the door behind him. The desk, and the paneling on the walls, are the same here as in the boardroom. Alina Sidorova is already present, as he knew she was. What surprises him about her, however, is the way she stands in the corner behind his desk, a drink in hand, staring at the man in the chair opposite like she's horrified. The man is Fedorov, Yuri can see that from his build, and Alina knows Fedorov. Yuri frowns, then steps up to him, on his left side.

The reason for Alina's expression soon becomes apparent. The left side of Fedorov's face glistens. The skin is pink and raw and shining. The hair on this side of his head has burned away, and the skin beneath looks tender. His left eye has survived the worst of whatever damage has befallen him, but the skin at its corner looks fused and twisted, and drags the lid down so it is half-closed. Yuri can smell the antiseptic cream that has been generously rubbed over all of the wounds.

"My friend," Yuri says, unable to tear his eyes away, "what has happened?"

Fedorov grunts. He grins. "Mr. Noakes found himself a

friend," he says. "Are you going to offer me a drink? I have been waiting, and I am very thirsty."

Yuri shoots Alina a look. "You have not offered Fedorov a drink all the while he is sitting here?" He stares at the glass in her hand. "I see you have taken care of yourself, however."

Fedorov laughs, waves like it doesn't matter. "Do not blame her, my friend," he says. "I am sure dear Alina has been caught off guard by my appearance. I am no longer as handsome as I used to be, and I'm sure this discovery has devastated her so."

Alina swallows. "I-I'm sorry, Fedorov. Yuri. I should have..." She waves her hands in front of her face. "Where are my manners? Vodka?"

"Please," Fedorov says with a tilt of his head.

"Two," Yuri says.

"Of course." Alina moves away from the corner, to the minibar opposite.

Yuri steps around his desk, watching Fedorov. The right side of his face is largely unharmed. Despite how painful the left appears, he seems to be in good spirits. "What happened?" Yuri says, taking a seat.

Fedorov takes the drink Alina brings him. He swallows it in one go. His lips pull back from his teeth, then he smacks them together. "*Ahh*. Well, where to begin, huh?" He tells Yuri what happened up the mountain.

Yuri listens intently, nursing his own drink. Alina has returned to the corner, and has adopted a neutral expression. She's listening to Fedorov's story, too, but she's trying hard not to stare.

"I sent Teddy and Reagan to pick him up," Fedorov says. He rolls his eyes, slaps the side of his head that's not burnt. "What am I thinking, yes? I think even these two cannot fuck this up. And yet, fuck it up they have." He shakes his head. "I am thinking to myself, it is Roger, yes? A mere accountant. What trouble can he cause them? I have bigger concerns of my own, things I need to get done. I do not need to trouble myself with an accountant, no? Their instructions are simple – take him up the mountain. Press a gun to his head, spook him. He knows there are dead bodies up there, he will speak, yes? All they need to do is *scare* him. They did not even need to make it all the way *up* the mountain – he could have got scared enough he gives it all up before they even get there! Instead, they get spooked themselves!" He looks at Alina, laughing. Alina forces a smile, though it's humorless.

Roger is an employee of Yuri's. Well, a former employee, now. Yuri hired him (by force, admittedly) for one purpose – to launder his money. Not all of his income comes from construction. Roger needed to get that dirty money clean. It was also his responsibility to keep taxes in order. He was good at it, until recently. Two nights ago, in fact. Yuri is a man who believes in rewarding loyalty, but he is sure never to misplace his trust. Roger is in charge of the laundering, but Yuri has made sure to know where his money is going. Where it is at all times. He has alarms set up on his accounts. Two nights ago, one of the alarms went off. Half a million dollars of his money disappeared.

Roger is the only man with access.

Yuri got in touch with Fedorov, told him what he needed to do – to get his money back. At the same time, Yuri wants to know *why* Roger has taken it. Before now, Roger has always done his job. He's stayed in his lane. The theft of half a million dollars is very out of character for him. Either Yuri has misjudged his character, or else someone has strong-armed him. Yuri knows he must be prepared for either scenario, hence why Alina is in his place of work. Usually, she is free to fill her days in her own manner. For the time being, though, Yuri cannot leave her to her own devices when there is the risk of an unseen, unknown enemy making a move upon him and his organization.

Fedorov continues with his story. He tells of Teddy and Reagan fleeing down the mountain, telling him of how they were ambushed. Tells of the attack on the cabin, the gunfight, and its explosive conclusion, which resulted in the damage to Fedorov's face.

Fedorov finishes, looks down into his empty glass as if wishing it had somehow refilled. Alina takes the hint. She plucks his glass, returns to the minibar.

Yuri is silent, mulling over the story Fedorov has told him. He gathers his thoughts before he speaks, going over every aspect of the details he has been given. "This mystery man," he says, "who is he?"

Fedorov shrugs. "I don't know, though I intend to find out."

Yuri considers this. He takes a drink in solemn silence. "I understand he's hurt you, and you want to hurt him for this, but is he truly part of everything that is happening? Are we sure he is a *friend* of Roger, or is he just a stranger who found himself in an unfortunate position? You said yourself, Roger left him behind, abandoned him. Going after him could cause noise we do not need."

Alina hands Fedorov a fresh vodka. He smiles, raises it to Yuri in salute. "My friend, I understand you are thinking of the bigger picture, but it is *my* duty to consider every loose end, yes? This man, whoever he may be, is a loose end."

"He's a waste of time," Yuri says. "We can deal with him later."

"I am not so sure." Fedorov takes a drink, sipping it this time, making it last. "Before I came here, I sent a couple of my men to Roger's home. He's not there, and neither is his wife, his child. He has fled. There is a chance his new friend could lead us to him. Lead us to him, and back to your money, yes?"

"And why do you think he would do that?"

"Roger took his truck."

"You think that is enough?"

"He killed six of my men. He blew up his own cabin. I am feeling he is not the kind of man to let this go so easy." Fedorov drains his drink. "And I am thinking there is more to him than first glance. A soldier, perhaps something more. There is professional pride. I believe this mystery man is our best chance of finding Roger. And if he is not, I will find Roger some other way."

Yuri thinks Fedorov is making excuses. He wants to go after the man who has burned his face and killed his men. He wants revenge, and he's making excuses to get it. "And if he does not lead you to Roger, you can kill him on the way, yes?"

Fedorov holds out his empty glass. "I see no other way around it." He knows Yuri knows the truth. He doesn't care.

Yuri sighs. "You handle things how you think is best, Fedorov." He needs his money back. He cannot allow it to have been stolen and for this deed to go unpunished. Pride is more at stake here than the money – both personal and professional. Especially professional. Word of this cannot be allowed to get out. He will lose standing if it does, here and in Russia. His masters in the Russian Mafia cannot find out. They would lose all respect for him.

He can imagine what Mikhail would say. *Your house is not in order, Yuri. If a man cannot keep his house in order, how can he be trusted with the responsibility of* our *interests?*

Yuri runs a hand down his face. Fedorov is his best chance of getting the money back. Of cleaning up this mess. Of clearing up these *loose ends.* "And what of the honey trap?" Yuri says. Fedorov's most recent project, before he was sent up to the cabin.

"The moment has passed," Fedorov says. The honey trap was for the Alaskan governor. "When I went up to the cabin, I took the girl off it. I did not want her to be proceeding without my guidance, or support. You know I am so supportive of all who answer under me, yes? I am afraid you are going to have to go ahead without the governor. I feel you have enough support without, though, yes? He will fall in line, along with all the others. They will persuade him you are the best man for the job, I am sure."

Yuri grunts. "I'd feel more confident with the governor." The theft of his money has thrown a wrench into his plans. It has slowed things down. He drains his drink, trying to keep his temper in check. Losing it will not accomplish anything.

He sighs. "Do what you need to, Fedorov. Get my money back. Get my accountant. Find this stranger. I will take care of everything else." He motions to Fedorov's wounds. His nose has grown accustomed to the smell of the antiseptic cream. "Do you need further treatment before you go?"

Fedorov grins as he gets to his feet. "No need," he says, handing his empty glass to Alina. "It will heal while I work."

17

Tom thumbs a ride into White Spruce Hill when he finally gets down off the mountain. The driver is an old man, on his own. Probably makes a habit of picking up hitchhikers, desperate to talk to anyone.

"Been hitching long, young'un?" he says.

"Long enough," Tom says, not thinking about how cold he is, nor how wet the cuffs of his jeans are. When he'd gotten far enough away from the remnants of the cabin, he'd found wheel tracks in the snow. They weren't from his truck. He guesses Fedorov, unless there was an eighth man who held back to see how things played out. Would he bother retrieving Fedorov's body? Was Fedorov injured, in need of some medical attention? Either way, Fedorov has gotten out in front of him, and Tom's not comfortable with that.

"Where you coming from?" the old man says.

"Up in the mountains."

"Oh, really?" This surprises the old man. "You don't look like you've been hunting. Look like you've been *fighting*, mind you." The man is referencing the marks on Tom's face from his hand-to-hand battle with Fedorov. Tom's face is so cold from the wind he doesn't feel them anymore. He looks at himself in the mirror. Had almost forgot the wounds were there. Is surprised the man stopped to pick him up when he's looking as rough as he does.

"I was walking," Tom says. He points to his face. "These are from the other night."

The old man laughs. "Hell of a place to take a stroll." It's getting dark now. He turns on his headlights. "How's the other guy look?"

"I'm not so sure," Tom says, thinking of the explosion. The other man should be dead, but Tom isn't certain he is.

"You ain't going looking for him now, are ya?"

"Wouldn't dream of it."

When they finally reach White Spruce Hill, it's dark. The man drops him off at the hill itself. Tom thanks him, then walks the rest of the way to Emma's. She's surprised to see him. "Back so soon?" she says, though she's smiling. "How was the blizzard?"

"I need to come in," Tom says. He's already checked the street before he came to her door. Walked straight past her house a couple of times to check there was no one suspicious around, no one sitting in any of the parked vehicles who could be watching and waiting. It's clear. "We need to talk."

"Sure," Emma says, perturbed now. When Tom steps into the light, she sees the cuts and bruises on his face. "Shit," she says. "What happened?"

"You might wanna take a seat."

They go into the kitchen. Emma offers to make him a hot drink, but Tom settles for water. He sits so that he's facing down her hallway, to her front door. He tells her what has happened. He sees her eyebrows rise as the story goes on, and sees how her face darkens when he gets to what has happened to the cabin. "Then I came straight here," he finishes. "They might check to see who owns the cabin, which will lead them right to you."

Emma blinks. It takes her a moment to process things. She holds up her hands. "Hold on, hold on," she says. "Let me get this straight – you laced the cabin with explosives, *just in case* something like this were to happen?"

Tom nods.

"I never saw them when I went up. They were there the whole time?"

"I hid them well. That was the point."

"Okay, okay – so, tell me, who exactly gave you permission to do that?" She stares at him.

"I'm sorry," Tom says. "Old habits die hard. I didn't intend, or honestly ever expect, to blow up your cabin, but..." He trails off. Holds out his hands. "Sorry."

She stares at him. "Do you – do you *know* –" She looks and sounds exasperated, struggling to marshal her angry and confused thoughts into sentences. "Do you know how long that cabin was in my family?"

"Yes," Tom says. "You told me."

Emma takes a slow, shuddering breath. "It's gonna take me some time to process this."

"We don't really have that time," Tom says. "I want to get out of here, now, and I want to take you with me. It's not safe, you being here."

"Tom, this is insane. I can't just drop everything and go off and, and – and *what*, exactly?"

"I'm going to make sure this doesn't come back on you," Tom says. "And I'm going to get my truck back. I need to borrow yours. Please."

Emma blinks at him. "You have got a *lot* of nerve, buddy."

"You can drive."

Emma rolls her eyes. She leans forward, takes Tom's hands in her own. "Listen, Tom, just let it go. Whatever this guy has got himself mixed up in, it's not worth it. It's not worth getting yourself involved – even if, as you claim, it is just to get your truck back."

"I'm already involved," Tom says. "And now, unfortunately, so are you. They *will* come here, Emma. I don't know who they are, but when an organization makes a move like they did up at the cabin, I don't believe for a second that they're going to leave any loose ends lying around. Keeping you safe is my primary concern right now. I want my truck back, sure, but it's not as important as you."

"I'm glad to hear I mean more to you than that beat-up old thing."

"Of course. But, y'know, if he'd hung around, I would've drove him back myself."

"What was his name – you said Roger, right?"

"Roger Noakes."

"I know everyone in White Spruce Hill," Emma says. "I don't know him. He ain't from around here. How are you even gonna find him?"

"I know his address."

"And where is that?"

"In Valdez."

"Jesus Christ – you know that ain't exactly right next door?"

"I know. He has a family, Emma. Maybe you're right – maybe I can just walk away from this and no one's gonna come looking for me, and no one's gonna come knocking at your door trying to find me, but I won't be able to rest easy knowing his wife and child are potentially in as much danger as he is."

Emma is silent at this. She stands, places her hands on her hips. Arches her back to stretch it out. "*Fuck,*" she says. She knows he's right.

"There's a chance that we get Roger back and we can wrap this whole thing up peaceably," Tom says.

Emma looks at him. "And what *are* the chances of that?"

"They're slim, admittedly." Tom shrugs. "But also I killed six men up at the cabin. The snow's gonna bury those bodies, but I'd feel a lot better if I had someone who could corroborate my story of self-defense, should they be found before then. I'd hate to have to go on the run again, so soon after I've just come off it."

Emma frowns, not sure she heard him right. "*Again?*" she says. "You and I are going to have a *long* talk on the way to Valdez."

Tom sees lights out of the corner of his eye, headlights thrown up against the closed living room curtains. He gets to his feet and goes to the edge of the curtains to get a better look. The lights are slowing, stopping. They die right outside Emma's house.

"What?" Emma says. "*What?*"

Tom goes to his bag, pulls out his Beretta. "Someone's coming," he says.

There's a knock at the door. Emma looks at Tom.

"Answer it," he says. "I'll be right behind you."

He follows her to the front door, then stands to the side, behind it, as she opens it. "Hello?" she says.

There are two men at the door. Their voices are familiar. Tom peers through the gap. Teddy and Reagan.

"Hello, ma'am," Reagan says, nodding.

"Sorry to disturb you," Teddy says, smiling as wide as he can. He's trying to look nonthreatening, but the smile makes him look crazed. "We know it's getting late, but we're trying to find a friend of ours. The last we heard, he was staying at a cabin up in the Chugach Mountains, and he was renting it from you."

While they talk, Tom looks past them, to the vehicle they

arrived in. There are more men in the back of it. They're sitting very still, but he can make out their silhouettes.

"Oh?" Emma says. "What was his name?"

"Roger," Teddy says without hesitation. "Roger Noakes. But we think he might have had a friend staying there with him, too? Maybe you're not aware of that guy. We think he was an old army buddy of Roger's."

Tom presses his gun to the gap of the door. "Stay cool," he says, speaking loud enough for Teddy and Reagan to hear. "I have a gun on you right now." He can see they recognize his voice as much as he recognized theirs. "Don't look at me," Tom says, "just keep smiling. Emma, invite them in. Don't look back, boys – I've spotted your buddies. They get out of that car, I start shooting, and the two of you will be the first I put down."

Emma steps back into the house, and Teddy and Reagan do as they are told. Emma closes the door.

Tom pats them down from behind, takes their handguns – more Glocks – from them. "All right," he says. "Time to talk."

Teddy rolls his eyes. Reagan has his hands raised. He mumbles curses under his breath.

Tom hands one of the guns to Emma. She looks at him like, *What am I supposed to do with this?* but she knows better than to communicate this verbally. Tom tilts his head at Teddy and Reagan, motioning for her to cover them from the front, as he does so from behind. Emma knows how to shoot. She's told him of how her adoptive father took her hunting when she was young, and of how her hunting trips predated even that. She's told him how there's a photo of her biological father holding her over a fallen buck when she's *very* young, too young to remember, and he's smiling into the camera. She said she was going to show Tom this picture, one of the few she owns of her birth father, but she's yet to have gotten around to it.

No, what makes Emma uncomfortable about this isn't the handling of a gun – it's pointing it at *people*.

"Why were you going to kill Roger?" Tom says.

"We weren't gonna kill him," Reagan says, "we were just gonna scare him, that's all. And then you showed up, sent the whole thing to hell."

"All right, so you weren't going to kill him," Tom says. "Let's say I believe that. Why were you trying to *scare* him?"

"To tell us what he's done with the money," Reagan says. Teddy shoots him a look, like he thinks he's talking too easily, but he doesn't say anything to stop him.

"What money?" Tom says.

"Yuri's."

"And who's Yuri?" Tom says. He notices how Emma's eyes have narrowed, like the name is familiar to her and she's trying to place it.

"Yuri Ivanov," Reagan says.

"Another Russian," Tom says. He addresses Emma. "You know him?"

"I recognize the name," she says. To Reagan, "He owns A1 Construction, right?"

"That's him," Reagan says.

"Two of you don't look like you work construction," Tom says.

Teddy snorts.

"I get the feeling that ain't the only pie Yuri has his finger in," Tom says. "What is he? A fallen oligarch fled to America? Russian Mafia?"

At the mention of mafia, Teddy and Reagan exchange glances. Tom has his answer. Emma sees it, too. Her eyes go wide.

Tom presses on. "So who's Fedorov?"

"Yuri's bodyguard," Reagan says. "His right-hand man. You don't wanna fuck with him."

Teddy decides it's time to speak up. "Except you already *have*," he says, peering back at Tom over his shoulder and smirking. "And now he's got a real hard-on for *you*, on account of what you done to his face."

Fedorov is still alive. As Tom suspected. Their paths will cross again, he's sure. The presence of Teddy and Reagan in Emma's house all but guarantees it. "He should be thanking me," Tom says. "It's probably an improvement."

Reagan tries not to laugh.

"What did Fedorov do back in Russia?" Tom says. "Army? Special forces? He's had training, more than you'd get in the Russian Mafia. That much was obvious."

"Um..." Reagan is thinking, trying to remember.

"Did it have an acronym?" Tom says.

"That's what he's trying to remember," Teddy says.

"Yeah? What about you – you remember it?"

Teddy smirks.

Tom presses the gun into his lower back. "I don't want to have to ask again."

Teddy sighs, blows air out hard. "SVR," he says.

"SVR?" Emma says.

Tom knows this isn't good. A tough bastard who no doubt has some experience with finding people, as well as expertise with computers and electrical equipment. "It translates as Foreign Intelligence Service," he says. "Their version of the CIA." Tom is aware they've been talking for a while now. The men outside, in the car, are no doubt becoming suspicious.

"Is he still with them?" Emma says.

Teddy grunts. "From what I hear," he says, "if you manage to get kicked out of the SVR, there's gotta be something *really* fucked up about you." He looks back at Tom. "Fedorov got kicked out."

Tom sees a shadow pass by the kitchen window over Emma's shoulder. It's a slight movement. It could be a bird. An animal. Or it could be a person. The top of the head of one of Teddy and Reagan's friends from the car, moving into position. It's a potential risk, and Tom needs to wrap things up here.

He grabs Emma, pulls her to the ground with him, then reaches up and drags Teddy and Reagan down.

"What is it?" Emma says, but she has the sense to keep her voice low and follow his lead.

"Maybe nothing," Tom says. "Or maybe we're being surrounded."

"Bingo," Teddy says.

Tom shoots him a look. From the side, Teddy on the ground, Tom notices something out the corner of his eye. The discrepancy of a small object on Teddy's lapel. Unseen when viewed straight on, only just apparent when seen from the side.

A microphone.

That expertise in electricals Tom had just been worrying about, coming to the fore.

The men outside, in the car, have been listening. They know Teddy and Reagan are being held captive. They know everything.

Tom covers the microphone with his hand. "How many of them are out there?"

Teddy grins. "Don't matter," he says. "*He's* here. He's the only one you need to worry about."

A window at the back of the house, from the kitchen, smashes as something is thrown through it. Tom catches only a glimpse of what it is, but that's enough. A flash grenade. He throws himself over Emma, covers her head in order to keep her face down, as he plugs his ears and closes his eyes tight.

18

Fedorov is excitable, knowing that the man who burned his face, almost killed him, is inside the house, within his grasp. Teddy and Reagan are in there with him. He sent them to talk with the woman. If the man is not there, fine – they can handle a woman, at least. And if he *is* – well, Teddy and Reagan are expendable. If the man gets as trigger-happy as he did up on the mountain, Teddy and Reagan are an acceptable loss, as far as he is concerned.

Fedorov would like to know his name. After all, his enemy knows his. The woman, Emma, does not say it. A shame.

He sits in the back of the SUV, listening to Teddy and Reagan inside the house. Their conversation. There are two other men stationed outside the house. He communicates with them via microphones and earpieces. He's instructed them to get into place. Number two has gone around the back to take up position. Number one is nearby, at the corner of the house, ready to move in through the front door should the time come. Fedorov wants the man alive. He has made this very clear. He pokes at the raw, burned skin on his face, feels how it stings. The stink of antiseptic cream is strong in his nostrils. He has not become accustomed to it.

Fedorov thinks the man has seen something. They all fall silent. He hears a thud, like they've all hit the floor.

"Number two," Fedorov says into his microphone. "I think they have made you, my friend. What is their position?"

"In the hallway, by the door, still," comes the response.

Fedorov hears a ruffling in his ear. The microphone has been covered. The man has spotted it. Fedorov sits up, stretches. "Time to move," he says. "Stun them, and then let us go inside."

Fedorov gets out of the SUV in time to hear the glass breaking at the rear of the house. The stun grenade is thrown inside. He twists his body side to side, feeling stiff muscles and joints pop. There is a truck parked in the driveway of the house. Fedorov goes to the back of it, kneels by its rear bumper. He affixes something to it, just in case, then straightens back up and nods at number one, still holding position by the front corner of the house. Number one nods back, readies himself. Fedorov pokes at his burns again. He is covering the front of the house with number one. He watches the door.

He can't hear anything inside. There's not as much noise as he expected, as he'd like. His men are armed with M16s. He'd thought there'd be at least one short burst. He looks at number one again, signals for him to move in. Number one hurries from his corner, eager to please. He pushes down on the door handle, then kicks it the rest of the way open. Fedorov follows him in.

Teddy and Reagan are on the ground, wincing and holding their ears, groaning, writhing. They didn't protect themselves against the grenade. Probably they were stupid enough to look straight at it.

There is no sign of the man, or Emma.

Fedorov pushes number one out of his way. He reaches down and grabs Reagan, the closest, and shakes him. "Where is he? Where has he gone?"

Reagan can't open his eyes. Can barely hear him.

"Out the back!" Teddy says, struggling to push himself up, rubbing his eyes with his other hand.

Fedorov looks toward the back. Through the kitchen. The window has been smashed. Number two is hanging inside. He has been impaled on the shards of glass remaining in the window frame. His blood drips to the tiled floor below. Emma and the man have escaped out the back. They probably crawled over number two's dead body. Number one runs to check him, but Fedorov can already see there is no point.

A vehicle roars to life outside. Fedorov goes to the door. The truck in the driveway – Emma's – is reversing at speed. It pulls forward, then stops abruptly in front of the SUV. The man leans out the window. He fires into the front of the vehicle, into the engine, disabling it. The truck speeds away.

Fedorov watches them go, disappearing down the road, into the darkness.

He grins.

19

"Holy fuck!" Emma says. She slams her hands down on the steering wheel, looking back over her shoulder. She's worked up. Tom watches the road ahead of them. "They're in my house! They attacked my fucking home!"

"They're not following us," Tom says, wanting her to watch where she's going. He has to grab the wheel to stop her from losing control when she almost steers them off the road.

She turns around, but not all the way. She looks at him. "What have you gotten me into?"

"I'm sorry," Tom says.

"You've said that a lot tonight," she says, "yet here I am, fleeing into the night from a bunch of armed maniacs."

"I'll fix it," Tom says.

"Uh-huh." Emma turns to the road finally. "You gonna fix the cabin that you blew up?"

"Yes," Tom says. "Eventually. I might need some help with that."

Emma shakes her head. "Jesus Christ..." She takes deep breaths, sucking the air down into her lungs, filling her chest.

"All right, so. What's next? Right now, I'm just driving. Where am I actually going?"

"We need to find Roger," Tom says, "like we were planning, before Fedorov turned up."

"Valdez?"

It would be easy to walk away, Tom knows. It always is. To just keep driving. To leave Alaska and never look back. Sure, there's the risk Fedorov is enough of a psychopath to come looking for him no matter where he goes, but he could deal with him down the line. Just leave the rest of the mess in his past.

Emma can't leave with him, though. She wouldn't. Alaska is where her life is. White Spruce Hill is her home. Right now, her home is in danger. *She* is in danger. Tom can't walk away from that.

"Valdez," he says. "We get Roger, make sure his family is safe, and then we figure out how to put an end to all this."

20

Yuri is at home. He showers, then shaves. He splashes on some cologne, and then heads through to his bedroom. Alina is already there. She showered earlier. While he was washing, she was drying and styling her long, platinum blonde hair. Now she sits in front of the vanity mirror in the corner, applying her makeup. She's dressed already. She's wearing a white dress with a plunging neckline, and short enough at the hem that if she bends over too far, her ass will be on show. Her legs are crossed over each other, and her bare feet tap out an unheard rhythm under the table while she curls her eyelashes. Yuri bought the dress for her. He insisted she wear it tonight.

Yuri starts getting dressed. A gray pinstripe suit. He sits at the foot of the bed after he has pulled it on, slips into his brogues and ties the laces. He watches Alina as she puts on a necklace and slides earrings into her lobes.

"You need to smile while we are at the dinner," he says, speaking Russian. "I expect you to make some effort tonight."

Alina doesn't respond.

"You will be charming. You will keep the wife distracted while we talk. Do you understand?"

She sighs the word, "*Yes.*"

Yuri stops what he is doing and watches her. Alina pretends like she hasn't noticed. Save for the heels she will wear, she's finished getting dressed. She remains in front of the mirror, though. Examines herself. Touches her hair, checks the jewelry from different angles in the light. Yuri clears his throat to get her attention. He sees how her hands freeze on either side of her face, and then lower. She turns herself around, faces him.

"You have been moping so much lately," he says. "You need to snap out of it. What is the problem?"

Alina hesitates. When she finally speaks, she can't look him in the face. She knows better than to meet his eye when she is complaining. "I don't understand," she says, "why, because some of your money has gone missing, I need to be on lockdown. It is not even much money. You have more – so much more."

Yuri stares at her until she finally looks up, flinches when she sees the expression on his face. "It is the principle," he says. "*No one* may take what is mine. If a man or a woman should take but a single dollar from me without my permission, I would gut them and parade them for all to see."

Alina says nothing to this. She knows it's true.

"And you, my dear," he continues, "must be on lockdown for your own safety, as well as for my peace of mind."

Alina has not been in America as long as he has. She has only been with him for the last three years. He met her in Moscow, when he had returned to the motherland to discuss business ventures with the Bratva – ventures that will soon, very soon, be finally coming to fruition – when she caught his eye. She was a waitress. She was the most beautiful woman in the room, her blonde hair so light as to be almost white, and he knew she'd caught the eye of every man present. He saw how Mikhail Petrov, his main contact in the Bratva, stared at her with open lust from across the room.

However, Yuri was the first to make his move. He was the one to talk to her, to ask her name. He was the one who invited her back to America with him – after a few nights spent in his hotel room, of course. A lavish room, where they dined on champagne and caviar, only the finest things, to give her just a taste of his lifestyle. His efforts won her over. The Bratva sent him back to America with Alina on his arm, a new plan on his mind, and their best wishes.

The time he'd gone to Moscow before that, four years before he returned with Alina, he came back with Fedorov. Yet another gift from the Bratva. *You will need him by your side,* Mikhail had said. *For our plans, you need someone whose hands can be dirty, while yours must remain clean.*

"Your peace of mind?" Alina says.

Yuri leans forward, clasps his hands together. "We need to know what possessed Roger to take the money, and why. This is very out of character for him. Until then, he had always been such an obedient dog."

"Sometimes even the most obedient dog may bite your hand," Alina says.

"Yes, and when it does, you make sure it never happens again. You bury it around the back. And you are certain the next dog knows better. You *ensure* it knows better." Yuri watches her, sees that she understands. "But if there is a risk that someone else has arrived, that someone else has been riling up our dog, encouraged him to bite us – we need to know who this someone else is. Until we do – until we know the truth of what has happened – we must be on alert. We must expect *everything*. Right now, it may not be safe for us. Depending on the size of the risk, we may need to flee to safety at a moment's notice. If that is to happen, I want to be sure that you are by my side. That we are together."

Alina looks down at her feet. She has painted her toe- and fingernails a pale shade of silver. She inspects it. "I miss my freedom," she says.

"You will get it back," Yuri says. "Just as soon as my money is returned. Think on that future, think on how happy you will be when it comes, and plaster a fucking smile on your face, huh?"

Alina stiffens. She nods.

"Show me," Yuri says.

Alina swallows. She takes her time raising her face. She finally does, looks him in the eye. The corners of her mouth twitch. She closes her eyes and takes a deep breath. When she opens them again, she is smiling. It looks natural. Yuri watches it for a while, checks for cracks. When he is satisfied, he says, "Good."

Yuri's phone begins to ring. It's Fedorov. "Put on your heels," he tells Alina. "And wait for me here."

She does as he says while he steps out of the room. Yuri answers. "How has it gone?" he says.

Fedorov tells him what happened at the house of Emma Raven, the woman who owns the cabin.

"Did you get a name, at least?" Yuri says.

"Nyet," Fedorov says. "So, they got away. We have no name. We lost a man. *But*, it was not a complete loss, no?"

"No?"

"No, I am not concerned. I slipped a tracker onto the woman's truck before we attempted to take them. Be prepared for every outcome, yes?"

"That is your department, Fedorov."

"Indeed. So, we can see them. We are not going to lose them. I have tracker. We're following them now. We're on the road. We're a few hours behind, because of course we have to get new vehicle and move the one they disable from the street. But, Yuri, I tell you, this is promising route, yes?"

"What is the route?"

"They're going to Valdez, my friend."

"Where else could they go?"

"I think I am right, my friend. They are looking for Roger, I am sure of it. While they were in the house, while I hear them speaking to Teddy and Reagan, the man, he is asking about Roger. Where he is, why we want him. Why else would he be curious? I am thinking they will go to Roger's house. If they do, I am right, yes?"

"Yes, you'll be right. I will give you a fucking medal."

Fedorov laughs. "I will like that very much. I will wear that medal with pride." Yuri can picture him grinning with those fresh burns, making him look even more terrifying than he already did. "So, I will see them go to Roger's, then we know for sure. Then *you* know for sure – I am already being very certain. And *then*? Then we are killing the two birds with the one stone, yes? We let them find Roger for us. Then, I will swoop in at end, and they are both mine."

"The man may know things," Yuri says. "If there is a potential risk to our organization, he may be a part of it. Do not kill him straight away, Fedorov."

"If you say so."

"Find out what he knows, *then* you may kill him."

Fedorov laughs again. "I was planning on taking my time with him anyway, my friend. He does not get to do *this* to my beautiful face and then escape all repercussions, oh no."

Yuri checks the time. "I leave it to you, Fedorov. I need to go. We have dinner with Councilman Manning, and it will take us an hour to drive there. I do not want to be late."

"Ah, yes, the good councilman, that is tonight."

"Mayor Pullman will also be there. This is an important dinner."

"I am aware. Send them both my regards, yes?"

"I'm sure they will be pleased to receive them." Yuri hangs up.

He steps back into the bedroom. Alina is dressed, ready to go. She is in her seat, sitting up straight, both hands resting in her lap. She looks at Yuri as he opens the door. She smiles again, just like before, to show how naturally it comes.

"Let us go," Yuri says.

"Yes," Alina says, still smiling. Showing she can be good. Showing she will do tonight what he's asked of her. "Of course."

21

"I keep expecting the cops to call," Emma says. She's still driving. "It wasn't exactly a *lot* of noise at my house, but it was more than enough, right? I mean, you shot into an engine right in the middle of the street."

"Maybe your neighbors were out," Tom says. "You don't have that many."

She shoots him a look. "All I'm saying is, I'm just surprised the cops haven't tried to get in touch. Someone must've seen or heard something."

"Don't hold your breath," Tom says. "In my experience, I've found that if you're dealing with someone rich enough and powerful enough, their influence often extends to the cops. Not always, and sometimes not all of them, but enough of them to make a bad kind of difference."

Emma's brow furrows at this. It's clear she doesn't like the thought of it.

"Of course, there's a chance Fedorov paid your neighbors a visit," Tom says. "He might have warned them off. Advised them it's smarter if they keep their mouths shut about anything they might have heard or seen. He's probably cleaned up the scene, gotten rid of the body hanging half-in and half-out of your kitchen window. Maybe he was nice enough to replace the broken window. He's a professional. He probably doesn't like to leave a mess."

"I'll believe it when I see it," Emma says.

They've been driving for a while now. They've almost reached Valdez. Emma has calmed significantly after the events of earlier in the evening. Had they not been attacked in her home, Tom thinks she'd still be a lot more annoyed about his blowing up her cabin.

"And don't think I've forgotten about the fucking cabin," Emma says, as if reading his mind. "You said you'd help rebuild it. Don't think I'm not gonna hold you to that."

"I wouldn't dream of walking out on a promise," Tom says.

Emma's eyes flicker to her mirrors. "Do you think they're following us?"

"There's no one behind us."

"I don't mean right now," she says. "I mean, do you think they're going to?"

"I'm sure they'll try," Tom says. "They don't know where we're going, though. They'll have to work that out first. They'll probably guess we're looking for Roger, but they're looking for him, too. If we get out in front of them, we should get to him with no problems."

They enter Valdez. They pull to the side so Emma can bring up the map app on her phone, then Tom recites the address to her from memory. Tom holds the phone and tells her the directions. Emma resumes driving. They head east.

It takes them another while to get where they're going. "It looked on the map like this place is right on the edge of town," she says. "Feels like we're driving out of it. Like it's barely in Valdez."

Tom looks at the phone. "Right on the outskirts," he says.

The roads and sidewalks here have been mostly cleared of snow. There is salt on the roads. The roofs of buildings and cars are covered, and there is no greenery to be seen on lawns or trees, but the walking and driving conditions are much safer than back in White Spruce Hill, where the retirees have not yet had a chance to get back out with their shovels since the blizzard.

They reach the street. "Stop at the end here," Tom says. "Kill the lights. Let's get a good look at it first. Tell me if you see anyone watching the house, or anyone sitting in a car."

"Like we're doing now?"

"Exactly like we're doing now."

Tom doesn't see anyone, and Emma doesn't speak up, either. The first thing he noticed as they reached the street, however, and counted up the doors to Roger's home, is that his truck is not present. It isn't here. Roger's house is in darkness, though the curtains are not drawn. It doesn't look like there's a single light switched on inside.

"All right," Tom says. "Get us a little closer, then we'll go inside."

Emma pulls forward, but she's frowning. "I hear you right?" she says. "You say *inside*?"

"I can knock on the door first if you like," Tom says. "But there's no one there."

"Okay, sure, so we leap straight to breaking and entering?"

"We need to know where he's gone. Only chance of an answer to that is inside the house."

They leave the truck and head up on foot. Tom makes to go straight around the back. Emma stops him. "I'd feel a lot better if we actually *did* knock first."

Tom obliges. There's no answer. No sound from inside, save for the echo of Tom's knuckles rapping upon the door.

"All right," Emma says. "I'm satisfied."

They disappear into the darkness down the side of the

house, go round the back. Tom checks the handle, but it's locked. He expected it would be. He pulls out his KA-BAR. Emma inspects the lock. "You know how to pop this?" she says, almost sounding like she might be impressed.

Tom has inspected the lock himself. He knows how to get inside. "Do you?" he says, curious.

Emma holds out her hand. "Give me the knife," she says. "And allow me to use a little finesse, as opposed to just sticking the pointy end into the frame, wriggling it about, and hoping for the best."

Tom grins, handing her the knife. This would not have been his technique, but he's intrigued to see her do it. He's never had her figured for a lockpick.

She slides the knife into the space between the door and the frame, above the door handle. "This kind of lock, it's a pin. That's all that stops the latch from going in when I turn the handle." Her other hand is on the handle itself, ready. "All I've gotta do is get a bite on the pin, pop it loose, and I can turn the handle." The door pops open. She turns to Tom, hands him back his knife. "*Voila*," she says.

Tom raises an eyebrow. "And where did you learn how to do that?"

"The product of a misspent youth."

They step inside the house through the door Emma has unlocked. They're in the kitchen. There's a small round table near the door. It's clear, as are the counters. The Noakes keep a tidy home.

"So what do we do now?" Emma says.

"The way you got that lock open, I figured you'd have some idea of where to go from there," Tom says.

"On the *rare* occasions I found myself needing to get into someone's house, it wasn't to try to find out where they might be."

"Why was it?"

She looks at him. "I was very young," she says. "It was to play pranks. Or, y'know, in some cases, it was to steal booze. That's as extreme as we ever got."

Tom grins. "All right. You look in here. I'll check the rest of the house – try to find anything that might give us some kind of idea as to where they've gone – particularly Roger. If it looks like the wife and kid have already gone somewhere safe without him, great, we'll leave them to it. And keep the lights off. We're gonna have to do this in the dark."

"I'm not an idiot, Tom."

He grins again, then leaves her in the kitchen. He does a sweep of the rest of the house, starting downstairs and working his way up. He sees framed pictures of the family. Lily and Elijah – Tom can now put faces to the names Roger gave him. The order of the picture frames on the wall down the hall leading to the front door makes Tom feel like he's taking a tour through Elijah's life, from birth up to the present. Tom remembers Roger saying he's six now. The most recent picture looks to be of the three of them on vacation somewhere. They're standing in front of a cabin, which is on a waterfront, all three of them smiling back into the camera.

Tom goes upstairs. He's sure the house is empty, but he takes his time, is quiet about it. Reaches the top of the stairs and looks around. Checks the boy's bedroom first. Is careful not to knock over the action figures stood posing on top of his drawers. Tom looks inside the drawers and under the bed. He's not sure what he's looking for exactly, but if Roger is hiding anything, there's a chance he's tried to conceal it in his son's room, likely thinking no one would look here.

The room is clear. He takes a quick look in the bathroom, checks the medicine cabinet, then goes into the master bedroom. Much like in Elijah's room, the bed is made. There are no dirty clothes strewn across the floor. The place looks like a show home. Tom checks under the bed and in the bedside tables. Looks in the wardrobe, too. There's nothing. On Lily's side of the bed (he knows it's hers from the contents of the bedside table), there is a framed photo beneath the lamp. It catches Tom's eye. He picks it up. It's the same location as one of the pictures in the hall downstairs. The same waterfront cabin. In this picture, Elijah is a baby. Roger is slimmer, and his hair is a little thicker. Lily has always looked the same. She takes care of herself.

Tom puts the picture back, but he holds the image of it in his mind. He wonders if they own it. If it's a holiday home. He wonders how many people know about it, and if that's where they are now.

He goes back downstairs, to the kitchen.

"How's it look?" Emma says.

"Clear," Tom says. "You get anything?"

"I know where he works." She reaches into a drawer she has left half-open and pulls out a handful of letters. They've already been opened, most likely by Roger, and stored away for safekeeping. They all have the same letterhead. It's the name of an accounting firm in Valdez. Tom takes one of the letters and checks the contents. It's an internal memo. Nothing of great importance. He slides the letter back inside the envelope and puts them back in the drawer.

"Good," he says. "That's where we'll go next, in the morning. I don't expect anyone's still gonna be in the office at this hour. We'll see if any of his co-workers have any idea where he might have gone to."

"We got a plan to get them to trust us enough to tell us where he might be, *beyond* just saying 'please'?"

"I'll persuade them," Tom says. "It won't be my first time."

"You're gonna turn on the charm?"

"I can be very charming. You know that."

"Uh-huh, and look where it's got me. Listen, I've got a better idea. I know a guy. He's an old friend. He can set us up with a...a *prop* that's gonna make Roger's co-workers trusting us a whole lot easier. And plus, it's getting late, and I'm tired, and he'll put us up for the night."

"Where is he?" Tom says. "He ain't back in White Spruce Hill, is he?"

"Nope," Emma says. "Not for a while now. These days, he's right here in Valdez."

22

Councilman Brandon Manning's house is the biggest chalet Yuri has ever seen. It looks like it belongs up in the mountains, catering to skiing tourists from far and wide. This is not Yuri's first visit. He has been a few times before, though not as often as Fedorov. Fedorov, however, has never come with an invitation. It's Alina's first time at the house, though. As they pull up in front of it, Yuri sees how she leans forward, closer to the windshield, her eyes wide to take it all in.

"One day," Yuri says, as he parks the car, "we will have a home far bigger than this."

"Yes?" Alina says, sitting back, facing him. "Are you planning on running for council?"

"I don't think they'd like my accent," Yuri says. "And Councilman Manning's wealth did not come from his political position. He was born into it. Besides, my ambitions are set far higher than that. Politicians all think they have power, but all they really have is the *illusion* of it. I have power. More than the councilman already, whether it be what he was born with or what he has gained in votes. And I will have more."

They get out of the car and go to the front door. Yuri notices that Mayor Pullman's vehicle is already here. No doubt the two of them are inside talking together. Talking about him.

Brandon himself answers the door when Yuri rings the bell. Brandon is in middle age, but has kept himself in good shape. He still has a full head of hair, and it is white – the proverbial silver fox. Holding onto his good looks is what proved to be his downfall. His expression falters a little, but he manages to smile for Alina's benefit. "Yuri," he says, nodding. "Ms. Sidorova, please come in."

Pullman, the mayor of Valdez, is seated on a chair by the roaring fireplace as they're directed into the lounge. He's younger than Brandon, but has not kept himself in shape as well as the councilman. His waistline is thicker, straining against the buttons of his shirt. His hair, however, has retained its natural color. There's a tumbler in his hand. It looks like he's drinking whisky. He doesn't make any effort to get up as they enter.

"Mr. Mayor," Yuri says to him, smiling.

Pullman nods.

"Has your lovely wife accompanied you tonight?"

"She didn't feel up to it," Pullman says. He's battling to control the way his mouth is twisting itself into a sneer. "She didn't feel up to being anywhere near *you*."

Brandon gets between them, holds up his hands. "*Please*," he says. "You're in my house. My wife is in the next room. Let's try to keep this civil, all right?"

As if she hears herself being referenced, Brandon's wife, Elizabeth, calls through. "Brandon? Is everyone here?"

Brandon shoots Yuri and Pullman a look, then calls to the door, "Yes, dear, everyone's here."

Yuri hears footsteps across the oiled wood floors. It sounds like Mrs. Manning is wearing heels. She steps into the lounge, beaming. She's wearing a loose flower-print dress. Her short hair is curled. Yuri sees she is indeed wearing heels, though they are barely an inch high. She has not aged as well as her husband. Despite being a couple of years younger than Brandon, she looks older. Any figure she may have once had is gone, and what it has become is concealed under billowing clothes. She's wearing a lot of makeup, but it cannot fully disguise the deepness of the lines around her eyes and mouth.

She comes to Yuri, smiling. "Mr. Ivanov," she says, "it's so good to see you again. It's been too long!"

"I thank you for welcoming me back into your home," Yuri says, returning her smile. "This is Alina."

Elizabeth takes Alina's hand, covers it in both of hers. "It's so nice to meet you, Alina. I've heard so much."

Alina plays her part. She smiles. "As have I, about you," she says. "It is so wonderful to finally be making your acquaintance."

"It's just a shame Mrs. Pullman is feeling under the weather," Elizabeth says, facing the mayor.

Pullman grunts. "She's also disappointed. She sends her apologies."

"Be sure to tell her I'm thinking about her. She'll be in my prayers."

"She'll appreciate that," Pullman says, then drains off his drink.

"And that she is in mine, also," Yuri says, winking at the mayor.

"Well," Elizabeth says, clapping her hands together, not noticing the way Pullman is staring daggers at Yuri. "Shall we eat? I sure hope you're all hungry. I know I am."

She leads the way through to the dining room. There's another fireplace in this room, keeping it warm. Yuri thinks there might be a fireplace in every room of the house. It's very cozy. He sees how Alina battles to stifle yawns in the heat.

They sit at the table, Brandon at the head. Yuri and Alina are to his right, Elizabeth is to his left. Mayor Pullman sits at the opposite end of the table. Elizabeth serves the food and fills their glasses. "I got vodka for you and Alina," she says to Yuri, pouring drinks. "I hope you like it. Brandon said that's what I should get."

"That's very thoughtful of you," Yuri says, lifting his glass. "Of both of you. But please, in future, don't put yourself out – I'll drink anything." He laughs, and Elizabeth and Alina join in. Brandon forces himself to chuckle. Pullman stares into the fire.

They have salmon, and make small talk while they eat. Elizabeth is very talkative. She doesn't know Yuri as well as her husband or Mayor Pullman do. Instead, in her blissful ignorance, she asks a lot of questions about Russia. About Moscow in particular. Yuri has to admit that he is impressed at the effort Alina puts in. Earlier, at home, he had not expected much from her. However, she is answering all the questions. She is smiling and attentive. She asks questions of her own, and looks suitably interested in the answers. She tells Elizabeth that the fish is delicious. Asks her if she prepared it herself.

"Oh, no," Elizabeth says. "I'm not any kind of chef. I certainly wouldn't want to poison our guests! No, we have a chef. He prepared it all. All I had to do was serve it!"

Pullman is not eating much. He pokes at his food, only occasionally puts something in his mouth. He is, however, putting away his drinks. He glances up at Yuri from time to time, when he feels his eyes upon him, watching, but he's quick to look away.

There is nothing wrong with Mayor Pullman's wife. She, much like her husband, is deeply uncomfortable being around Yuri. Their family has been threatened. The children have been sheltered from it, but Mrs. Pullman is aware. Fedorov paid them a visit, let them know how things would be going forward. Made it *very* clear to them. Yuri needed the mayor to play ball on a new apartment complex. He was blocking the contract, claiming its erection would destroy an area of natural beauty. This was a couple of years ago now. The complex is built, and the apartments are mostly all uninhabited. Yuri doesn't care about that, though. Selling them is not his business. Building them is.

Things wouldn't have had to get so nasty as Fedorov making threats, though, if the mayor only had some dirty laundry in his closet. A mistress, perhaps, or an affinity for boys. He didn't, though. His personal life was clean, much to his own detriment.

With Councilman Manning, however, it was not so difficult. There were rumors he was a womanizer. All Fedorov had to do was set the honey trap. Brandon fell into it with ease. The girl Fedorov hired to be the bait was sixteen. The whole sordid incident was photographed and recorded. Yuri still has the pictures, the video, and the audio. It didn't take much for the councilman to do as he was told, with the threat of these details hanging over him. Sure, the girl was legal in Alaska, and maybe she *did* look older than sixteen, but Brandon is in his fifties. He'd lose everything.

Funnily enough, since the blackmail began, the councilman seems to have discovered a whole new loyalty to his wife. Fedorov has been keeping tabs on him. He has not cheated, not once. He has resisted all temptations, as if doing better now will somehow erase what he has done in the past.

Yuri watches Elizabeth. Thinks how different she would be acting tonight if she were to see the pictures, or the video. If she were to hear the things her husband was saying to a girl young enough to be his granddaughter.

Elizabeth sees him looking. She smiles at him, before continuing her conversation with Alina. She's so sweet. She has no idea of how she has been betrayed.

They finish eating. Further polite small talk is made around the table while Elizabeth clears away the plates. When she is out of the room, Yuri looks at Alina, nods. It's signal enough. She understands what she has to do. She waits until Elizabeth returns and sits herself back down.

"Mrs. Manning," she says, her voice practically a purr, "you have such a beautiful home. If it is no trouble, I would love to take a tour of it?"

Elizabeth's smile never falters, but she glances at Brandon. She understands. "Of course, dear," she says, standing back up and coming round the table to take Alina by the arm. "Let's leave the men to talk shop while I show you around."

Yuri watches them leave. He can hear Elizabeth's voice as they pass through the foyer. She's telling Alina about the house's architecture. Yuri goes to the door, closes it. "Gentlemen," he says, turning back to the room.

"I'm gonna need another drink for this," Pullman says, scraping his chair back and stumbling to the drink cabinet in the corner of the room.

Yuri thinks he's had enough, but he doesn't waste his breath telling him so.

"All right," Brandon says, not shifting from his chair at the head of the table. "What'd you call us here for? What do you want?"

Yuri returns to his seat, and waits for Mayor Pullman to get back to his. He's taking his time. Yuri clears his throat to prompt him. He sees how Pullman's shoulders hunch at the sound.

Yuri would have liked to have had the governor present for this. He'll make do with the tools available to him. He always has.

Pullman sits back down, taking a long drink as he does so. There are thick beads of sweat on his brow. Yuri begins. "The Trans-Alaska Pipeline System," Yuri says.

"The pipeline?" Brandon blinks. "What of it?"

"I won't ask if you know of it," Yuri says. "Of course you do. Several hundred miles of feeder pipelines. Eleven pump stations. Since it first began operating in nineteen seventy-seven, it has transported billions of gallons of crude oil from Prudhoe Bay all the way down to Valdez. Our home. *Adoptive* home, in my case."

"We don't need a history lesson," Pullman says, his voice gruff with the alcohol. "We're well aware of the fucking pipeline, and it's just as easy for us to get online and check the stats as it is for you."

Yuri continues, undeterred, as if making a presentation to his board members. "As with all progressive endeavors, it has not been without controversy. Ecological groups, environmentalists – the usual." Yuri waves his hand in the air. "They cause trouble, as they always do. There have been talks of expanding the pipeline over the years, but they have always met pushback and protests, yes?"

Pullman sighs. He's not impressed so far. This isn't anything he doesn't already know.

"Due to the length of the pipeline," Yuri continues, unperturbed, "it is impossible to secure, which leaves large sections of it unattended, sometimes for days at a time."

Brandon's eyes are narrowed. He's uncomfortable. It looks like he's worked out what Yuri is getting at faster than Pullman has.

"So, gentlemen, listen closely, please." Yuri leans on the table, looks at them both, makes sure he has their attention. He stares at Pullman until he finally looks up. "Here is what is going to happen. A section of the pipeline is unfortunately going to fall victim to sabotage – perhaps the work of one of these environmentalist groups? Who can say? But, when this has occurred, there will be a need for emergency and immediate rebuilding. When this happens," he indicates Brandon, "you will insist on calling in A1 Construction Services to save the day. As will the mayor." He indicates Pullman now. "With the sabotage happening so close to Valdez, you will feel *very* strongly about seeing to this matter as soon as possible. But do not worry, gentlemen, when you say the name of A1 Construction Services, you will find yourself with the support of a surprising number of your peers." Yuri grins. "The two of you are not the only ones Fedorov has paid a midnight visit to."

Neither of them say anything for a while. Pullman's mouth works like a fish out of water. Brandon is stony, ashen. They exchange glances.

Brandon is able to speak first. "The...the sheer damage this will cause..."

"My company shall also be employed to clean up the damage and the mess that shall no doubt occur."

Pullman is spluttering. "I can't – I can't even begin – I don't know what the *fuck* to say to any of this."

"You don't have to say anything, Mr. Mayor," Yuri says. "All you need to do is understand how much money you are to make from this. As I do, and as my friends back home do. Because, gentlemen, as we undertake the repairs, *that* is when we shall push forth on expansion. It shall finally come to fruition, and again A1 Construction Services shall be granted the contract to install it."

"This is insane," Pullman says. "You're out of your goddamn mind!"

"Mr. Mayor, please, lower your voice," Yuri says, speaking softly. "And do not ever talk to me in such a tone."

Pullman bites his lip.

"Do you even..." Brandon stops, swallows. "Do you even *know* anything about pipework?"

"Me? No, of course not. But that is why, six months ago, I bought a company that does. They have been integrated into A1 Construction Services. Like any good business, we are always looking for ways to expand."

Pullman has buried his face in his hands. He's shaking his head and muttering, "You're mad, you're mad," over and over.

Brandon covers his mouth and stares into the flames.

Pullman drags his hands down his face. "No," he says. "This is ridiculous. This is the craziest damn thing I've ever heard. Do you have any *idea* the ecological damage this will cause? No, of course you don't, because it's unimaginable! And even if you *could* somehow fathom it, I'm sure you wouldn't fucking care!"

"Mr. Mayor, please, I have asked you once already not to speak like this –"

"And you," Pullman says, rising to his feet and pointing at Brandon. "How can you be so quiet through all of this? Have you heard what he's proposing?" Pullman's voice is rising, getting louder. Soon, Alina will not be able to pretend to Elizabeth that she is sure it is something else.

"It is not a proposal, Mr. Mayor. Now please, calm down," Yuri says. "I have asked you many times already."

"Not a proposal?" Pullman says. "*Not* a proposal? Then what the hell is it?"

"They were instructions, Mr. Mayor. I told you, expected you to be paying attention."

Pullman throws up his arms. He wheels on Yuri, his eyes wild, a pointing arm outstretched, and he's about to say something, more than likely shout it, but before he gets a chance, Yuri is on his feet and has him by the throat. Anything he was going to say is choked off. Brandon watches them both, alarmed.

Yuri maintains the same even, calm tone he has kept throughout the evening. "Just because Fedorov is not here," he says, "do not make the assumption that I am lost without him."

Pullman's eyes bulge. His face is turning bright red.

Yuri squeezes. "Have you calmed yourself, Mr. Mayor?"

Pullman can't speak. Only choked little cries and gasps are able to escape him. He nods.

Yuri pushes him back down into his seat and lets go. Pullman sucks down air, rubbing his throat. He's wheezing. He starts coughing. Yuri straightens his suit, then sits back down. He takes a deep breath through his nose, then smiles at the mayor and the councilman once more.

"Now," he says. "Councilman, it would seem Mr. Mayor was not paying as much attention as he should have been. I'm sure you can fill in any blanks he may have after I have left. We will be going ahead with this plan in just a few short days, so be prepared at a moment's notice."

Brandon says nothing. He looks like he wants to throw up. Pullman is still rubbing his neck. His face remains red. The color is fading very slowly.

"I am sure that with this brief passage of time, you will begin to see things my way," Yuri says, standing and tucking his chair back in. He has said all he needs to say, and now he's ready to leave. "If not, well, ecological damage will be the least of your concerns."

mma's friend is called Steven Kane.

"This is his place," she says, pulling to a stop in front of a small, one-level home in a nondescript neighborhood. Tom follows as Emma gets out of the truck and leads the way to the door. He checks up and down the road and into the windows of the neighboring houses. The curtains are all drawn. It's late. It's likely that most of the people who live here are asleep.

There's a light on inside Steven's home, however. Tom can see it through the glass at the top of the front door, coming from the back of the house. He can hear music playing inside, too. It's turned up loud, but muffled through the wood. It's electro-heavy. Sounds like a rave in there. Tom doesn't recognize it. It's not the kind of thing he listens to. Emma knocks, hard.

"I don't think he's going to hear you over that," Tom says.

"You might be right." Emma pulls out her phone, searches her contacts until she finds Steven's number. She calls him. "Yo," she says, "turn down the music and answer the fuckin' door, will ya? It's freezing out here."

Inside, the music comes to an abrupt stop, and Tom can hear movement approaching. When it opens, a man as broad as he is tall, with long black hair and a thick beard, fills the frame. "Emma goddamn Raven," he says. "When I saw your name come up on my phone, I was all like, what the *fuck*?"

"It's been too long, Steve," Emma says, smiling. "I keep meaning to come visit, but you know I get busy back at home. Ain't nothing stopping *you* coming through that way, though, maybe visiting your folks like a good son or something."

"Uh-uh," Steven says, "I told you, when I got out of there, I was *out*, and staying out, and I intend to stand by that. And my folks can always come see me. They know exactly where I am – ain't my fault if they're too cheap to pony up for the gas."

They embrace each other in the doorway, and Emma introduces Tom. He and Steven shake. "Nice to meet you, man," Steven says. "Any friend of Emma's, et cetera. Come on in, you said you were cold."

Tom steps inside, looks over what he can see of the house. The living room is to the right, off the hall, and opposite it are two doors into what Tom assumes to be bedrooms. There's another door beside the living room, but it looks like a small area, and Tom imagines it has to be the bathroom. The light Tom could see through the glass is from the kitchen at the rear of the house.

"Come on through," Steven says, leading them to the back. "Make yourselves comfortable. You want anything? Drink? Food? I ain't got much, ain't been to the store in a while, but I got enough for us to have a good time."

The kitchen window is wide open, letting in cold, clean air, but Tom can still smell the marijuana that Steven has been smoking.

Steven notices him sniff. "We can smoke up, too, you like," he says. "That's the one thing I got plenty of." He grins.

"Not for me," Tom says. "Thanks."

Steven takes a seat at the table, leans back in it. He's so tall and wide the chair looks tiny beneath him, though it's of average size. "So," he says. "To what do I owe the pleasure?"

Emma takes the seat opposite him. Tom remains standing. He goes to the window, looks out into the backyard. The grass is covered in snow. He can see the outline of the houses behind Steven's.

"We need a favor," Emma says.

"Sure," Steven says.

"We need a couple of fake IDs."

"Way you're talking, I thought it was maybe gonna be something difficult," Steven says. "Having said that...are they for *you*? I'm just saying, buddy –" he looks at Tom "– you look old enough, and Emma, I know your age."

"We need PI licenses," Emma says.

Steven is intrigued now. "Private investigators? What're you up to?"

"We just need some people to talk. And they're maybe gonna be more liable to talk if they think it's for something official."

"It's maybe best we don't tell you too much about it," Tom says.

"All right," Steven says. "Sure. I can do that. It's gonna take a few hours, though."

"We've got all night," Emma says. "We need them by morning. Speaking of, it all right if we crash here?"

"Of course," Steven says. "You ain't even gotta ask. You can take the spare room. It's pretty clean. Been a while since anyone last stayed in there." He drums his fingers on the table. "I just need to get my tools, then I'll get started."

"What do you need from us?" Tom says.

"A picture," Emma says.

"Ah, she remembers," Steven says. "But a polaroid camera is one of my tools. Come with me, and let's get this thing done."

They follow Steven into his bedroom. He pins a white sheet to a wall in the corner of the room and positions them, one at a time, in front of it. Gets them to take off their jackets, get down to just T-shirts. He takes headshots from a distance.

"Still doing this the old-school way, huh?" Emma says.

"Why fix it if it ain't broken?" Steven says. "And to be honest, I don't get that many requests for fake IDs these days. Last one I had was a couple of weeks ago. This blonde chick, European, I think, she –"

"A *chick*, Steven?" Emma says. "Really?"

"It's been a while since we hung out at length," Steven says. "You're gonna have to forgive me. I've slipped back into sexist speech patterns." He looks at Tom, winks.

"I don't necessarily think it's sexist," Emma says. "I just think it's very demeaning, and I'm sure the lady in question wouldn't appreciate hearing herself referred to in such a manner."

Steven pauses. "Uh-huh," he says. "You want me to show you to the spare room, or do you think you can find it yourself?"

"I'm sure we'll manage to find our way around your mansion," Emma says.

Steven holds up the developing pictures. "I'll get to it, then," he says. He retrieves a bag from the back of his wardrobe. Tom guesses it to be the tools he earlier referenced. He takes a laptop from his bedside table, too. Carries it under his arm. "Don't worry, man," he says to Tom as he passes. "I'll be sure to photoshop out all those bruises you're wearing."

Tom and Emma go next door, into the spare room. There's a bed pressed up into the corner, but little else.

There's a poster of a naked cheerleader on the wall by the door. She has one pompom on her hip, and another behind her head. Emma is unimpressed. "Asshole," she says.

"How do you know him?"

"High school," Emma says while she takes down the poster. "I'm not staring at this all night." It's thumbtacked to the wall. She's not gentle about tearing it down.

"Was he making fake IDs back in high school?"

Emma chuckles, rolling the poster into a tube and standing it up in the corner. "Yes," she says. "He learned how to do it from his uncle. Who, coincidentally, is in jail now for fraud, but that's a different story. Me and Steven had a little business going together. He made them, I sold them. I made sure to put the word around, and kids from Valdez would come all the way to White Spruce Hill to buy them. They had to sit on the bus for a *long* time just to reach us, all so they could drink a beer in their local bar."

"You've always had an entrepreneurial spirit, then," Tom says.

"You've gotta start somewhere," Emma says.

Tom goes to the window. It looks out into darkness down the side of the house. There's not much to see. He'd feel more comfortable if he had a view of the street. "We should sleep in shifts," he says. "To keep an eye on things. We don't wanna get caught unaware."

"All right," Emma says. She sits down on the edge of the bed.

Tom realizes how long it has been since he last slept. He's running on fading adrenaline. The bed looks very appealing. "I'm gonna take a walk around the neighborhood," he says. He needs to push through his exhaustion, just for a little longer. "Check it out, see how things are, make sure there's nothing outta place. When I get back, I'll take first shift."

Emma shrugs one shoulder, then lies back on the bed,

pulling the blanket over herself. "Suit yourself," she says, then rolls over and closes her eyes.

24

Fedorov travels with Teddy and Reagan. He sits in the back while they're in the front, taking turns to drive. Fedorov watches the tracker, gives directions. They are on Emma and the man's trail.

Fedorov has told Teddy and Reagan, "The two of you, this is your final chance, yes? You fuck up on a *drive*, then we will be having very serious conversation after."

They understand their situation. They've been decent heavies over the years, but they claimed to aspire to more. Fedorov has given them the opportunities, starting with taking Roger up the mountain, and they have done nothing but disappoint him so far. He has a feeling they will put extra effort in now. They don't want to upset him. They don't want to face his wrath.

The tracker has been stopped for a while now. It's in Valdez. It went by Roger's house first. Fedorov had already sent men by after Roger disappeared from the battle at the cabin. He knew there was nothing worth seeing there. He instructed Teddy and Reagan to keep their distance, and left Emma and the man to it. Let them look – he was satisfied just to know that he is right, that they *are* looking for Roger. This left him more intrigued as to where they were going next, wondering if they'd found some kind of clue that his men had missed.

And now they're there, wherever it is.

They reach the street as the man steps out of the house. "Stay back!" Fedorov says. "Don't let him see you."

Teddy is driving. He kills the lights and rolls into an empty driveway, like they're just getting home. Fedorov looks back. He sees the man walking down the street, away from them, his hands in his pockets. He's subtle about it, but Fedorov sees how he turns his head, how he's looking into every car, into every house. When he disappears around the corner, Fedorov instructs Teddy to take a drive by the house, but then to turn them around.

"I want to take a look at it," he says.

Teddy does as he's told. While they approach, Fedorov reaches into his electrical bag on the seat beside him. He takes out a wall listening device. It will allow him to hear through the walls and through the windows. It has a recorder in it. They won't need to hang around. Fedorov is hopeful that tonight is the night he will learn his enemy's name. They get to the house. They can see Emma's truck parked outside.

"Go on down the road," Fedorov says, getting out of the truck. "Get far. Do not let the man see you. I will catch you up when I am done here."

Fedorov goes down the side of the house, starting on the right. None of the curtains are drawn. He can see into the living room. It's empty. Around the back, he looks into the kitchen. There is a man at the table with long dark hair. He's wearing headphones and nodding his head along to the music. He's working on something at the table, leaning in close over it, his hair concealing what it is.

Fedorov goes down the other side of the house. The left

side, if he were facing it straight on. He can see into one bedroom, but it's empty. The room next to it, the curtains are drawn. There is a light on inside. He's able to see through a gap in the fabric. He can see the back of Emma's head. She's curled up on the bed, sleeping. There is no sign of Roger. Whatever this place is, it is not where he is hiding out.

He takes the wall listening device from his pocket and attaches it under the sill beneath the window. He turns it on, then goes to leave.

Footsteps are coming down the street, returning to the house. They're very light, but Fedorov has been trained to listen for such things. He glides back into the darkness, disguises himself in the shadows.

It's the man. His enemy. He walks by the house. Fedorov does not hear the door open. He doesn't go straight inside. He's checking the perimeter.

Fedorov smiles to himself, feels the burns on his face pull tight. It would be so easy. To just stay right here, in the shadows. To ambush him. Kill him. Were it not for the explosion at the cabin, the man would be dead already. He runs his tongue over the burns on the corner of his mouth.

But Yuri wants Roger. The man will lead Fedorov to Roger.

Fedorov resists the temptation. He slides back out of the alleyway down the side of the house, back out onto the street. He keeps walking, until he finds Teddy and Reagan waiting for him.

"We do not need to hang around here," he says, getting into the back. "They will be spending the night, I think. We will watch them on the tracker, make sure they are not surprising us."

"What're we gonna do instead?" Reagan says.

"I am hungry, boys – are you not hungry? Come, we go

eat. I see a gas station on the way here, with a diner next to it. We go there."

Fedorov keeps an eye on the tracker as they go. It doesn't move. It takes them twenty minutes to go back to the gas station they passed on the way in. He gives Teddy and Reagan the tracker and sends them into the diner. "Watch this," he says. "I am going to use bathroom." He starts off across the gas station forecourt.

"They'll have a bathroom in the diner," Teddy says, confused.

"I will use this one. Order for me when you are in. Hamburger." He continues on. He has his electrical bag with him. It contains the cream for his burns. He does not want anyone to walk in on him while he is applying it. He thinks the gas station bathroom, down the side of the building, will be quieter.

It's empty when he walks in. It's plain to see that there is not much care taken of this bathroom. If it has a cleaner, they do not come by regularly. It stinks of piss and shit. The tiles on the ground are wet, and the walls are covered with graffiti. They are not the most sterile conditions, but Fedorov does not intend to roll around in them. All he needs is privacy, and a mirror. Even the cracked one he settles on will do. He balances his electrical bag on the edge of the sink, unzips it and takes out the cream. He squeezes some out onto his hand and begins rubbing it into his burns. They sting at first touch. They always do. They soon go numb.

The door opens. Fedorov pretends not to notice. He does not want to be seen at his most vulnerable, but if he must, then he will not rise to it with embarrassment.

Footsteps traipse across the wet floor. Fedorov can see the man in the mirror's reflection. He is on his way to the urinals. There is something off about his movements. He's drunk, or at least he's had a few drinks. Enough to impair his faculties.

He stops, seems to realize Fedorov is there. He turns, watches him, watches what he is doing. He leans in for a better look.

"Well, *shit*, man," he says. "Who gave you the Freddy Krueger treatment?"

Fedorov grunts. "Just an accident, my friend. Merely an accident."

The man frowns. "That accent," he says. "You a Russki?" He's grinning. "Holy shit, *comrade*. What're you doing all the way out here?"

"All the way out here? We are not so far from Russia, my friend."

"This some Red Dawn kinda shit?" The man chuckles, clearly finding himself very funny. "You infiltrating, that it? You one of the scouts, leading the way?"

"Mm," Fedorov says, continuing to apply his cream. "This is exactly right, my friend."

"You keep saying that, man. I ain't your fuckin' *friend*. Why'd I wanna be friends with a fuckin' Russki?" He shakes his head. "What happened to you, anyway? You making vodka? It blow up in your face?"

"Something like that," Fedorov says. He's staring at the man now.

The man sees his eyes in the reflection for the first time. They cut him silent, if only for a moment. "Whatever, man," he says. "Fuck you. I'm just making conversation. You ain't gotta be such an asshole about it." He continues on to the urinals.

Fedorov sucks his teeth. He rubs in the last of the cream while the man pisses. Fedorov looks to the urinal. The man is zipping himself back up. Fedorov steps close behind him.

"You need to clean up, *comrade*," he says. "Allow me to help you."

He grabs the man by the back of the head, slams his face into the tiles. He hauls him away, toward the stalls. Throws him through the door. The man loses his legs, goes down. Fedorov sees into the piss- and shit-stained toilet bowl. He grabs the man again, forces his face into the water, and begins to flush it, over and over, drowning him.

The man's thrashing body starts to go limp. Fedorov pulls him out, hauls him up to his feet. "Goodness, my friend," he says, shaking him. "You were so close to drowning. It is such a good thing I am here to pull you out, yes?"

The man is gasping. He can't see for all the water in his eyes. He's coughing it up from his lungs. Fedorov drops him, leaves him on the ground next to the toilet.

Fedorov exits the bathroom. Grabs his electrical bag on his way past. Outside, in the clean air, the smell of the antiseptic cream is strong in his nose. It always is when he's freshly reapplied it. It will not take long for him to get used to it again.

He strides into the diner, whistling to himself. Teddy and Reagan have a booth at the back. His food has already arrived.

"It just came," Reagan says as he sits.

"Excellent," Fedorov says. He notices how they sniff, smelling his cream. They don't say anything about it. "I have worked up such an appetite, yes?"

25

Tom would like to leave straight away, but knows there's no point. It's still early, and there won't be anyone at the office.

Steven makes breakfast. "I've got eggs," he says. "And they're still fresh, so we're in luck."

While they eat, Tom checks the IDs Steven has made for them. He's managed to get rid of the bruises and cuts on Tom's face, just like he said he would.

"Impressive, huh?" Steven says, wriggling his eyebrows.

"It looks like it'll pass," Tom says.

"They always do," Emma says.

They say their goodbyes, Emma and Steven embracing at the door, Tom shaking his hand, then they get back on the road. They head to Roger's workplace. The IDs, and their story, get them through reception with ease. Gets them directions up to the floor where Roger's office is. They step out of the elevators and walk down the center of the floor, lined on either side by cubicles and offices. They find Roger's and flash the IDs at his secretary. She looks concerned. "Yes?" she says. "Is this about Mr. Noakes?"

"That's very astute, ma'am," Emma says, her voice deep and official. Tom feels she may be laying it on a bit thick, but he leaves her to talk. He sees the way the secretary side-eyes him, and the wounds on his face.

"Where is he? Is he all right?" the secretary says. "No one's heard from him. We're getting worried now. This isn't like him. He never even takes a sick day."

"Have you called the police?" Emma says.

The secretary blinks. "You're not the police?"

Emma shows her the ID again. "Private investigators, ma'am."

"Oh. Oh, well, not yet – do you think we should? It's probably been long enough, right? They say you have to leave it at least twenty-four hours, but it's been longer than that now."

"Well, how about you just hold tight for the time being, wait and see what we can turn up." Emma pockets her ID again. "A distant aunt of Roger's has died, a Ms. Cecilia Noakes. She lived in Oregon, and we understand they hadn't seen each other since Mr. Noakes was a boy. But, in her will, she divided up the inheritance between all of her surviving nieces and nephews, having no children of her own. She's left him a substantial amount of money."

"Oh?" the secretary says.

"That's right," Emma continues. "We've been hired to find him and to relay the good news, but we went by his home and he's not there."

"Well, I wish I could help –" the secretary says.

"You don't know where he's gone?" Emma says.

"What about where he *might* be?" Tom says.

She looks at him. It's clear she's alarmed by the cuts and bruises. They scare her.

"As my colleague suggests," Emma says, seeing the look the secretary gives Tom, "is there perhaps anywhere you know of, perhaps somewhere Mr. Noakes doesn't like too many people knowing about, in case they should try to contact him while he's on vacation?"

The secretary avoids looking at Tom while Emma is talking. "I'll have to think..." she says.

"If you could," Emma says. "It would be a big help to us."

Tom thinks Emma is going to give the secretary a number where she can get in touch with them later, when she's had a chance to try to remember. Tom would rather they got some kind of an answer now. They don't have the time to wait around. He thinks about the pictures he saw back in Roger's home. The family portraits in front of the cabin – Elijah growing up in each subsequent one.

"What about a cabin?" Tom says. "A holiday home? Somewhere nice and quiet, secluded, hidden away."

The secretary frowns at first, but then he sees a light go off behind her eyes. "Well," she says, "there *is* Mr. Robinson's cabin – he's one of Mr. Noakes's clients. He lives in Canada most of the year, but he has a place in Anchorage. He's very fond of Mr. Noakes. He lets him use the cabin. Mr. Noakes takes the family there at least once a year."

"That sounds like a good place for us to start," Emma says. "Do you have an address?"

The secretary starts searching in her desk, pulling open drawers. "It'll be here somewhere," she says. "Just give me a second."

Emma and Tom exchange looks, like this might be a good lead. Right now, it's their only one.

"Ah, here's my address book," the secretary says, straightening back up in her chair. She flicks through it. She starts reading it out loud.

Emma cuts her off. "How about you just write it down for us."

"Of course," the secretary says. She finds a piece of paper, writes down the address, and hands it over. "If Mr. Noakes *is* at the cabin," she says, brow furrowed, "why do you think that might be? It's not his vacation time. If he's ill, he should still be at home. Why do you think he might've run all the way to Anchorage and not told anyone?"

"I wouldn't like to guess," Emma says, pocketing the address. "But I'm sure his reasons aren't as bad as anyone might worry."

"I hope not," the secretary says. "If you find him, please tell him to get in touch with us. We're all worried sick. I even drove by his home last night, just to see if he was there."

"We'll be sure to let him know how everyone is feeling," Emma says.

26

They leave the office and get back on the road. Emma sets up the map on her phone again. "I need to stop somewhere and buy a charger," she says, "something I can plug into the lighter, otherwise I'm gonna run out of battery."

"I'm sure there's a shop somewhere around here," Tom says.

Emma finds an electrical store and goes inside. Tom stays in the truck. He watches the road. It's quiet. No one is coming. Keeping one eye on the side mirror, he reaches into his bag. Checks his burner phones. They have signal here. No one's tried to reach him. The Santa Muerte pendant catches his eye. He takes it in his hand, holds it. Strokes the scythe she carries. She makes him think of Alejandra. He has avoided thinking of Alejandra while he has been with Emma. He has not looked at her picture so much, though he has it with him, here, in this bag. Within easy reach.

He thinks of a crazed Russian with a half-burnt face, looking for them.

A Russian who, had Tom not laced the cabin with explosives, would have killed him.

Tom puts the pendant over his neck, tucks it under his shirt. Feels its hard edges press cold against his chest. He zips up the bag as Emma returns to the truck.

"Got one," she says, plugging it into her phone and then into the lighter.

"I can drive if you like," Tom says. "You've been behind the wheel a while now."

"Uh-uh," Emma says, pulling away and getting back on the road. "I've seen how you handle other people's things."

Tom checks the map on her phone. "Says it's a five-hour drive to Anchorage."

Emma nods. "Yeah, but let's be honest – condition of the roads, the traffic, the weather, it's probably gonna take us longer. Best we try to get comfortable, and in a couple of hours we keep our eyes open for somewhere to eat."

"You spent much time in Anchorage?"

"Not really," Emma says. "I've been once or twice, but I've never had much reason to go. You?"

"Not to Anchorage, no." Tom keeps an eye on the mirrors as they drive, watching the vehicles that appear behind them.

"Uh-huh. I've been thinking – it was pretty much non-stop yesterday, so I ain't had a chance to ask. You were *supposed* to tell me on the way to Valdez, but don't think I didn't notice how you managed to stay quiet on that. But we've got a long drive ahead of us now. I think maybe it's a good idea for you to tell me a little more about yourself than you've shared so far."

"Like what?"

"Like how you learned to handle explosives." She shoots him a look. It's too soon for her to be over it. Tom probably has a lot more of these looks waiting in his future.

"I was in the army," he says.

"Well, let's talk about that."

"I don't like talking about it."

She looks at him again. "Then it's gonna be a *long* drive."

"You could always turn the radio on."

Emma does not turn the radio on. They drive in silence for a while.

Eventually, she speaks again. "How long ago did you leave the army?" she says. "You go straight into traveling right after you got out, or...?"

Tom sighs. "You're not gonna let it go, are you?"

"You blew up my cabin, Tom. I think you owe me a story, at the *least*."

"All right, fine. You have a point with that."

"I should've played the destroyed cabin card sooner."

"You wanna be careful not to overplay it."

"No such thing, my friend. You know why? Because you blew up my cabin, that's why." She's grinning while she says it.

Tom laughs. "All right. This isn't gonna be as long a story as you're hoping." He doesn't intend to tell her everything. The past is the past, and that's where he'd rather leave it. He's done a lot of things he's not proud of, and seen a lot of things he'd rather forget. "I left the army a long time ago. I was recruited into the CIA."

"Well, *shit*," Emma says, eyes wide. "You have my attention, Mr. Rollins."

27

Alina sits on the leather sofa pressed against the wall in Yuri's office. She sips a drink and flicks through a fashion magazine. She looks bored.

Yuri ignores her. He has a lot more on his mind than worrying about how Alina is managing to entertain herself. He has boredom enough of his own. Currently, he catches up on paperwork. He signs his name, over and over again. When he's done with this stack, he has the checks to fill out. It will be a long day of signing his name.

His phone rings. It's Fedorov. An update, no doubt, and a welcome interruption. "Yes?"

"I have a name," Fedorov says, his tone jovial. "*Tom*."

"No surname?"

"Tom *Rollins*. Emma, she called him Mr. Rollins last night, while they were talking."

Yuri frowns. "How did you hear this?"

"They went to a friend's house, stayed there. His name was Steven. I placed a bug outside the window, picked it up this morning. I've just finished listening to the recording it made."

"Are they on the move?"

"We're following them. They stopped by Roger's place of work, and then they continued on the route. This is promising, yes? We've been driving a couple of hours now. It seems they are going to Anchorage."

Yuri considers this. "You think Roger may be there?"

"If he's not, I hope Tom Rollins finds it to be very beautiful, for it will be the last place he sees. I will kill him. I will kill both of them, him and the woman, for wasting my time."

"Then how would you find Roger?"

"I will find him somehow. Do not worry. It will take a long time, perhaps, but I will find him eventually. But, that being said, I am thinking he will be in Anchorage. It is good place to hide, yes?"

"It's a very good place to hide," Yuri says.

"I feel this may be end of line for our journey."

"How are your burns, Fedorov?"

"Ah, they are fine," Fedorov says. "They are nice and crispy now, yes? Ha, no, the cream is keeping them soft, but I think they are healing."

"Okay. Well, you will keep me updated. Let me know how it is going. Let us hope Anchorage is the end of the line."

"I will talk to you again soon, my friend."

They hang up. Yuri feels a sense of satisfaction come over him. Fedorov is closing in. Soon, he will have both Roger and this Tom Rollins. He'll have the woman, too – Emma Raven – though Yuri does not have much use for her, nor for Roger's family. He supposes, as Fedorov would say, they are loose ends. He will leave Fedorov to deal with them. He will not think on them too much.

He looks at Alina. She is still focused on the magazine. If she was listening in, she is doing well at hiding it. "Did you hear?" he says.

She looks up slowly, finishing the line she is reading. "Hear what?"

"I was talking to Fedorov."

"Oh." She grunts.

"He thinks he is near the end of his journey. Soon, we will know."

She's silent a moment, then says, "That's good."

"Indeed. Once it is over, you will not need to accompany me into the office every day. You will get your valued *freedom* back."

She forces a smile, though it is on her face for only an instant.

Yuri watches her. She starts to turn her attention back to the magazine. He runs his tongue around the inside of his mouth. "Of course, I have enjoyed having you with me," he says. "Perhaps we should draw it out a little longer?"

He doesn't get as much of a reaction as he was expecting. Alina already looks defeated, and nothing changes about this. "As you wish," she says.

Yuri's eyes narrow. He is losing patience with her. She always looks so miserable. He cannot stand it. "I did not bring you to America to just sit around with your face like this all day."

"With my face like what?" she says, putting the magazine down now and turning to him fully.

"As if you see nothing but dark clouds. As if your life is some great hardship, and I do not give you all that you ask for and more."

"Mm." Alina is silent for a moment, as if she's deciding something. She drains off her drink, still thinking. Finally, she places her hands on her knees, her decision reached. "You brought me here to decorate your arm. You brought me here to impress your friends, and raise the envy of your enemies. You brought me here to fill your bed, and to fulfil all the duties being in it entails. And sometimes it feels like you brought me here to hold me as a prisoner."

Yuri does not appreciate her candor. He feels his patience evaporating, his temper rising. "You don't like it, go back to Russia. Go back to the shithole dirt town you came from before I found you."

"I was in Moscow. I did not need you," she says. "I was making my own way. But you promised me sunshine and freedom. You promised me a new way of life. You promised me I could be myself, and not some ideal of what you want me to be."

"You do not need sunshine," Yuri says. "The cold is in your blood, as it is in mine. And you have freedom – you have too much freedom, that you think you can talk to me like this."

Alina glowers at him. "I talk to you as you talk to me. What? You do not like it?"

Yuri stands, his fists slamming down on his desk as he does so, the papers before him ruffling, some of them scattering. "Do not push your luck, Alina." He feels the earlier sense of satisfaction, after the call with Fedorov, ebbing away, almost gone. "You will talk to me with respect. You will know your place."

"I know my place," Alina says. "On my knees, at your feet." Her lips twist into a sneer, and she reminds him of Mayor Pullman the night before.

Yuri comes around the desk, marches across the room to her. "I will not warn you again."

Alina remains seated. She looks up at him. Her sneer turns into a small smile. A provocative smile. "But you adore warning me, Yuri," she says. "Sometimes, I feel like if you are not warning me, we are not talking."

He strikes her. The back of his hand connects with her

face with a resounding clap that echoes around his office. She is thrown back into the sofa, her face turned away from him.

Yuri waits, his eyes on her. He is breathing hard, angered. He grabs the back of her head by her hair, hair so fine it is like silk. He almost rips it from her skull, turning her round to face him. There is blood at the corner of her mouth, where his knuckles have mashed her lips against her teeth. It is incredibly red against her pale skin. "*Know* your place, Alina," he says. "Do not talk to me like that. Do not look at me like that. Do you see what you are making me do? If you were to behave, I will not need to be so stern with you. Are you understanding?"

She manages to nod. Her eyes are lowered, avoiding looking into his. He lets go of her. She lowers her face now, keeps it away from him.

Yuri looms over her. "Go and clean yourself up," he says. "Do not let anyone see you. Then come back here – *straight* back here. I will be timing you, Alina. Five minutes."

He does not move as she stands. She has to squeeze by him. He watches her go, a bad taste in his mouth. He goes to the bar and pours himself a drink. A vodka. It burns the taste away. He checks his watch. She has a few minutes. He returns to his desk. His mind is racing too much to return to the paperwork just yet. He clasps his hands and watches the door. Keeps track of the time. Waits for her to return. He's all worked up.

She makes it back within the window he has granted her. She avoids his eye. She continues on to the sofa, back to her magazine.

"Come here," he says.

Alina does as she's told. Her face remains lowered. She stands before him at the side of his desk, right next to his chair. He gets to his feet, then turns her away from him. He bends her over the desk. She knows what is coming. She grabs the edges of the desk to brace herself.

Before he begins, before he even lifts her dress, Yuri leans in close to her. His mouth is by her ear. "You belong to me, Alina," he says. "You are mine. Do not ever forget that." He waits a moment for this to sink in. "Have you never asked yourself, what became of the woman you replaced? She did not go back to Russia. She has never left America, though you could never find her."

She is stiff beneath him. Her eyes are closed. She sniffs. He sees a tear fall onto the desk below, onto a sheet of paper, soaking it through.

"Say it," he says.

"I..." There is hesitancy. She has to swallow, to clear her throat. "I am yours," she says. "I belong to you."

Yuri strokes the side of her face. "That is right," he says. "Good girl."

28

I t hasn't been easy, but Roger and Lily have been doing their best to pretend, for Elijah's sake, that nothing is wrong. That everything is normal. That it's not at all out of the ordinary for them to up and take a spontaneous vacation to Mr. Robinson's cabin in Anchorage. They can hide the truth from him. He's a child. It's easy. Maybe he gets the sense that something is wrong, but he's not going to question it. He's happy to go along with whatever they tell him.

Lily, however, is not so easily misled. Roger had to come clean to her, as soon as they reached the cabin and put Elijah to bed.

"Tell me," she said, in the truck – Tom's truck – on the way here. "We've got a long drive. Tell me."

Elijah was sitting between them. He wasn't sleeping, despite how long they'd already been traveling. He was alert, watching through the windshield, seeing the snowy fields they were passing by.

"Not right now," he said, nodding at their son between them.

Lily shot him a look, unimpressed. She wanted to know the truth.

So he told her, last night, when Elijah was asleep. Told her everything he had kept from her so far. How he'd been forced into laundering the money of a gangster with connections to the Russian Mafia. "They made me do it," he said. "There was a gun to my head, Lily – a literal fucking gun to my head, the first time. So I did it, because, I mean, what choice did I have?" He held out his hands, helpless, then let them fall.

"You could've said no," Lily said, as if it were that simple. "You could've gone to the police."

Roger laughed, though it was without humor. "That what you think, huh? You think that would've made it all go away? Ha, you think Yuri doesn't have connections in the police? You think they wouldn't cover for him? And hell, even if they *were* to do something, his men would still be out there. They'd come after us. It isn't so straightforward as just saying no, or going to the cops. The fact they chose me in the first place sealed our fate – *all* of our fates. Mine, yours, and Elijah's. I had to do this, to keep us all safe."

"*Why'd* they pick you?" she said.

Roger shook his head. He'd asked himself the same question so many times. "Just bad luck, on my behalf," he said. "A1 Construction Services came with an account, and it was given to me. Yuri obviously liked my work." In truth, he'd invited Roger out to dinner. Roger hadn't thought anything of it. It wasn't uncommon to be rewarded for a job well done – as evidenced in the usage of Mr. Robinson's cabin. At the dinner, Yuri asked him strange questions, asked him if he knew about laundering money. If he understood how it worked. Of course Roger knew. It was his job to know about such things.

Looking back, Roger should've played dumb. Should've made like he didn't know a thing about it. *Sorry, Mr. Ivanov, but all my customers are law-abiding citizens, and I've never had any need to know about such things.*

After the meal, Yuri insisted on driving Roger home. Roger said he'd call a taxi, but Yuri wouldn't hear otherwise. As Roger got into the back, Fedorov was already there, waiting. He was smiling. There was a gun in his hand.

"You will be laundering my money for me going forward, Mr. Noakes," Yuri said, following him into the car and sandwiching Roger between the two Russians. "I trust there will be no issues with this arrangement?"

Lily was silent for a while, before she finally asked, "Did they...have they threatened Elijah?"

Roger took his time answering. "Yes," he said. "There's no point lying to you, not now. They threatened him, and they threatened you."

They slept in the same bed that night, at first, but Lily kept her back to him. Roger left her alone. He couldn't sleep. He lay awake all night, listening to the house, terrified every time he thought he heard a footstep outside, crunching through the snow, or the creaking of a floorboard. In the middle of the night, Lily got up and left the bed. She left the room. She went next door, into Elijah's room, and climbed in with him. Roger imagines this will remain the set-up going forward.

It's morning. Roger is alone in the kitchen, making coffee. Lily sits with Elijah in the next room, the two of them watching television.

"How long do we have to stay here?" Lily says, suddenly in the kitchen with him.

Roger gives a start. "I don't know," he says, catching his breath. "But we're safe here."

"For now, sure," Lily says. "But hiding out isn't any kind of plan. We need to get back to our lives eventually, Roger."

"Look, I just need some time to think, okay?"

"You've had long enough to think."

Roger does his best not to raise his voice. "Why do you think everything has such a simple solution? There's no quick fix to this, Lily. You think I've been doing anything *but* thinking about how we can resolve this?"

She doesn't say anything to this.

"I can't just go back to Valdez and put my hand on a Bible and swear to him I didn't take his money. That's not enough, even if I could prove who *did* take it. He's not gonna believe me anyway. Whatever happened to it, he's already made up his mind that I was involved. He's already tried to have me killed once."

"*Did* you take the money?"

Roger looks at her. It's clear she's wanted to ask this question since he first told her why they've had to go on the run, why they're having to hide out. "You think that if I took that money we'd still be in Alaska? We'd be *long* gone, Lily. Half a million dollars wouldn't last forever, but it would sure get us *far.*"

Lily chews the inside of her lip. Her arms are folded, like she can't shake a chill in the air. It's not cold in the cabin. It's warm. Almost hot.

"Do you want coffee?" Roger says.

She shakes her head, then drifts away, through into the living room with Elijah. Roger watches through the open door. He sees her sit down beside their son. Sees how Elijah smiles up at his mother.

Roger sighs, then finishes making coffee. He sits down at the table with it and rests his head in his hands. What he said to Lily was true – he hasn't stopped thinking about their next move. What it could be. What it *should* be. So far, he's got nothing. His head feels full of clouds. It can't get clear. Nothing comes through. Nothing makes sense. He wishes it could be so easy as just hiding out here, in Anchorage, finding a way to make this work, but he knows it can't. The cabin isn't even theirs, and Lily is right – they need to get back to their lives. Of course, if they go back to Valdez, they won't have much of a life to go back to.

"Roger," Lily says. There's concern in her voice. "Roger, come here. Quick."

He lets his hands fall from his face, and he sees stars from where he has been forcing his palms into his eyes. He goes into the living room. Lily is sitting up, turned to the window. "There's someone outside," she says. "A truck has just pulled up."

Roger's heart begins to hammer, and he can feel the coffee he just drank trying to crawl back up his throat. He goes to the window, to the side of it, and peers out. He sees the truck. The way the sunlight hits the windshield means he can't see inside it.

"Who is it?" Lily says, unable to hide her fear from Elijah. "What should we do?"

Roger hears his own breathing, ragged in his ears. The truck's doors open, on either side. A woman gets out from behind the steering wheel. She's Native American. He doesn't know her. He doesn't know any Native Americans. He clenches his jaw. Then he sees the passenger, the man.

It's Tom Rollins.

Roger isn't sure if this should make him any calmer.

Tom Rollins is looking right at his own truck, parked down the side of the cabin.

"Shit," Roger says.

29

Tom looks the area over and sees that his hunch was right. This *is* the waterfront cabin from the framed photographs back in the Noakes' house, and there's his truck parked down the side. Emma sees the truck, too.

"This must be the place," she says.

A door down the side of the cabin, near the truck, opens cautiously. Tom and Emma freeze. Tom's hand reaches back to the Beretta tucked into his waistband, ready to grab it.

Roger Noakes pokes his head out. "Hey," he says. He holds out an arm, and at the end dangle the keys to Tom's truck. "Are you here to take your truck back?"

Tom strides up to him and grabs the keys from his hand. He shoots him a look and Roger withers, shamefaced. "Yes," Tom says. "But we're also here to talk."

He notices the surprise on Roger's face, like he expected him to grab the keys and be on his way.

"May we come in?"

"Uh," Roger says.

A woman appears in the frame behind Roger. Tom recognizes Lily from the pictures in the house. No doubt Elijah is back there somewhere, too.

"Who is it?" she says. "Roger?"

"Just – just stay there, Lily. They're coming in." He steps back, into the house.

Tom follows him in, and Emma is behind him. "Let's all get ourselves acquainted," Tom says, then looks at Roger and adds, "and reacquainted."

Roger is looking at Emma. "Yeah," he says. "Let's."

They make their introductions. Tom and Emma shake hands with Lily. They avoid shaking Roger's. Neither of them is very pleased with him. He looks like he knows this, as he clasps his hands in front of himself and turns his face to the side.

"Look," Lily says, "I think it's best if I'm in the room to hear whatever we're about to talk about, but I don't want to take a risk on Elijah overhearing anything he shouldn't. So everyone just hang tight until I get back, okay?"

Tom nods. Lily leaves the kitchen and goes through to the living room. She tells Elijah he needs to play in his room for a while, and she accompanies him up the stairs to get him settled.

Roger rocks back and forth on his heels. "Um," he says. "Can I get either of you a coffee?"

"Water will be fine," Tom says.

"Same," Emma says.

Roger hurries to it, grabbing a pair of glasses and pouring them water from a bottle kept in the refrigerator. "How, um," he says, handing over the glasses. "How did you find me?"

Emma flashes her fake PI license. "We have our ways."

Roger leans in close. "Are those," he says, "are those *real*?"

Emma laughs.

"They're very convincing," Roger says.

"Your secretary sure thought so," Emma says.

"Ah," Roger says.

"Don't hold it against her," Emma says. "She's worried about you. Said she's even driven by your house."

"Oh, really? She said that?"

"Said she was gonna call the cops," Tom says. "We talked her out of it, for now. Something tells me the cops ain't gonna be much use in this situation."

"That's what he told *me*," Lily says, returning to the kitchen. "You agree with him on that?"

Emma tilts her head toward Tom. "That's what he seems to think."

Tom nods.

Lily looks between them. "The two of you want to sit? I think I want to be seated to talk about this."

They all sit together around the kitchen table. Tom clasps his hands atop it. Emma clasps hers loosely, an index fingernail scratching at the side of a thumb. Tom notices how Roger and Lily both sit with their hands under the table, between their thighs, their shoulders hunched. They're both wearing thick sweaters, despite how warm it is in the cabin.

"This place is, uh, it's bigger than I was expecting," Emma says, looking around the kitchen from her seat and through into the living room. "All the while we were on our way here, I kept imagining this dinky place, maybe smaller than mine."

Roger seems to realize something. "Oh," he says. "Was that *your* cabin?"

"Uh-huh," Emma says. "Made the mistake of renting it out to this guy." She motions toward Tom.

"How is it?"

"It's not there anymore," Emma says. "Well, I guess bits of it probably are, and they've probably stopped smoldering by now. I wouldn't know. I haven't been up there. Haven't had the chance yet. Been too busy trying to find you."

"I thought I heard – when I was going down off the mountain – I thought I might've heard an, an explosion. I wasn't...I wasn't sure..."

Tom watches him.

Roger can barely look his way. "How, um... How did you manage to...to get out of there?"

"He blew it up," Emma says. "Ain't you been listening?"

Lily looks between them all, her mouth slightly open. Tom doesn't think she's heard the story of the battle up at the cabin. In fairness, Roger wasn't around for most of it. He was just the instigator. He doesn't have any of the juicy details to tell.

"That's not important right now," Tom says. "What's important is what happens next."

"And what's going to happen next?" Roger says.

"That depends on you," Tom says. "What's *your* plan?"

Lily leans forward, to face her husband. Roger avoids her eye. Tom gets the feeling she's been asking him this exact same question. It's clear they can't hide here forever, especially not now that they've been tracked down once.

Roger doesn't say anything for a while. His hands are clasped together in front of his face now, his elbows on the table, like he's praying. Tom doesn't think he's praying. He's thinking. He finally lowers his hands, opens his eyes, takes a deep breath. "I don't...*know*, exactly, what I'm going to do next. Listen, okay, just hear me out. If I could, I'd go back to Valdez, I'd talk to Yuri, I'd tell him I didn't take his money – hell, I'd tell him I could probably even find out for him who *did* take it – but the truth is, he's not gonna listen to me. That's not how he operates. If he gets one thing in his head, he'll stick to it. As far as he's concerned, I'm the only one who had access to his money, therefore I'm the only person who could've stolen it, and because of that, he's not going to brook any excuses or reasoning."

"He'd rather kill you than take a chance on finding out

where his money actually is, and maybe getting it back?" Emma says.

"It's all about reputation," Roger says. "For him, half a million dollars is chump change. He's not really going to miss it. But he can't let it be seen that someone is able to steal from him and get away with it, even if he's blaming the wrong fucking person."

"Language," Lily says.

Roger waves her off. "He's not here, he can't hear us."

Tom assumes he's referring to Elijah.

Roger looks at them across the table, at Tom and Emma both. "Look, I'm sorry, but you're part of this now. You're in it. By now, he's going to know who both of you are. He's going to be looking for you, too."

"I'm guessing he's not planning on giving us a slap on the wrist, neither," Emma says.

"It could be worse," Roger says. "If Fedorov were still alive –"

"Fedorov's still alive," Tom says.

Roger looks at him. "But – but he was at the cabin! I assumed – I mean, I figured that since you're still alive, it must've meant that...that..."

"It very nearly went in his favor," Tom says.

"Who is *Fedorov*?" Lily says.

Roger ignores her. "Shit," he says. "If he's still alive, he's gonna be mad as hell that you got away from him."

"I didn't get away," Tom says. "I tried to take him out. I failed."

"What did you do?" Roger says.

"Jesus Christ," Emma says. "He blew up my cabin – how many times am I gonna have to say it?"

They talk around the table, but Tom isn't listening now. He's heard all he needs to. He's thinking. Out the corner of his eye, he sees Emma. He looks at her fully. She's in danger.

They're all in danger – Roger, Lily, even Elijah, upstairs, doing whatever it is he's doing. Whatever it is six-year-olds do when they're sent to their room and have to entertain themselves while the adults talk. It's Emma he fixates on. He thinks of Alejandra. Of how he wasn't there to save her. How he couldn't help.

"We're going back to Valdez," Tom says.

The table goes silent. All eyes turn to him.

Tom looks at Roger. "You and I, we're going back to Valdez. We're going to see Yuri, and we're going to straighten things out."

"Have you...have you not been listening to anything I've said?" Roger says. "He's not going to listen."

"He'll listen to me."

"What makes you so sure?"

Tom doesn't answer. He looks at Roger. Roger swallows.

"One way or another," Tom says, "this whole thing is going to come to an end."

Roger and Lily look at him for a while longer. A decision has been made. Something is going to happen. Roger has to clear his throat. "Wh-when?"

"Now," Tom says. "Sooner the better."

30

Tom takes Emma to one side while Roger and Lily talk in the living room. He thinks Roger is trying to persuade her that this is for the best, that everything is going to be okay. That before they know it, they'll be back in their own home, back to their lives. Lily is probably telling him to be careful, to watch out for himself. Telling him that she'll be worried about him. That she'll be thinking about him.

"I want you to stay here," Tom says to Emma. "With Lily and the kid."

"You don't need to try and protect me, Tom," she says. "I can take care of myself."

"I know," Tom says. "That's why I want you to stay here. Because I know you can look out for *them*, too."

The corner of Emma's mouth twists to the side. "You're trying to keep me out of the way. Trying to keep me safe."

Tom shakes his head. "No. Where I'm going, I'd rather have you by my side than *him*. But we've got to go, and we've got to leave them behind, and I'll feel a lot more comfortable

– and I'm sure he will too – knowing that there's someone back here who can watch over them."

Emma inhales deeply through her nose. "All right," she says. "Fine. You've convinced me. I'll stay here – but this time, you use your own truck. I'm not letting you trash anything else of mine."

Tom grins. He takes the Beretta from his waistband, hands it to Emma. "You know how to use this?"

"Yeah, I know."

"I hope you don't have to."

Emma takes the gun, tucks it into her own waistband. "You and me both," she says. She nods her head toward the living room, to Roger. "So how do you expect to smooth things over with his Russian boss?"

"Well, we could find out who's really responsible for stealing the money, but from what he said, it doesn't sound like that would make much difference. Yuri and his men would just keep coming until they get to make an example."

"So what's the alternative?"

"I go see this Yuri Ivanov in person, and persuade him that it's in his interest to back off. He has far more to lose in continuing to come after the Noakes, you, and me, than if he just cuts his losses now and backs off."

"You think he'll go for that?"

"I'll put the offer on the table. What happens next is up to him."

Roger comes back into the kitchen. "Okay," he says. "I'm, uh, I'm ready to go. I mean, if you are."

Tom nods. Emma leans in close and kisses him on the cheek. Into his ear, she says, "Be careful."

31

Fedorov looks ahead, to the cabin, where the tracker has stopped. It's been stopped for a while now. "Do not go any closer," he tells Teddy. "Hold back." He watches the cabin. Studies it. Something looks off. Emma's truck is there, setting off the tracker. It's the only vehicle present. There's nothing else. There's the chance Roger and his family got rid of whatever they came here in – or maybe even that they've gone out to get groceries, but there's nothing around here for miles and miles, and it will be gone for a while.

Fedorov opens his door. "Stay here," he says. "I am going in for a closer look."

He goes closer, stepping lightly over the snow, moving window to window on the ground floor. He finds them in the living room, watching the television. Little Elijah is lying on his belly on the floor in front of the roaring fireplace, filling in an image in a coloring book. Lily is on the sofa, chewing on a thumbnail, facing the television but not really watching it. Beside her is Emma Raven. She has her feet up on the table in front of them.

Fedorov thinks to himself that this is interesting. He is finding these two worlds colliding, but there is no sign of Tom or Roger. He has missed them, but they've left the women behind. Presumably they're planning on coming back at some point. He can't take a chance on how long that may take.

He can always ask the women where they've gone, and how long they intend to be.

He goes around the other side of the cabin, to where Emma's truck is parked. There are marks in the snow where another truck has recently departed. He imagines it driving off down the road. To where? Back the way they've already come? There is no tracker on this vehicle. Fedorov's best option is to talk to the women, but, as the Americans say, he doesn't want to put all his eggs in one basket.

He goes back to Teddy and Reagan, pulls open the door on Reagan's side. "They are gone," he says.

"Shit," Reagan says.

"Shit indeed," Fedorov says. "It looks like they went that way." He points. "Follow them."

Teddy and Reagan look at him like they think he's joking.

"I am not joking, my friends. Go after them."

"What –" Reagan says. "I mean, what are they driving? How are we supposed to know?"

"The truck Roger took from the cabin, yes? You remember it? I remember it."

"So we just go and hope for the best?" Teddy says.

"Stop talking now," Fedorov says. "Stop wasting time. Follow them. I want you on the road. We cannot let them get too far. You go after them, I will stay here. I will talk to the women – they are still inside. I will find out where they are, and I will be in touch with you. You go now, and you keep in touch with me. Keep me updated. Be fast – perhaps you will catch up to them."

Teddy and Reagan exchange glances.

"Do not look at each other – listen to me. Do as I say. Go. *Now.*"

Fedorov slams the door closed, and Teddy and Reagan finally set off. He watches them go. He'll give them an hour, to see if they are able to catch up with Tom and Roger. To see if Tom and Roger return to the cabin. After an hour, it will be dark.

And then, he will go inside.

32

Tom drives his truck back to Valdez. Roger sits beside him and looks awkward, keeping his hands clasped in his lap like there's a risk he might try to steal the truck again. They don't talk. Tom doesn't have much to say. He's helping, but he hasn't forgiven Roger for abandoning him at the cabin in the middle of what was his mess, and stealing Tom's truck to boot. He's helping because his conscience will not allow him to walk away from Roger's wife and small child being in danger.

"I'm, um, I'm sorry I took your truck," Roger says. He has no doubt guessed the cause of the uncomfortable silence between them.

"I've got it back now," Tom says. "No harm done."

"And I, uh, I mean..." Roger composes himself. "Thank you for helping us. Me, and my family. I – that is, *we* – we all really appreciate it."

"Save your thanks until we've seen this thing through," Tom says.

"Right," Roger says. "Okay. I get that. Don't count your chickens, right?"

"Right," Tom says. As always, he keeps an eye on the mirror, on the road behind them.

Roger stares out the window, then at the road ahead. His head is on a swivel. He drums his fingertips on his thighs. It's clear that he's nervous going back to Valdez. Clear that he's nervous in general. "I can find who took the money, y'know," he says, turning to Tom.

"That so?" Tom says. He doesn't take his eyes from the road.

"Yeah, absolutely." He leans forward, excitable suddenly. "If I thought Yuri would listen, I'd tell him as much. I could find out who really took his money. I could let him know. Then he could deal with who's really responsible. But like I said, he's not going to listen..."

"What would you need to find out the truth?" Tom thinks it might be worth having this information in their back pocket, just in case.

"A computer," Roger says. "I usually did all my work at the office. The laundering, I mean. I didn't want to do it at home."

"There a reason for that?"

"I just... I just didn't want Lily to find out."

"All right. When we reach Valdez, we'll head to your office."

Roger nods. "I can find the truth," he says. "I can. I'm sure I can..."

33

It's getting dark outside the cabin. Inside, the fire is still roaring. It's warm. It's cozy. Under different circumstances, Emma would very much like to sit back and relax and comfortably snooze in front of the television. But these aren't those circumstances, so instead she's on her feet, pacing the floor.

Elijah lies in front of the fire. He's been there for hours, filling in a coloring book, or writing stories in a little notepad, or flicking through a comic book. He's very well behaved, and seemingly unfazed by all that is going on around him. Lily confided to Emma, earlier, when they were both on the sofa, that Elijah doesn't know what is happening. He thinks they've just gone on a spontaneous vacation.

"He's always loved it here," she said, leaning in close to Emma, their shoulders touching. "Whenever we've come up in the past, he hasn't wanted to leave. He's asked us before, why can't we live here instead." Lily watched her son while she spoke. She was smiling.

Emma steps up to a window, looks out, down to the water. It's a lake. It's very still. She can imagine in the summer, when the sun is shining, that the lake is full of swimmers and boaters, perhaps a couple of Jet Skis. She can see it vibrant with life. Right now, it's dead. It's quiet. There is no life upon the water.

She sighs. She hopes this will all be over soon. She wants her life back. She wants to get back to how things were – running her business, spending her evenings in the bar listening to bad music performed by bad bands, and occasionally running into a handsome drifter with whom she can pass a few pleasant evenings.

She'd like her cabin back, too. But one thing at a time.

"It'll take them a few more hours before they get back to Valdez," Lily says. She's on the sofa still. She hasn't moved in a while. She's putting on a good show of being calm, most likely for Elijah's sake.

Emma nods. She knows this. "That doesn't make me any less antsy," she says.

"Just sit down and try not to think about it," Lily says. "That's all we can do now. Try not to think about it, and hope everything is back to normal soon. By the time we wake up tomorrow morning, it could all be over and done with, right?"

"I doubt I'll be able to sleep tonight," Emma says. "And I don't know what Tom is planning, but I'll be surprised if he's able to get this all resolved by morning."

"I live in hope," Lily says. "Though my hope only stretches so far, and I agree that I'll probably struggle to sleep tonight, too." She falls silent and chews her lip, staring into the distance, thinking about something. Emma waits, feeling like there's something she wants to say. "What...what makes you so sure Tom can handle this? I got caught up in the moment when he was here – like, there was a confidence about him, y'know? He sounded like he knows what he's talking about. But now they're gone, and...and I guess I'm just having doubts."

Emma reaches out, squeezes her arm reassuringly. "Tom's not the kind of guy anyone wants to mess with," she says. "He sounds like he knows what he's talking about because he *does*."

Lily nods. It's hard to tell if this has put her mind at rest.

Emma folds her arms. She looks down at Elijah. He looks more like his mother than his father. "What's your husband like?" she says, turning back to Lily. "I wasn't around him for too long. I didn't get much time to gauge him."

Lily looks unsure of the question. "How do you mean?" she says. "Do you mean what's his personality like?"

"Sure," Emma says. "What's he like as a person? And as a husband?"

"Oh, well." Lily thinks. "He's very...he's very hard-working. He always has been, though the last couple of years he's taken it up a level. So many nights he got home late, long after Elijah had gone to sleep. Especially lately. I guess a lot of that probably had to do with Yuri. That man doesn't sound like someone he'd want to keep waiting."

"I'm not gonna sugar-coat it, Lily – it doesn't sound great when the most you can say about him concerns his work ethic."

"I don't mean it like that," Lily is quick to say. "I'm just beginning to understand why he's been so distant for a while now. So...absent. So *cold*. But he wasn't always like that. He's a sweet man, really. He's very loving. He loves *us* – he has to, to put himself in danger like he did, to try and keep us safe."

Emma figures that maybe there wasn't much to gauge of Roger's personality in the brief time she met him because there wasn't much personality on show. Stress has concealed the real him, buried him deep. He's become a different person. She wonders, once this is over, if and when he's no longer in the employ of Yuri, will he revert back to how he was? Will it be like he's a different person again?

Emma crouches down in front of Elijah. "What're you coloring in there?" she says, tilting her head to try to make out what the image is from upside down.

"Robot," Elijah says. "Fighting a giant squid." He doesn't look up from coloring one of the squid's tentacles a bright green.

"That right?" Emma says. "They put something like that in your coloring book, huh?"

"No," Elijah says, still coloring. "I drew it."

"You did?" Emma turns her body some more, leans in closer, makes out that the outline is not as clear and steady as she first thought. "Oh, yeah," she says. "It's very good. You're quite an artist, and that's quite an imagination you've got there." She means the latter part of what she says, but not so much the former. Even after being told what she is looking at, she's still struggling to see it. It's just a mass of twisted colors, two shapes vaguely crushed up against and wrapped around each other.

"It's getting late," Lily says. "I think it's gonna be time for your bed soon, Elijah."

"Okay, Mom," he says, his pencil never leaving the paper.

"Five minutes," Lily says.

"Okay, Mom."

Emma gets back to her feet.

"I really think you should sit," Lily says.

"I've got too much energy to sit," Emma says. "And nowhere to put it."

"Why don't you go for a walk?"

It's not a bad idea. Emma would like to do it, but she can't. She can't leave them alone. She needs to stay here, in the cabin. Needs to watch out for them. The cold metal of the Beretta pressing into her lower back is a stark reminder of this.

"Maybe in the morning," she says. "It's dark right now,

and I don't know the area." It's a feeble excuse, but it will have to do. Lily probably knows Emma is here to protect them. She's probably seen the gun already, and guessed at the reason she was given it.

They're not safe here. No matter how secure they may think they are, people are looking for them, and those people could find them at any time.

Lily places her hands on her thighs and pushes herself up to her feet. Her knees click as she stands. "That's five," she says.

Elijah does not protest. He does not need to be told twice. He puts down the coloring pencil and gets straight up.

"Are you going to say goodnight to Miss Raven?" Lily says.

"Goodnight, Miss Raven," Elijah says.

"Goodnight, Elijah," Emma says. "Sleep tight. And just call me Emma."

Lily pats him on the back and ushers him toward the stairs. "Wash your face, brush your teeth, and pyjamas on. You know the routine. I'll be right up behind you." She stays behind as he heads up the stairs, turns back to Emma. "We won't be long," she says. "Think you'll be able to keep yourself entertained while I'm out of the room?"

"I'll find a way," Emma says.

Lily smiles, then goes up after her son. Emma can hear taps running in the bathroom upstairs.

Emma takes Lily's advice. She tries to sit. She sat earlier. She sat for a while. Every second of it was torture.

She faces the television. It's been years since she last watched anything. She keeps herself too busy to sit in front of the screen every night. It's playing a game show. Emma tries to watch it, but she can't tell what's going on, and what little she's able to work out bores her.

Upstairs, she can hear the movements of Lily and Elijah. She can hear the taps still running in the bathroom.

There's movement out the corner of her eye, at the window. Emma's head snaps toward it. She looks out into the dark, trying to figure out if she saw movement outside the glass, or if it was a reflection from the television. She sits, frozen, watching, waiting for something more to happen. She holds her breath. It's burning in her lungs. She feels a cold chill run through her insides. Nothing else moves outside, but she can't shake the feeling that she saw something out there in her peripheral vision. It could have been an animal, a low-flying bird passing by.

Except she's sure it wasn't an animal.

She thinks it was a man.

She stands, takes a step toward the window with one arm reaching behind herself, toward Tom's Beretta. She reaches the glass and presses her face up to it, scans the outside, down to the water. She can't see anything. She can't hear Lily and Elijah moving around upstairs anymore. She isn't listening to them. All of her attention is focused on the outside of the cabin, on trying to find the person she is sure she saw pass by the window.

She pulls out the gun, holds it down by her side. Takes deep breaths. She goes to the back door. It's locked. The key is in the lock. She needs to be sure that there's no one out there. She unlocks the door, steps outside. She holds the gun two-handed out in front of herself, pointing at the ground. She's more used to firing rifles, hunting up in the Chugach Mountains. The only time she's used a handgun has been at the firing range. She's never shot anything with a handgun before. Only targets. She knows to aim for the center of mass. Nothing fancy. Just stop whoever is coming at you.

The evening air is chill. Her breath mists. She can hear the lake lapping gently at the shore, and a gentle breeze whistling through nearby trees. There's nothing else to hear.

No footsteps. No one stepping through the snow. No vehicles, no voices.

Emma looks around. She checks for footprints, especially under the window where she saw the movement. There are prints, but they could belong to anyone. They don't look like they're fresh. There's nothing out of place.

Everything is as it should be. She can't see anyone. Still, she can't shake the feeling that something is wrong. That there is someone out here. There is the chance that her paranoid mind conjured the shape, but she doesn't think so. Emma isn't given to hysterics. She's not prone to imagining things that aren't there. If she thinks she saw someone, then chances are that someone is out here.

"Who's there?" she says. She holds the gun up, points it out into the dark. "Step on out – I know you're there."

There's no response. No movement.

Emma clenches her jaw and holds her breath. She turns slowly, staring into the dark. Her eyes have adjusted to the shadows, but she can't see anyone.

"Anyone out here, you better show yourself now," she says.

Again, no response.

Emma doesn't drop her guard. She doesn't put the gun away. She keeps it raised as she moves down the side of the cabin, to the corner. Again, there are footprints in the snow. Man size. It's hard to tell when they were made. They could belong to anyone. They could be Roger's. She wishes she'd checked the area earlier, wishes she'd come out and checked the snow around the outside of the cabin, examined the prints already present. She knows it's the kind of thing Tom would have done.

At the corner of the cabin, she stops. The outside of the cabin is made up of logs. She sees snow on one of them at the corner, like someone has pressed their boot to it. She can see the print of the sole. She looks round the corner, on the other side. There is another boot print, but higher on this side. She looks up and sees another print, but fainter now, the snow almost all gone. Emma feels her heart leap into her throat. Someone has climbed up the side of the cabin, using the corner of it for purchase, stepping from log to log.

Emma takes a step back, looks up. A window is open. Wide open.

Emma hurries back to the open rear door, then steps inside. The Beretta is raised, pointed out ahead of her. She moves through to the living room.

"Hello, my dear." The man's accent is Russian. The left side of his face is burnt. Emma guesses this is Fedorov. She's heard so much about him, but this is their first time meeting. He's holding Elijah to his chest so that the boy's feet are dangling a foot from the ground. Fedorov holds his own handgun against the side of Elijah's face. Lily is on the sofa behind them, her face pinched, her hands balled on her thighs. She can't take her eyes off Fedorov and Elijah. She can't sit still, either. She keeps starting to stand, then sitting back down, too concerned for her son. She looks like she's about to cry and throw up at the same time.

Emma points the gun at Fedorov.

"I do not think that is such a clever idea," he says.

Fedorov is right. She knows he's right, she knows she can't shoot, but she keeps the gun up regardless.

"Please," Lily says. Her voice is very small. It's not clear, at first, whether she's talking to Fedorov or Emma. "Please don't hurt him, *please*..."

Emma bites her lip. She could shoot, but it's a big risk. Even if she were able to hit Fedorov right between the eyes, there's nothing to stop him from squeezing the trigger first, blowing Elijah's brains across the room. Across his mother.

Fedorov smiles at her hesitation. "Pass me your weapon,

my little darling," he says. "And then we shall all return to Valdez together, yes?"

Emma doesn't want to give him the gun. But she doesn't want to keep Elijah's life in danger, either.

"Now, my darling," Fedorov says. "Let us not stay here waiting. We need to go and catch up to Tom and Roger, yes?"

Emma swallows. She closes her eyes. It's longer than a blink. When she opens them again, she loosens her grip on the gun. She lets it dangle from a finger. "Drop it," Fedorov says, "and kick it to me."

She does so. Keeping hold of Elijah, he leans down to retrieve the Beretta. Only when he has it does he put Elijah down. Elijah runs over to his mother. She grabs him in both arms, squeezes him tight. She's crying now. The tears are running shiny down her cheeks.

"Over there," he says, motioning Emma to where Lily and Elijah are. "All of you, together."

Emma does as she's told. Fedorov covers them all with his gun. He tucks the Beretta down his waist, the same place Emma was carrying it. "Do you have the keys to your truck?" he says to Emma.

She nods.

"Good." He grins. With his burned features, it is hideous. "Then let us go."

34

Yuri is at home, in his study. He places a call through to Russia, to Mikhail, assures him that everything is proceeding according to plan. He does not mention anything about the missing money, or Roger, or Tom Rollins. When he's done, he goes downstairs, gets himself a drink in the kitchen. Alina is in the sitting room, in front of the fire. Her feet are up on the coffee table. There's a drink in her hand. She's been drinking a lot lately. Yuri feels he may need to address this at some point, but for now, he lets it slide. She's staring into the fire. Watching the flames.

"What are you doing?" he says, standing in the doorway.

She gives a start, not hearing his approach, lost in her own world. "Nothing," she says. "Just keeping warm."

"Mm." Yuri takes a drink.

Alina takes her feet from the coffee table, tucks them beneath herself. "How did your call go?" she says.

"Fine," Yuri says. He takes a seat in the chair opposite her. It faces toward the window. The curtains are not drawn. His home is atop a hill, and he has a view of Valdez spread out before him. The roofs below are white, covered with snow, all of them blending into each other.

The sitting room is full of shadows. The only light is from the fireplace. It flickers against the back wall, behind where Alina is sitting. There is a lamp within Yuri's arm's reach. He does not turn it on. He is enjoying the quality of the light in the room. It is soothing. The warmth envelops him. He forgets all his worries.

And then Alina speaks.

"Why...?" she begins tentatively, second-guessing herself. There is a hesitancy before she continues, likely brought on by the way Yuri has opened his eyes, is looking at her. She clears her throat. "Why...why are you doing this?"

Yuri frowns. "Doing...*what?*"

"The sabotage you are planning to the pipeline – why?"

"Why?" He almost laughs. "It's going ahead the night after next, and you're asking me *why?*"

"What is...what is to be gained from it?"

He looks at her like she's stupid.

"Money, yes," Alina says, answering her own question, "power, yes, you've explained this to me already – but why the pipeline? You were already making money. You were already gaining power."

"Not this kind of power," Yuri says. "With the pipeline, we will control the oil. We will control the state. We will control so much more than that."

"But the damage –"

"I don't care about the fucking damage," Yuri says, his relaxed feeling gone now. The warmth of the room, the soft lighting, none of it matters now that Alina has opened her mouth and disturbed his peace. "This is what the Bratva want, this is what they shall get. It is the way of the world, Alina. Surely you are not still so naïve?"

Alina says nothing to this.

Yuri raises his eyebrows. "Are we done now, yes? Is this discussion at an end?"

"It's just, as we get closer to it, as the prospect of it all happening suddenly becomes so much more real, I find it so difficult to comprehend."

"To comprehend what, exactly?"

"How you, or they, could care so little?"

Yuri chuckles. "Oh, we all care a lot. Just, evidently, not about what you think we *should*."

Alina opens her mouth to say more, but she stops. There is a buzzing. It's Yuri's phone. He looks at the screen. It's Fedorov. Yuri's stomach sinks a little. This can be either good or bad news, and while he hopes for the former, he knows he must be prepared for the latter.

"Yes?"

"Good news, my friend," Fedorov's boisterous voice says. He's speaking English. "All the pieces are moving into place, though they shall arrive separately."

"How do you mean?" Yuri says.

"Tom Rollins, he is taking Roger to Valdez. They are on their way there now. Teddy and Reagan are following them."

Yuri frowns. "Where are you?"

"I am with their women – and the boy! He is a big boy, for his age. He is asleep now. He is asleep on my lap – there is not so much space in this truck for us all to be squeezed in together like this! His mother now is looking at me as if I should not be speaking so loud!" He laughs.

"I don't care about the women, Fedorov. I thought I made that clear."

"Loose ends, my friend, loose ends."

"Then you should have snipped them already." He sees how Alina is watching him. Sees how the flames from the fireplace dance in her eyes. He wonders how much she can hear of Fedorov's side of the conversation. "You don't need them."

"They may come in useful," Fedorov says, switching to Russian. "There is no need to get rid of them so abruptly. We might need them later."

"I'm not so sure, but I will leave it up to you."

"That is for the best, my friend. That is why you pay me." He laughs.

"And I pay you well," Yuri says. "What plan do Tom and Roger have?"

"They are going to find out who took your money."

"Roger took the money."

"He denies that."

"I don't care if he denies it. There's no one else. This Tom Rollins is a fool to be suckered in by his lies."

"Well, that is what the women have told me they are going to do."

"You believe them?"

"I believe it is what they have been told. The wife, Lily, she is not the kind to lie. She is frail. She's scared. She's worried for her son. She will tell me the truth of anything I ask."

"What about the other one?"

"A little tougher, this one." Yuri can hear the grin in his voice, and though he's still speaking Russian, he can imagine Fedorov has directed this comment toward her.

"Are you still in touch with Teddy and Reagan?" Yuri says.

"Another piece of good news, my friend – they have caught up to Tom and Roger. They saw them at a gas station. They rang me, asked instructions. They are learning, yes? Finally. I tell them to hold back, to pursue, keep them in view. I do not want to run the risk of them fucking anything up, not now, when we are so close to having them."

"That is wise," Yuri says.

"Yes. We are all on our way to Valdez. We will have everyone in our grasp by morning, I think. If not then, end of day."

"See to it."

"I will. And all in time to fry our bigger fish, yes?"

"Yes." Yuri hangs up. Alina is still watching him. "You shouldn't eavesdrop," he says.

"Then you should leave the room," she says. Before he can respond to this, she adds, "What will you do with Roger, when you have him?"

Yuri smiles at her. It is not a pleasant smile, he knows. He feels the way it twists his mouth. "I will find out where my money is," he says. "And I will get it back. And I don't care how many limbs and appendages Fedorov has to break or remove to get his answers."

"What about the others?"

"Fuck the others," Yuri says. "They do not concern me. Fedorov wants this Tom Rollins to satisfy what was done to his face, but that is a personal endeavor. It has nothing to do with me. So long as it does not interfere with his regular work, I do not care."

"The women," Alina says, "the child. What about them?"

Yuri stares at her until she looks away. "I told you already," he says. "Fuck them."

He can't see Alina's face, but he does not think she reacts well to this statement. It looks almost as if she is realizing something for the first time. Yuri doesn't know, or care, what it could be.

They remain in silence for a few minutes, the only sounds now coming from the burning wood in the fireplace. Alina gets up. She keeps her face turned away.

"Where are you going?" Yuri says.

"I'm going to bed," she says, her voice straining to be soft.

"It's still early," he says.

"I'm tired," Alina says. She leaves the room. He hears her going upstairs.

Her abrupt exit makes him think there were things she wanted to say, but knew it was best to keep to herself. She did not want to get hit again, hurt again, like last time. Yuri sits back. He enjoys his drink. He enjoys the warmth and the light of the room again. He relaxes into his chair. It is good that Alina left. It is good that she fled, rather than take a risk on being struck. It is good that she kept her mouth shut.

It means she is learning.

35

It's a quiet road. There are bumps, caused by the snow, but nothing severe. There's nothing on either side of them – just trees, filled with darkness.

Roger is dozing in the passenger seat, his head pressed against the door frame. It rattles, but it doesn't wake him. He's been asleep since they left the gas station just over a half hour ago. Tom lets him rest for now, but he will wake him soon. There are headlights behind them. They have been there for a while now. They keep a safe distance. They don't come up too close. Tom has slowed the truck. He's allowed them an opportunity to catch up, to overtake, to have the clear road ahead all to themselves. They did not catch up. They maintained their distance. Tom could see, in the darkness behind them, how they braked hard to avoid coming too close. Tom is suspicious. He's continued on his route, has given them a chance to turn off. They haven't. They've persisted. Soon, he's going to have to be sure. He's going to have to do something about them.

He nudges Roger's shoulder, pushing him a little harder than he maybe needs to. The top of Roger's head bounces off the window. He wakes up wincing, rubbing his scalp through his thinning hair. "Ow," he says, though he doesn't seem to realize Tom pushed him. "We hit a pothole or something?"

"Sure," Tom says. "Stay awake."

Roger pushes himself upright. He blinks hard, then rubs his eyes. He squints into the darkness ahead. "We almost there?"

"No," Tom says. "Someone might be following us."

Roger curses, then looks into his side mirror. "How can you be sure?" he says. "They're so far away."

"I'm not sure," Tom says. "But they've been behind us for a while now."

"What're you gonna do?"

"I'm gonna *be* sure."

Roger looks like he wants to ask more, to get some details about this statement, but he keeps his mouth shut. He's fully awake now, watching the mirror. "I dunno," he says, when he does finally speak again. "They're really staying back. Maybe they just don't want to hassle us? It's not like the roads are in a safe condition. They could just be trying to avoid an accident."

"If you're following someone, and you're not trying to run them off the road, you keep your distance," Tom says. "If I were in their position, and I wanted to know where the person up ahead was going, I'd hold back, too. Except, on a night like this, and the road being as quiet as it is, I'd do it with the lights off."

Roger side-eyes him, then says, "I'm still not so sure."

"Yeah, well, we'll find out together." Tom sees a bend in the road up ahead. They're still surrounded on either side by tall trees, looming over them. There's no end to this woodland in sight.

Tom gets round the corner, loses sight of the vehicle behind them. He pulls off the road over a shallow bank, kills the lights. He pulls into the trees, then maneuvers so the front of the truck is pointing back toward the road.

"Oh, Jesus," Roger says. "Oh, shit." He holds his breath.

"You don't have to hold your breath," Tom says, looking back toward the corner they have just rounded. "They won't be able to hear you."

He hears Roger exhaling, though trying not to be obvious about it.

Light is thrown up on the corner as the following vehicle nears. It comes around the bend. The light gets brighter. It does not reach the trees where Tom and Roger are parked – they're too far back, too close to the corner. The vehicle – an SUV – passes by. Tom tries to see inside as they go, but it's too dark.

"Okay, so they're past us," Roger says. "You happy?"

"Not yet," Tom says. He pulls out of the trees, follows the SUV, the headlights still off.

Roger grabs onto the door handle and the bottom of his seat. "Jesus Christ!" he says. "Are you crazy? It's pitch black!"

"I can see just fine," Tom says, following the lights ahead.

He keeps a safe distance. The same kind of distance they were keeping when they were behind. They slow. They start to brake. They stop in the middle of the road, and Tom does the same.

Roger is watching them. "What're they doing?"

"They've lost us," Tom says. "They're panicking."

The SUV stays in the middle of the road for a moment longer, and then it crawls to the side. It stops. The people inside are probably debating what to do next. Working out if there were any junctions they passed after they came around the corner, a road they may not have noticed. They might be on the phone, calling in their lost target.

"I'm going in for a closer look," Tom says.

"What? No, just leave them. They'll drive on, and then we can continue. Just leave them."

Tom ignores him. He turns off the truck's interior light, then opens the door. The engine is still idling. He looks at Roger, then at the keys in the ignition. He kills the engine, and takes the keys with him. "Sit tight," he says.

Tom ducks low and creeps up. He uses the dark trunks of the trees for cover. The only engine he can hear on the road is from the SUV up ahead. He can't hear anything else approaching. He pulls out his KA-BAR as he nears.

From the rear window, he can see the back of two familiar heads. Teddy and Reagan. Reagan is in the passenger seat. He's on the phone, but he's not talking. Teddy is banging his head on the steering wheel. Tom moves down the driver's side of the vehicle. He moves fast, to avoid being seen in the side mirror. He pulls open the driver's door, puts an arm across Teddy's chest and the KA-BAR to his throat. Reagan gives such a start he almost drops the phone.

"Kill the call," Tom says.

Reagan does as he's told.

"Guns," Tom says. "Hand them over. Nice and slow or I cut his throat."

Reagan complies, pulling a Glock from an underarm holster.

"I can't move," Teddy says. "You're gonna have to lighten up if you want mine."

"Nice try," Tom says. He grabs Reagan's gun, then presses it to the back of Teddy's head. He takes the arm from his chest. "All right," he says. "*Now* you've got all the space you need."

Teddy hands over his own Glock. Tom releases the magazine, pops the bullet from the chamber. He throws the gun into the trees, but keeps the magazine. He keeps Reagan's gun trained on Teddy, then pats him down, searching for any other weapons. There aren't any. He finds his phone, though. He drops it to the road and smashes it under his boot, then throws that into the trees, too.

"Pass me yours," he says to Reagan, holding out his free hand.

Reagan hands it over. Tom smashes and disposes of it in the same fashion as Teddy's.

"Now the keys," Tom says.

Teddy begrudgingly complies. Tom tosses them.

"We need to stop meeting like this, gentlemen," he says. "One of these days it's not going to go well for you, and, frankly, I'm getting bored of going through the same routine every single time." He goes around the front of the vehicle, pointing the gun at them through the windshield. He gets to Reagan's side, opens the door, pats him down. Like Teddy, he does not have any concealed weapons. "I don't have the space in my truck for the two of you to come along with us, so you're just gonna have to sit tight here until someone comes by and helps you out. It's gonna be cold, so I recommend you keep the doors shut."

Reagan looks defeated. Teddy glares.

"How'd you find us?"

"Dumb luck," Teddy says, cutting off Reagan as he opens his mouth. "Well, I say that, but I don't suppose there's anything so lucky about it when there's as many of us out looking for you as there are. Ain't that right?" He nudges Reagan.

Reagan swallows. "Someone had to come across you eventually," he says. He doesn't look at Tom.

"Uh-huh," Tom says. "So there's more of your buddies out on the road?"

"We shouldn't tell you this, but what the fuck we got left to lose, right?" Teddy says. "We're out on the roads toward every major city and town in Alaska. We were on our way to Anchorage when we spotted you back at the gas station."

"That so?" Tom says.

"Yeah. You may have spotted us, but you're a marked man – your truck, Emma Raven's truck, we know what we're looking for. You ain't even gonna know we've found you until we've run you off the road." Teddy grins, shows all of his teeth.

"Okay," Tom says. "And if that happens, I'll deal with them just like I've dealt with you. Something tells me I might have to be a bit more careful with your buddies though, right? Surely they can't be as dumb as the pair of you."

This wipes the smile off Teddy's face. "Fuck you," he says, sounding like a petulant child.

"Where's our mutual Russian friend?" Tom says.

Teddy snorts. "Kentucky Fried Fedorov is coming for you, too," he says. "You ain't gonna be so fuckin' chirpy when he gets his hands on you."

"I like that," Tom says. "I like that name. That's a good one. You call him that to his face? No? I didn't think so. Where is he?"

"He's in Valdez," Teddy says. "We're supposed to take you to him."

"Yeah, well, that ain't gonna happen. Guess I'll have to find him in my own time. When I do, you mind if I use that Kentucky Fried line? I really like it, I do, but I don't wanna take the credit for your wit."

Teddy clenches his jaw and sits back, stares straight ahead. Reagan looks ashamed to have failed, to have been caught out by Tom once again. He keeps his face lowered.

"I'm gonna shoot your tires out," Tom says. "Just in case you go looking for those keys, and you're successful. So don't be alarmed when I start firing."

He closes Reagan's door, then shoots out the passenger-side tires, both of them. He does the same on the driver's side. Teddy stares at him all the while. When he's done, Tom keeps the Glock. He goes back to his truck.

"I take it from the gunshots they *were* following us, then?" Roger says, eyes wide.

Tom starts the engine. "Our old friends Teddy and Reagan," he says.

"Shit, really?"

Tom nods. He starts driving, back on the road.

"They still alive?"

"Why wouldn't they be?"

"Um... I dunno, I just thought, maybe..."

"They're just a couple of heavies. They're not trained assassins. If it came down to it and it was us or them, sure, I'd put them down, but a situation like this, when they're just showing themselves up as the pair of amateurs they are? There's no need."

As he passes by the SUV, lower now on its wheel rims, Roger tries to see inside. He looks back as they pass. "Fedorov send them?"

"Yeah," Tom says.

"Poor guys," Roger says, turning back round. "He's not gonna be happy that you made them, that you took them out of commission. They might even start to wish you *had* just killed them."

"Well," Tom says, "that's their choice. I'd rather keep my conscience clear."

36

Emma's jaw aches. She hasn't unclenched her teeth since she was first forced to start driving her own truck back to Valdez. Lily is beside her in the middle seat. Her hands are balled in her lap. Her knuckles are bone-white. Her head is turned. She hasn't taken her eyes off Fedorov and Elijah since the journey began.

Fedorov is by the window, his body twisted so he can see both women. So he can see Emma, particularly. Make sure she drives the route. Make sure she doesn't try anything stupid. Emma wouldn't, not when he has Elijah in his lap, and not when he has the gun in his hand. Elijah is clearly scared of Fedorov. He looks uncomfortable with the Russian's thick arm across his chest. On the few occasions she has looked over, Emma has seen the way Elijah avoids looking back at Fedorov. She thinks it's to do with the burns on his face. They frighten him. Fedorov is a bogeyman come to life.

Emma does not care for Fedorov, for reasons that go beyond the obvious one. He has not stopped talking since the journey began. He's loud and obnoxious. He laughs at his own jokes. His constant monologue has stopped only once, when he made a phone call. Even then, he spoke like he wanted them to hear – until he switched to Russian. Emma wonders what was said then. What needed to be so secret that they couldn't be allowed to understand? No doubt it related to them – to herself, and Lily, and Elijah. Maybe to Tom and Roger, too.

"Perhaps, when we are in Valdez, if we are not too busy straight away," Fedorov says, "we shall get something to eat, yes? I am hungry. I am sure you are hungry, too. You, little one, you are hungry, yes?" He jostles Elijah on his knee. Elijah doesn't say anything. "Hungry and *shy!*" Fedorov laughs. He speaks to Lily. "So quiet, this little one. So shy. Like you, when you were young, yes?"

Lily swallows before she speaks. Emma hears the click in her throat. "He's scared," Lily says. "Let me hold him. Let him sit with me."

Fedorov laughs. "No, no, my dear. I am not so foolish, yes? The boy stays with me. We are very comfortable here together, in the corner. Yes, little one?"

Elijah makes a sound in his throat, but it's hard to tell what it's supposed to be, or mean.

Fedorov doesn't seem to notice, or care. "Do you like cereal, little one? It is more for breakfast, yes, but you can have some tonight. Although, by time we reach Valdez, it may be morning already, yes? Time for cereal! Wherever we go, whatever time it may be, I am sure we will be able to find some cereal. I will send my men out to get some. I will send them to get us all some food. We will be hungry in Valdez. I am hungry now!" Again, he laughs. "I would like to take you ladies to a restaurant, but I cannot entrust that you will not do something regrettable. And so, we must wait. We must wait until we can eat in."

Emma tries to tune him out. He isn't saying anything worthwhile, nothing that could perhaps come in useful at a later time. He's talking for the sake of talking. He's just making noise. He likes the sound of his own voice.

They pass through woodland. It is dark here. There are no other cars on the road. There are no streetlights. The moon is out, but it struggles to get through the interlocking canopy of branches overhead.

"Emma – Emma Raven, I am talking to you." Fedorov's voice breaks through her attempt to ignore him.

"I didn't hear," Emma says. "I'm concentrating."

"I said, do not be afraid to speed up a little, yes?"

She shoots him a look. "I *am* afraid to speed up," she says. "These roads aren't as bad as they get, but they're not great, either. I don't wanna turn us all upside down, run the risk of breaking our necks."

"There is nothing wrong with these roads," Fedorov says. "They are fine. You can go faster. I am thinking you are too scared of reaching our destination, yes?"

They round a corner. Emma starts to respond, but up ahead, at the side of the road, something catches her eye. Fedorov notices her looking. He turns his attention ahead, too. He does a double take, narrows his eyes, then mutters something under his breath in Russian. "Slow down," he says. "Pull up alongside it."

Emma does so. The SUV is off the road. She doesn't have to cross lanes to stop next to it. Closer, with the headlights on it, she sees how the tires are deflated, how it is sitting on its rims.

Fedorov winds his window down. He signals to get the attention of the two men inside the SUV. They are sitting hunched up, their coats pulled tightly around themselves. They're shivering. They look freezing. The driver notices

Fedorov. He opens his door. The windows are electric, and the SUV does not seem to have any power.

Emma recognizes the driver, and the passenger beside him. They were in her house. Teddy and Reagan.

Fedorov sounds angry. "What have you assholes done?"

Emma can't hear much of Teddy's response. It's obscured by Fedorov blocking the window, and by the way Teddy's teeth chatter. She makes out one phrase, though – *he spotted us*. She can guess exactly who the *he* is.

Fedorov sounds like he's about to explode. She hasn't seen or heard him angry so far. He's been talkative and affable. He's been over the top with his friendliness. "Get in the back of the truck – *now!*"

"It's – it's open," Teddy says. He's clearer now, speaking up to try to make his point. "We're already so cold. We'll – we'll freeze –"

"Good, I hope you do!" Fedorov says. "You will deserve it for being such fucking idiots! Such *failures*! And do not forget my bag! Do not forget my bag, you fucking failures!"

Emma cannot see the bag he is talking about. While he's distracted, she looks to his gun. It's still inside the truck. Only his head and shoulders are leaning out the open window. Her breath must quicken as she considers making a move, grabbing for the gun, turning it on him, because Lily turns to her, guesses at what she is thinking. Lily swallows, shakes her head. "No," she says, her voice small.

Emma looks at her. Her hands are still on the steering wheel. Her jaw is still clenched. She's starting to get a headache from it now. She looks back at the gun. She'll have to leap over Lily, and then squeeze past Elijah, but she could reach it. She could grab it. She could tear it from his grip, and press it to his head. Pull the trigger before he even knows what has happened.

"Don't," Lily says, keeping her voice as quiet as possible. "It's not clear. You won't make it."

Teddy and Reagan have gotten out of the SUV. Fedorov is still screaming at them, nodding his head at the back of the truck, telling them he hopes they freeze, and when they reach Valdez he'll thaw them out by pissing on them.

"He'll kill us all," Lily says.

Emma looks at Elijah. Fedorov's arm is still around him. It's high, choking him a little. Elijah is looking back at her. Like his mother, he seems to understand her intentions, too. Like his mother, he's pale and terrified.

Emma looks at Lily. She nods. She turns back to the road ahead. She breathes out and feels her body shudder. Her arms are shaking. Fedorov pulls his head back into the truck as Teddy and Reagan climb up onto the flatbed.

"These fucking assholes," he says. "I cannot trust them to do *nothing* – *nyet!*" He simmers for a moment, breathing hard through his nose. He shakes his head and mutters in Russian again. "What are you waiting for?" He wheels on Emma. "Drive! Let us go!"

Emma gives a jolt at his bark, then pulls away from the crippled SUV.

Fedorov sits in silence for a while. He watches the SUV as they pass by it. He looks back at Teddy and Reagan, sneering. Emma glances in the mirror. She sees how they huddle together, their collars pulled up high, covering their faces and their ears.

Fedorov jostles Elijah on his lap suddenly. "Such fools they are, yes?" he says, and his old tone is returning now. The anger has drained away. "Such disappointments. I am thinking I will get some use out of them, and then they will not be much longer for this world."

"Don't tell him that," Emma says.

"No?" Fedorov says. He grins. "I do not think he minds,

my dear. Now, if you want to talk with me, talk with me, but until now you have not. If you have nothing agreeable to say, then perhaps you should keep your mouth closed and just drive, yes?"

Emma drives.

37

"Is there security in the building?" Tom says.

They're parked across the road from Roger's workplace. The building is in darkness. The parking lot is empty.

"No, there's no security," Roger says.

"That surprises me," Tom says. "Handling people's money as you do."

"Yeah, but none of it's *in* there. It's all online. There's nothing physical."

Tom watches the building.

"How long are we gonna sit here for?" Roger says.

"Until I'm sure it's clear."

"You're not sure already? We've been watching for, like, an hour now. I don't see anyone."

"I'd rather trust my own eyes than anyone else's." He scans the area, looks up and down the road. Checks for people on the sidewalks. Checks passing and parked vehicles. There aren't many people about. It's late, and it's cold.

Roger yawns. "I know I slept on the way here, but Christ,

I'm tired. Long journeys, they'll take it out of you, right? Even if all you're doing is sitting in the passenger seat."

Tom doesn't answer. He's confident no one is at the building. That there's no one lying in wait, ready to ambush them. He drives his truck over the road, into the parking lot, pulls into the space nearest the entrance. They get out and go to the door. Roger unlocks it, and they go inside. He pulls out his cell phone and uses it as a flashlight rather than turn on any of the strip lights overhead.

"You've been here before, right?" Roger says.

"Yes," Tom says. They head to the stairs, go up to Roger's office. "It looks different in the dark."

"Sometimes, when I work late, it's darker than this when I leave. I'm not gonna lie, I spook myself on the way out. Start jumping at every little shadow."

"Anything grabbed you yet?" Tom says.

Roger starts to say no, but then he grins and says, "Couple of times."

Tom looks at him. "Anything I should know about?"

"No, no, I was just joking." Roger waves it off. Tom thinks he meant something by it, though. He's not sure what.

"Anyone else likely to be working late?"

"I don't think so," Roger says. "All the times I did it, there wouldn't be anyone else here."

They get to Roger's office. Roger goes to his desk, starts up his computer.

"It feels like I've been gone for years," he says. "It's hard to believe it's only been a few days."

"Uh-huh." Tom steps up beside him. The computer has loaded. Roger types in his password. "How long will this take?"

"Might take a while," Roger says. "You might want to make yourself comfortable."

Tom grunts. "All those nights you worked late," he says, "your boss was never curious what you were doing?"

Roger shakes his head while he starts logging onto programs. "We keep the details of the accounts we handle to ourselves," he says. "To be totally honest, it wouldn't surprise me if there's a lot more laundering going on in here than anyone realizes."

"Your bad luck to get caught up with the Russians, huh?"

"Sure seems that way." Roger's fingers glide over the keys, tapping at them. There is a stream of information on the screen, but Tom can't make sense out of any of it.

He peels away from the desk, goes to the window. There's not much to see down below. Roger's office is at the back of the building. He can see a road, but it's quiet. He sees someone crossing it on foot. They're moving slow, and laden with bags. Homeless, probably, with nowhere else to go. They continue on down the sidewalk without a backward glance.

"Keep at it," Tom says, heading for the door. "I'm gonna check the windows."

"Sure," Roger says without looking up. His fingers are moving fast over the keys. It reminds Tom of Cindy, of how she works, how fast her fingers move while she's on the computer, too. He hasn't spoken to Cindy since he reached Alaska, since before he got out of the questionable facility that passed for a backstreet hospital down in Arizona. She hasn't reached out to him, either. She's probably busy. Not for the first time, he wonders how she spends her days, and figures it's probably best he doesn't know.

He walks past the desk of the secretary he and Emma spoke to, who gave them the route to Anchorage. He moves past the empty offices, down to the other end of the building. He glances back at Roger, illuminated by his computer in his office. He's lost in whatever is on the screen.

The truck remains the only vehicle in the parking lot

below. Tom watches the road. A couple of cars go by, but nothing suspicious. No one hangs around. No one is watching the building. Most of Valdez's inhabitants will be sleeping now. The moon is out and provides extra light, which is reflected by the snow on the ground. In a few short hours, it will be dawn.

Tom looks back. Roger is still behind his desk, but he's sitting very still. He's staring at the screen. Frowning. Tom walks back, watching his face. It doesn't change. He looks up as Tom enters the office, gives a start. He taps a couple of keys, then starts typing again.

"What is it?" Tom says.

"Um," Roger says.

Tom steps around the desk, behind his chair, looks down at the screen. Again, he can't make any sense of it. "Speak to me," Tom says.

"I...um..." Roger continues to tap keys. "So, uh, the money's definitely been taken." He laughs weakly.

Tom looks at him.

"I..."

"Can you see who took it?" Tom says. "Can you see where it's gone? How to get it back?"

Roger's shoulders sag. He deflates. He shakes his head. "I can't," he says. "I can't...I can't trace it. I've been trying."

"You said you'd be able to," Tom says. "You said you were sure."

"I, um, I never said I was *certain*..."

"I'm not interested in semantics, Roger," Tom says, his voice hard. "Why can't you find the money?"

"I don't – I don't know – it doesn't make any sense – it's like everything I would do to cover my own tracks has been done –"

"That sounds suspicious, Roger," Tom says.

Roger looks up at him, earnest. "If I can't trace it, that proves I didn't take it, right?"

"I'm not sure that excuse will fly with Yuri."

Roger shakes his head. "No, I don't think it will..."

Tom spins Roger around in his chair, places his hands firmly on his shoulders and looks into his eyes. "Roger," he says, "this is the last time I am going to ask you. Did you take the money?"

"No! I swear, I didn't take it! I have no fucking idea who did!"

Tom holds his eyes. He has his hands high on his shoulders, close to his neck, close enough to feel his pulse. It has quickened a little, but most likely this is down to Tom turning him around abruptly, getting into his face. It's nothing major. He holds Tom's gaze. His look is just as earnest as his voice.

Tom lets go of him, straightens. "Is there anything to be learned from this?" he says, pointing at the computer. "Or have we already wasted enough time?"

"I've done everything I can," Roger says.

"Then turn it off," Tom says. "Let's go." He heads out of the office, for the exit, frustrated but keeping it to himself.

Roger hurries to keep up. They descend the stairs. "So, um, uh, so, I mean –"

"Spit it out," Tom says.

"What *now*?"

"We go see Yuri."

"Okay," Roger says, handling this better than Tom expected him to. "I figured as much. So what happens when we reach him?"

"I talk to him," Tom says. "And see if I can't dissuade him from his current course of action."

38

It's morning. Yuri and Alina arrived at the office ten minutes before. They got here early. The workday has not yet begun. The offices beyond Yuri's own have not filled with people, and there are no workers on the workshop floor. Yuri drinks coffee, black, and Alina sips at a tea. She sits against the wall, flicking through a magazine. Yuri is sure it is the same magazine she's been flicking through for days now. No wonder she looks bored.

Yuri, despite how relaxed he'd felt in his sitting room earlier in the evening, struggled to sleep last night. His thoughts raced at the upcoming prospect of the pipeline's sabotage, and everything that is to come after. There is a lot on his mind. He imagines it will be a while before rest comes easy.

He yawns, stretches his arms wide and then back, behind him. His shoulders pop.

"You are tired?" Alina says.

Yuri takes another drink of the strong coffee. "It will pass," he says.

"I did not hear you come to bed."

"It was late. You were already sleeping."

"I slept well."

Yuri is jealous. If his tiredness gets too much, he will take a nap later. There's nothing stopping him. He's the boss. To distract himself, he turns on his computer.

His phone begins to ring. It's Fedorov.

"We are in Valdez," he says. "On the outskirts of town." There's a pause. Something is off in Fedorov's tone. He's less upbeat than usual.

"What is wrong?" Yuri says.

"It is that obvious, yes?"

"I can always tell when something is troubling you. You do not hide it well."

"I never have." Fedorov sighs. "There is a problem."

"Tell me. Do not keep me waiting."

"Teddy and Reagan were spotted by Tom Rollins. He accosted them. He has continued on his way without a tail."

"So you do not know where he is?"

"No," Fedorov says. "I do not know."

Yuri grits his teeth. He does not say anything.

"I will find him," Fedorov says.

"You keep saying that," Yuri says.

"And I mean it. I will find him. I will find both of them. I still have their women."

"How many times do I have to tell you, Fedorov – I do not care about their fucking women."

"They are a means to an end," Fedorov says. "They will have their use, I am sure of that. I am to keep them in safe place, and then I will find Tom and Roger."

Yuri can feel his temper boiling over. "I am disappointed, Fedorov," he says, struggling to keep his patience in check. "I am very disappointed in how you have handled all of this."

Fedorov does not respond. Yuri knows that his statement will have cut him deep. "I am... I am sorry, Yuri."

Yuri glances at his computer screen. There are a few emails in his inbox. He clicks on the icon, maintaining his silence with Fedorov.

"I will put the women in a safe place," Fedorov says. "I will do it now. I will secure them, and then I will complete my mission. All my men will be on it. They are in Valdez, I am sure of it. There is nowhere else they can be. They cannot escape me now."

Yuri starts to tell Fedorov he had best not fail him again, that he had best redeem himself, but he doesn't say anything. An email catches his eye. It cuts him silent.

Fedorov continues to talk. Yuri has to tell him to stop.

"Be quiet," he says. "I'm trying to read something. It may be important."

Fedorov shuts up. Yuri reads the email through. He blinks. He reads it again to be sure. It has clearly been written in a rush. Some of it is garbled, but he is able to understand what it is saying.

Alina has been roused by his silence. She's watching him now, her eyes narrowed.

Yuri feels himself begin to smile. His temper is cooling. His impatience is replaced by excitement, by the same kind of relaxed joy he felt yesterday, in the sitting room, with the fireplace roaring and the light low.

"Fedorov," he says.

"Yes?"

"Get rid of the women. You do not need to look for the men." His smile widens. "I know where they are."

39

Tom follows Roger's directions to Yuri's home. The route is taking them out of Valdez, on a little-used road, the sides of which are high with snow. It's narrow, barely enough space for two vehicles to pass. So far, no one has tried. They're the only ones on it.

When they first started heading this way, a couple of hours ago now, it was still early morning. "By the time we get there," Roger said, "Yuri isn't going to be there. He'll be at the office." They haven't passed him on the way to the house, but Roger says he's taking them in the back way.

Yuri not being home, despite drawing this whole thing out, is not the worst thing. It will give Tom a chance to look the area over, to check it out. To get into position and to have a plan prepared for when Yuri *does* return.

The road is thinning up ahead. Now there's space for just them. It doesn't look like anyone has driven down this part in a while. The snow is melting on the dirt road, but it's still high on the sides, high enough to brush against the doors of the truck.

"This is the way you usually came in?" Tom says.

"I've only been a few times," Roger says. "Wasn't much need for me to come to his house. If ever I needed to come around, it was just for private business, which was why he'd tell me to come in from the back."

"Didn't want the neighbors to see."

"He doesn't have many – and to be honest, none of them are close enough to see anything anyway. Probably just a power thing, really. It always is with Yuri."

"How long is this road?"

"Uh..." Roger looks around. There aren't any markers or landmarks. Nothing but fields, covered in snow, until they reach the trees. Tom isn't sure what he's looking for. "At a guess, I'd say we've probably got about another mile to go. But his house is right at the end. Can't miss it."

Tom grunts. He holds the steering wheel with both hands. The truck bounces. It's slow going.

40

Teddy and Reagan are shivering uncontrollably by the time Fedorov directs Emma to a stop at a cabin on the outskirts of Valdez. It's set back among the trees. There is a car parked down the side of it, almost buried under snow. Emma wonders what this place is – if it's Fedorov's home, or if he has it for the occasions when he needs to keep people out of the way. Like now.

Fedorov hands Elijah over to Lily, sits him in her lap. She wraps her arms around her son, squeezes him close and tight, kissing the top of his head. Fedorov holds an open hand out to Emma. He wants the truck's keys. She gives them to him. He gets out of the truck. He moves fast, like he's in a rush. Teddy and Reagan have gotten down off the back. Their arms are wrapped around themselves. Their lips look almost blue. Emma can see frost on the surface of their jackets, which are not thick enough for riding in the open air. Reagan is clutching Fedorov's bag to his chest. She wonders what is inside the bag.

"Inside, boys!" Fedorov says, slapping Reagan on the arm. Reagan flinches, like this hurts more than it ordinarily would.

"Start a fire, warm yourselves up!" He claps his hands together, hurries them on. "Be quick about it, go! Go!"

They trudge on through the snow, toward the cabin. Emma watches their backs as they go, how they have their shoulders hunched up. They can barely move for shaking. They look like they want to curl up and die.

Fedorov turns his attention to the truck. He's about to motion for them to get out, to follow Teddy and Reagan in, but he stops and looks to the cabin again. Watches as Teddy drops to a knee and pulls out a key from under a snow-coated doormat. He tries to jab it into the lock, but he keeps missing.

Fedorov says something loud, in Russian, then marches over to them. He shoves them aside, unlocks the door, then pushes them in. Emma can hear him shouting at them, but it's all in Russian. She wonders if they understand Russian.

"How long do you think they're going to keep us here?" Lily says.

"Whether it's a day, or more than a few," Emma says, "it's too long." She looks at the cabin. The three men are inside. She turns back to Lily. "I can hot-wire the truck," she says.

Lily looks at the cabin now.

"I just don't think I can do it fast enough," Emma says. "I don't think I can get us far enough away to outrun their bullets. I don't want to take a risk on any of us getting shot through the back of the head."

"Then why tell me?" Lily says.

"Because...because I feel helpless," Emma says. "Because..." She trails off. She's not sure why. Because she wants Lily to know she's not useless? She doesn't know.

Fedorov re-emerges from the cabin. He waves for them to come inside.

"Let's go," Lily says. "At least it'll be warm." She keeps hold of Elijah as she gets out of the truck, and carries him inside.

Emma doesn't follow, not straight away. She remains where she is, behind the steering wheel. She grinds her teeth. Watches as Lily and Elijah pass by Fedorov. He grins and ruffles Elijah's hair as they pass. He turns back to her, now. He stares at her.

Emma gets out the truck and goes inside. Teddy and Reagan are getting the fire started. They huddle in front of it, waiting for it to build, to start giving off warmth. Fedorov closes the door. "When it gets going," he says to his men, "be careful you do not get frostbite." They ignore him. They don't move away from the fire. They're both sniffing, over and over.

"Over there." Fedorov points Emma, Lily, and Elijah to the sofa in the corner, pressed up against the wall under a window. They go where he sends them. Emma perches on the edge and looks around. The room is sparse. There is a plain rug in front of the fireplace where Teddy and Reagan are huddled, and another sofa behind them. There is a closed door, behind which Emma assumes is the kitchen, and another doorway leading down a hall, to bedrooms and the bathroom. There is no television. No radio, either. No bookshelves. If this is Fedorov's home, Emma cannot see anything with which he would entertain himself. She returns to her second theory – a safe house. Somewhere to hold prisoners.

"Are you warm?" Fedorov punctuates his question by kicking Teddy, knocking him over. "You are warm now. Stand up, both of you. Over here." He steps to the corner of the room, as if he is going to share secrets with them, but when he speaks, it is at the same volume as always. "You are going to watch them, yes? And this time –" he places a hand on the back of each of their heads, draws them in close, so their foreheads are all touching, "– you are not going to disappoint me, yes?" He lets them go. "They are only two women and a child."

Teddy and Reagan don't look much warmer than when

they first arrived. They are still trembling. They still have their arms wrapped around themselves. Emma knows that kind of cold. The kind that, when you've been out in it for too long, it feels like it's seeped down into your bones. Like you're not sure you're ever going to be able to get it back out again. It'll take another few hours – maybe even days – for them to thaw out completely.

Fedorov leaves the room, goes down the hall to the back of the cabin. He returns with two handguns and a cell phone. He presses the guns into Teddy's and Reagan's chests, holds them there until they take them. He gives the phone to Teddy. "I am assuming you have lost yours, yes? Only I have the number to this one. If it rings, it will be me. Do not keep me waiting." He's carrying something else in a box under his arm. Emma can't see what it is, but it looks long and thin. "I may want you to bring them along to me later, so that we have all of our new friends in one place. I will decide when I get there – in the meantime, the two of you will have chance to warm up, yes? If they try anything foolish, however, kill them."

He looks back now. His eyes lock with Emma's. He's grinning. His burns look dry and monstrous. "But I hope you behave yourselves, my dears. I would like so very much for us all to be able to meet later, and then we shall eat together, yes? We shall have cereal, yes?" He directs this last at Elijah. "I have somewhere I need to be. I will return soon." He throws the keys of Emma's truck up into the air, catches them, winks at her, then leaves.

Teddy and Reagan crouch down in front of the fire again. It's roaring now, and the warmth is spreading through the cabin, spreading through the bodies of these near-frozen men. They reach out to it with both arms, their hands so close they're almost touching the flames. Their trembles finally begin to calm, and the color returns to their faces.

"Don't do anything stupid," Teddy says, talking to Emma and the others without turning. "I'm too fucking cold and too fucking tired to be dealing with any bullshit, you hear me?"

No one answers. Reagan doesn't have anything to add. He stares into the flames, his brow furrowed, and he continues trying to get warm.

41

T he house at the end of the driveway looks empty. It's not as big as Tom expected Yuri's home to be. Snow lies thick on its roof, and its windows are almost covered. It's enclosed on both sides by trees.

Tom looks the area over for a good place to park. He rolls into the trees, far back. It should not be visible on the road up to the front of the house. If Yuri does not come until he finishes work, it should be dark by then. He gets out of the truck and goes to the back of it, sweeping over the marks his tires have left, until they can't be seen from the house. Again, if it is dark when Yuri returns, he won't be able to see anything anyway.

Roger is still at the truck, though he's stepped out of it now, is standing by his door. He stretches side to side, twisting. "I need to piss," he says when Tom is close enough.

Tom is not willing to let him out of his sight. He can't imagine where Roger could escape to from here, especially not without a vehicle, but the abandonment back at the cabin is sticking with him. "Let's go, then."

"We can go inside."

Tom tilts his head.

"Sure," Roger says. "I know where he keeps a key. We can get inside. Hide out in there, where it's warm."

Tom looks back at the house. The front looks out onto a wider road, which leads up to it and looks as if it has been in more recent use than the road at the back. They will have a better vantage point from upstairs, which will be in their favor. Tom can check the rooms, too, see if there are any weapons inside. Right now, all he's armed with is his KA-BAR and the Glock he took from Teddy and Reagan.

"Is there a landline at the cabin in Anchorage?" he says. "I want to check in with Emma. I've not been getting any signal."

"There's a landline," Roger says. "And there's one in *there*, too. You could use that one."

"All right," Tom says. "We'll go inside."

Roger smiles, then leads the way. He goes to the back of the house. There is a security box. Roger punches in the code, opens it up. He takes the key from inside and unlocks the door. They step into a kitchen. Roger continues on through, to the front of the house. The floors are made of wood. Tom follows. They pass through the hall. They go by the front door. Tom notices drops of water sitting on the surface of the varnished wood, likely caused by melting snow. He looks to the side. He sees the watery shape of a boot's heel, twisted as if it's going through to the sitting room.

Tom grabs Roger by the collar, pulls him back, away from the sitting room door. "Stay back," he says, reaching for his KA-BAR.

Someone steps out of the room opposite, the dining room. Tom doesn't recognize him. He's armed with an M16. It's pointed at Tom and Roger.

A voice comes from the sitting room. A Russian accent,

not as thick and gruff as Fedorov's. "It's too late to try and run, Mr. Rollins."

Tom reaches, slowly, for the Glock.

The armed man sees him. "Uh-uh," he says. "You think I'm the only one here? Head through there." He points with the end of the M16 toward the sitting room.

Tom follows the directions. He doesn't have much choice. Roger is close behind him. There are another half a dozen armed men in the sitting room. A couple of them are pointing their rifles at him, along with the guy behind who has it trained on his back. The rest of them aren't aiming, but they're ready to be raised should he try anything.

On the sofa in front of the armed men are a man and a woman. The woman is very blonde, almost white, her hair like fine silk. The man smiles at Tom. This must be Yuri. Their first meeting.

"What a pleasure it is to finally make your acquaintance, Mr. Rollins," he says. "I'm sure you can guess who I am?"

Tom nods.

Yuri flicks a wrist toward him, a gesture Tom remembers Fedorov performing up at the cabin. "Restrain him," he says.

The man behind and the two with their rifles raised come forward. They take Tom's weapons, then grab him by the arms, one either side, the man behind with the barrel of his rifle now pressing into Tom's back.

Roger steps away from Tom, his hands raised. He speaks to Yuri. "Look, I brought him to you, like I said I would, right?"

Tom looks at Roger. Roger avoids looking back at him.

"I did what I said I'd do," Roger says. "I kept up my end."

Yuri's face is impassive. The girl shifts uncomfortably beside him. She keeps her face lowered. She looks like she'd rather be anywhere else than here.

Roger gets jittery under Yuri's gaze. "I said I'd bring him

here, right? The guy who's been causing you so much trouble – Tom Rollins. Here he is, served up on a silver platter. I said I'd do that, it's done – and I told you I could get your money back. I just need a laptop, that's all."

Yuri takes his time responding. He makes a show of picking lint off the leg of his trousers. "I never responded to your email, Roger," he says. "I never agreed to your request."

Tom hears Roger's audible gulp.

"You took a big risk coming here, Roger." Yuri gets to his feet, steps closer to him. He looks him up and down. When he speaks next, it is a whisper. "Do you really think I believe that you did not take the money?"

"I didn't think you would." Roger, despite his sudden bravado, sounds like he's about to piss his pants. "I've told everyone who'll listen that you wouldn't believe me, but I know, deep down, that you're more reasonable than that, right? I can get your money back. I can find whoever took it. I swear, I just need some time, I –"

Yuri punches him, doubles him up. Roger falls to his knees, then to his side.

Tom watches the girl. She sneaks looks, unable to remain completely ignorant. She winces.

Yuri, looming over Roger, inspects his fingernails. "I have you now," he says, "both of you, so I see no harm in permitting you a little extra time to see if you can 'find' the missing money." He crouches down. "Let us say, oh, twelve hours? That seems more than *reasonable* to me." He smiles, showing his teeth, looking like a predator about to devour its prey. He snaps his fingers. One of the armed men steps forward. There is a case slung over his shoulder. It looks like it contains a laptop.

"Take him upstairs," Yuri says. "Get him set up. Keep an eye on him."

The man reaches down, hauls Roger to his feet. Roger

whimpers. Yuri returns to his seat beside the woman. He places a hand upon her thigh, squeezes. She closes her eyes. She looks like she wants to cry.

"Gentlemen," Yuri says, looking at both Tom and Roger in turn. "Fedorov is on his way. He will be here soon." He smiles, an ominous message to them both. He flicks his wrist again, and the armed men drag them from the room.

Roger avoids looking at Tom again as he's led up the stairs, but he speaks in passing. "I'm sorry," he says, speaking low, "but this is my only way out."

Tom keeps his anger in check. Compartmentalizes it. This is a second betrayal. This one will not go unpunished.

The armed men are not taking Tom upstairs. They're taking him down the hall, no doubt to restrain him until Fedorov arrives. He pretends to trip over his own feet. He falls, cursing on the way down, managing to catch himself before his face hits the ground. The men laugh at him. They poke him with the toes of their snow-wet boots.

"Get your ass up," one of them says. "You ain't even got a *reason* to be weak-kneed yet, buddy."

Tom wraps a hand around the Santa Muerte pendant at his neck. He snaps it loose and puts her into his mouth, tongues her to the back, storing her, holding her in place with his tongue. He pushes himself back up, and lets them lead him on.

42

Roger is not sure where they have taken Tom. He's upstairs, in a room, alone, typing away at the keys of the laptop and still coming up with nothing. The guard assigned to him is outside the room. He checked that all the windows were locked before he stepped back out.

It's been a couple of hours now. Roger is sweating – sweating hard. His mouth is dry. He hasn't heard Fedorov arrive yet. He's glad. The presence of the mad Russian will stress him further, especially knowing what Fedorov will do to him if the twelve hours runs out and he still doesn't have an answer.

Part of him – a small part for now, which may grow over time – regrets betraying Tom Rollins. Giving him up to Yuri just to buy himself some time and good grace. From the moment Tom and Emma tracked Roger and his family down to the cabin in Anchorage (which reminds him – if he comes out of this unscathed, he's going to fire that fucking secretary), Roger has been obscuring the truth. Not outright lies, not exactly, but enough to play on Tom's apparent hero complex. Enough to persuade him to help – for *Lily's* sake, for *Elijah's* sake, for *Emma's* sake.

Truth is, Roger knows Yuri's temperament can go either way. Getting the money back, and pointing out who actually took it, might – *might* – get Roger back into his good books. And, if it doesn't, Roger still has a Plan B. There are plenty more millions in Yuri's laundered accounts, and Roger still knows how to access them all.

He emailed Yuri from his office while Tom was at the other end of the building, looking out the window to watch the street below. He wrote the message fast, but he deliberated over sending it for a while. In fact, he didn't hit send until Tom surprised him, re-entering the office. Tom has a very light step.

Roger needed to take a gamble – Fedorov wants Tom for what he's done to his face. Giving Tom up to Fedorov, Yuri's loyal right-hand man, that would buy him some time with Yuri. Coming in with a bargaining chip like Tom Rollins, the mountain man who's already killed so many of Yuri and Fedorov's men, that would surely stay the bullet Yuri no doubt wanted to put into him on sight.

Roger's diaphragm still aches from where Yuri hit him, but if this is the worst he walks away with, he'll count himself lucky. There's a bruise forming there, he's sure. He prods at it, feels how a dull pain blooms there, trying to get himself to focus harder on the task in hand.

The problem immediately facing him is actually getting to the bottom of this riddle. Finding out who really took the money, and where they've put it. He still has a while to crack the code, but he's going to have to think outside the box. So far, it already feels like he's tried every trick he knows. He chews on the corner of a thumbnail and probes at the bruise with his other hand, staring at the screen.

He looks up, distracted. There are voices outside the door.

Someone is talking to his guard. Someone come to replace him, give him a break? But then he realizes it's a woman's voice. A familiar voice. *Alina.*

The door starts to open. Alina appears, then presses a finger to her lips. Roger nods that he understands. She crosses the room to him, sits beside him. Her eyes flicker between him and the door. "I told the guard Yuri sent me to check on you," she says, her voice a whisper. "Are you insane, bringing him here?"

She's talking about Yuri, he knows, and not Tom. "Relax," Roger says. "I've been out here with him too. He knows I know about it."

Alina gives him a look like she's not so sure. This empty house belongs to Yuri. It is not his home, not like he told Tom. Yuri uses it to house visitors from Russia. Fellow Mafia. Roger was brought out here to meet a couple of them once. He remembers the main one, Mikhail. Roger was nervous, kept shaking. Mikhail almost crushed his hand when he shook it. He laughed at how pale Roger looked: "This is the man handling your money?" he'd said, in a mocking tone. Yuri didn't rise to the bait.

Mikhail and the other men were loud, like Fedorov. They laughed a lot, and slapped Roger on the back to punctuate every time they said something they thought was funny. They drank a lot of vodka, and insisted he join them. Roger thought he was going to poison his liver. He almost passed out a couple of times, but they kept shaking him awake. He had a hangover that lasted a week. He told Lily his boss had invited him out to drinks to celebrate landing a big account, and they overdid it. Lily had no sympathy for him. She gave him the silent treatment for a couple of days for being gone all night without a single call, before finally stroking his forehead and bringing him painkillers and soup, and plenty of water.

This house, however, holds far fonder memories. It is where he and Alina would meet in secret. Where they would indulge their affair.

He looks at Alina, and smiles at her. It feels like it has been forever since he saw her last. She doesn't smile back, but he doesn't take this personally. She's stressed. Perhaps bringing Yuri here, to their love nest, was a mistake, but Roger thought Yuri would appreciate it more than if he took Tom Rollins directly to his house.

She's still as beautiful as the first day he laid eyes on her. That must have been two years ago now. *Time flies*, Roger thinks, *when you're having fun – and when you're in love with the most beautiful woman you've ever seen.*

The first time he saw her was a few months after Yuri had brought him in to launder his money. They were at Yuri's house, sitting at the big table in the dining room. Alina merely passed through. She was wearing some kind of thin robe – it was summer then – and it billowed out behind her as she glided through the room on her way to the kitchen. Or perhaps that is just Roger's memory playing tricks. Perhaps the robe did not billow anywhere near as much as he remembers. The whole scene is slowed down in his mind. Like in a movie. He remembers having to remind himself not to stare, that this fleeting image of beauty was the girlfriend or wife or mistress of the Russian gangster who held his life in his hands. He had to force his mouth closed, too. He clenched his jaw together, scared of it falling loose again.

He thought about her a lot after that initial sighting. That's all they were, though – just thoughts. Then he'd see her more. She'd be at Yuri's office when Roger had to call around to talk business. She'd be at his home. She started to hang around more. She'd talk, and her voice was so delicate, her accent so soft and singsong. She'd smile at him. She'd laugh at his pathetic attempts at jokes. It was a genuine laugh, too, not the head-thrown-back, almost mocking laughter of Yuri or Fedorov.

Roger started to think about her more. More and more. He'd think about her when he was alone in the shower. He'd think about her when he was with Lily. Daydreams would come unbidden in the middle of the day, while at work, in meetings, driving his car.

And then, as if in a dream, his sexual fantasies became a reality.

He was working late, on Yuri's accounts, of course. They were the only accounts he worked late on. Alina came to him. He didn't know how she'd gotten into the building – she told him later that one of the cleaners let her in after she'd told them Roger had called her, that he needed to see her urgently to discuss her account. They believed her. Why wouldn't they? She's so charming. A beauty that could unnerve anyone. She came into his office, a vision made flesh.

"Hello, Roger," she said.

He was surprised to see her, of course. As much as he'd longed for such a moment, he'd never expected it to actually come true. The small talk that followed does not matter. Roger barely remembers it. He can't forget what came next. The seduction. She came onto him. They had sex, right there in his office, in the chair where he had spent so many years of his life slaving away over other people's money.

It wasn't one and done, as he thought it might be. It was a regular thing. Alina told him, directly after, that she'd like to see him again. Privately. And so it continued. She'd come to the office after hours. She'd sit on his lap while he finished his work, nearly always working on Yuri's money. She'd show interest, asking him what he was doing, and she'd chew on his ear while he answered.

Or, if not at the office, they'd find a quiet place in town and get in the backseat of his car or hers. And then, sometimes, they'd come *here*, to this empty house. Alina always knew whether someone was staying here or not.

"Are you having much luck?" Alina says, nodding at the laptop.

Roger sighs. "No," he says. "The top and the bottom of it is *no*, I can't find the fucking money. I don't know who's taken it, or how they did it."

Alina watches the screen. She always watched him while he worked, as if she understood what he was doing. Her brow would furrow, her eyes narrowing in concentration, as they're doing now. "Have you checked his other accounts?" she says.

"Of course," Roger says.

"Show me," she says.

"What's the point? There's nothing there."

"Show me," she repeats. "Perhaps a fresh pair of eyes will see something you cannot?"

Roger has never been able to say no to her, so he shows her what she wants to see. She watches, rapt, as he enters the accounts. "See?" he says. "Nothing. Everything's in place. Untouched."

"I see," Alina says. "And that is how you access them? Those are the codes?"

"Yeah," Roger says. "And the only people who know them are me and Yuri. And you too, now, I guess." He doesn't care about the other accounts, though. The other accounts are not missing any money.

Roger closes the laptop, puts it to one side. He twists toward her, reaches out and takes her hand. "Listen," he says. He leans closer, strokes her knuckles. "I can't find the money. I don't think I'll ever be able to find the damn money. But fuck the money. I have a plan."

"A plan?"

Roger nods. "Well, a Plan *B*. Let's go. Let's get out of here. I was buying time coming here. I didn't know Yuri would bring you with him, but this is ideal. It's perfect, in fact. I don't have to try to find you – we're together already, so let's just *run*."

Alina blinks. "Run?" she says.

Roger points at the laptop. "All of his money is at my fingertips. *All* of it. *We* can transfer it – set up an account of our own – and we can *run*. Get out of here, get far, far away. We can be together, finally."

Alina slips her hands out of his. She bites her lip. She's considering it – Roger can see that she's giving the idea serious thought. "Where...where would we go?" she says.

"It doesn't matter," Roger says. "Anywhere, so long as we're together."

"Somewhere...*hot*," Alina says.

"Yes, exactly, somewhere hot," Roger says, smiling, giddy now.

"Greece, perhaps?"

"Sure, Greece, sure," Roger says. Greece would probably have been one of the last places to occur to Roger as an option.

Alina's eyes narrow. "What about your family?"

"They'll be fine," Roger says. "They'll be fine without me. Lily's parents moved to Florida a few years ago. She'll go and live with them. Everything will be all right for them. They'll be okay."

Alina is silent for a moment. She looks toward the door, the guard sitting or standing outside. "Have you ever thought about us running away together before now?"

Roger licks his lips. "I've... It's crossed my mind." Another fantasy that, until this moment, he never expected had a chance of coming true.

"When I was a girl," Alina says, glancing at the door again, her voice still low, "when I was very young, my parents died. My grandmother raised me. Every summer, we would go to Corfu. Do you know of Corfu? It is a Greek island. Five summers we went there together, two weeks each time. We would spend our days on the beach. We would swim in the sea. At night, we would go to the bar, and my grandmother would sneak me cocktails." She smiles, remembering. "They were the happiest times of my life. And then my grandmother died. I have not been back to Corfu since, but I have thought about it often."

Roger blinks. "Okay," he says. "I already said fine, we'll go to Corfu. I'm easy. So long as it's with you."

She looks at him now, looks him deep in the eyes. "Yuri does not know that story. I have never told him. I have never wanted him to know. He will never think to look for me in Greece."

"That's good," Roger says.

She reaches behind her back. Roger isn't sure what she's doing. Her hand begins to rummage, like she has an itch. "We are not going to run away together, Roger," she says.

He isn't sure he's heard her right. "What's that?"

"I am going to be free, Roger," she says. "I do not need another man for my freedom. I am not the helpless blonde bimbo in desperate need of your rescue. All I needed from you was to learn how to get the money. With me in your lap and my tongue in your ear, you were only too eager to tell me what to do."

"What're you – what're you talking about?"

Alina leans in close. Her hand is still behind her back, though it's still now, no longer rummaging or scratching or whatever she was doing. "How could I ever run away with a man so easily prepared to leave his family behind, to abandon them to such danger?"

Roger's eyes widen. "*You?*" he says. "You stole the money?"

"I would already be gone, Roger, but you never told me Yuri had an alarm on his accounts."

"I – I –" Roger can't think straight. His Plan B has frittered away before his very eyes. "I'll – you *bitch* – I'll tell him. I'll tell Yuri it was *you* –"

Alina's hand returns from behind her back. She strikes Roger in the side, below his rib cage. He feels a sharp pain. A stabbing in his chest. "You will say nothing," Alina says. "Half a million would have been enough, but now I will take it all, and you have shown me how I am to do that."

Roger looks down as she pulls her arm back. She's holding a switchblade. The length of it is red with his blood. She presses a hand over his mouth. Roger can taste blood. He can taste the moisturizer earlier rubbed in to the palm of her hand. His eyes are flickering. The image of her blurs. He can't make out her face. The angel has become a devil. His killer. She has killed him.

She whispers into his ear. "Thank you, Roger," she says. "I could not have done this without you."

43

The men took Tom into the basement. They stripped his shirt from his torso, no doubt in preparation for Fedorov's arrival. While they looped rope through the beams overhead, Tom slipped the Santa Muerte pendant from his mouth to his hand. He holds it still while he hangs from the beam, his arms bound above his head. The toes of his boots dangle inches above the ground. There is a fiery pain in his shoulders, but he grits his teeth and ignores it. It will numb.

Two of the armed guards remain in the basement with him. They grin at the way he winces, at how uncomfortable he looks. Tom feels the ropes, checks their thickness. He presses the pendant to it, presses her scythe to the fibers. The scythe is not sharp, but it has sharp edges. They will have to do. He does not attempt to cut through just yet. The guards are watching too closely. They will notice if his hand starts sawing.

Tom is near the back of the basement. There is a wall behind him. Directly opposite are the wooden stairs down which he was led. To the left, near where the armed guards are leaning against the wall, there is a small table. Currently, there is nothing on it, but Tom knows it is there to serve a purpose. It is likely waiting for Fedorov. To Tom's right there is a furnace, but it's not on. There is a chill down here. He can feel the bare flesh of his chest prickling.

The door leading into the basement opens. Yuri comes down the steps. He's holding Tom's KA-BAR, studying it. "I believe," he says, reaching the bottom and coming closer, holding up the knife, "that this is Army issue, yes?"

Tom does not answer.

"Come now, Mr. Rollins, this is no interrogation. There is no need to be so tight-lipped – it was a straightforward question, was it not?"

Tom does not answer.

Yuri sighs. He places the KA-BAR on the table to Tom's left. "Please yourself," he says. He looks Tom over. "You keep in shape, I see. Your body is a temple, yes? I imagine Fedorov will take great pleasure in destroying it."

The door at the top of the stairs opens again. This time, it is the woman who comes down. She comes up next to Yuri, but she avoids looking at Tom.

"Alina," Yuri says, "where have you been? You were gone so long I came down to visit our guest."

Alina responds in Russian. Her voice is low.

Yuri grins. He turns to Tom. "Do you know Russian, Mr. Rollins?"

"Only a little," Tom says.

Yuri's grin grows wider, almost becomes a smile. "Alina has just told me that I should not ask a lady why it has taken her so long to go to the bathroom."

"I'd be inclined to agree with her," Tom says.

Yuri laughs.

"I would like to leave now," Alina says, in English this time. "I do not want to be here when Fedorov arrives."

Yuri pats her head. "You have such a delicate constitution, my dear. Very well. We shall leave." He motions Alina toward the stairs, but he looks back at Tom before he goes. "Goodbye, Mr. Rollins. Fedorov will arrive soon, I am sure. You will not have to wait for long. The two of you will have a most wonderful time together." There is a gleam in his eye. "I do not imagine that we will ever see each other again."

Tom does not give him an answer.

Yuri does not wait for one. He turns on his heel and follows Alina out of the basement. She is already out the door. It closes when Yuri passes through. Tom glances at his two guards still present. They do not look as concerned about what is to come as Alina did.

They look excited.

44

Elijah is sleeping. Lily sits close to him, her arm wrapped around his shoulders. She's trying to stay awake, but her head is nodding, threatening to doze off.

It's stuffy in the cabin, but Emma manages to keep herself alert. She bites down on the inside of her cheek. She can taste blood. She watches Teddy and Reagan. They look bored. Teddy paces the floor in front of the fire, every so often stopping to drop another log into the flames, to keep it going. Reagan is on the sofa opposite. He's hunched forward, looking down at his clasped hands. Next to him is the bag that Fedorov insisted they take from their crippled SUV. They're keeping it close, but there's still no sign of what is inside it.

It's getting dark outside. Emma sees a few flakes of snow falling, swirling by the window, but nothing serious. Nothing heavy. There is no threat of another blizzard.

"This is bullshit," Teddy says, stopping his pacing and standing in front of Reagan with his hands on his hips. "How long are we supposed to stay out here on fuckin' babysitting duty?"

Reagan shrugs without looking up. "Until Fedorov tells us otherwise."

"*Fuck* Fedorov," Teddy says. He snorts. "Fuckin' Russki. He thinks we're a fuckin' joke, you know that, right? Wouldn't surprise me if he just forgets all about us, leaves us out here."

Reagan shrugs again. It's hard to tell if he's listening to his friend. He's lost in thought.

"You know what we need to do, right?" Teddy goes on, regardless. "We need to prove to him that we're *not* a joke."

Reagan looks up finally. "Then we should just sit tight, right? How else are we gonna prove it?"

Teddy does not like the sound of this. He blows out air. Runs his tongue around the inside of his mouth. He looks over toward Emma, sees she is watching, listening. He doesn't like it. "Mind your fuckin' business," he says.

Emma does not look away.

Teddy rolls his eyes. "Just go to sleep or something, will ya? Jesus Christ, stop staring at us like some crazy bitch."

Emma raises an eyebrow, but she continues to stare. Her mind is running, looking for inspiration, an opening, a way out of this situation.

Reagan sits back, lets his head rest on the rear of the sofa. He closes his eyes. It's a moment before Teddy notices and kicks his boot. "Stay awake," he says.

"Just resting my eyes," Reagan says, not moving.

Teddy kicks him again, harder. "Open your fuckin' eyes, damn it."

Reagan does so, with a sigh.

Teddy shoots a look at Emma again, then sits down next to Reagan, his back to her. He lowers his voice, but Emma can still hear him. "What the fuck's the matter with you?"

Reagan shrugs.

Teddy imitates the gesture, raising and lowering his shoulders in comic exaggeration. "What, you can't speak now?"

"I'm just tired, man," Reagan says.

"No, that ain't it. I know you, Reagan. Something's up."

Reagan shrugs again.

Teddy is about to say something, but he looks down at his leg suddenly, at his pocket. He stands, pulls out the phone Fedorov gave him earlier. He looks at the screen, then at Emma. He scowls. "Watch them," he says to Reagan, then leaves the room, goes into the hallway to answer the call.

Reagan sits forward, but he does not look over. He sniffs. Clasps his hands. His thumbs rub against each other like a one-man thumb war.

It does not take long for Teddy to return. He's grinning, slipping the phone back into his pocket and pulling out his gun. "That's the call," he says. He looks at Emma, and this time, he continues to smile when he sees her looking back. "Let's go."

"Go where?" Reagan says.

"I got directions," Teddy says. He waves the gun at Emma. "Wake them up," he tells her. He turns back to Reagan. "Fedorov's there." He grins, and it's one of the most malicious-looking things Emma has ever seen. "And he's got his man."

Emma feels her throat constrict. Her stomach sinks. It's hard to breathe, suddenly. *He's got his man. Tom.*

Teddy notices she has not moved. "I said wake them *up*, crazy bitch!"

Emma turns, presses her hands to Lily's shoulders and tries to rouse her. Her mind has clouded. She can't think straight. Tom and Roger have been captured – they can't be talking about anyone else. Teddy directed the statement at her. It was for her benefit. He wanted her to know.

Wanted her to know there is no one coming for them. They're on their own now.

"Get your gun out," Teddy says. "I'm gonna drive. You watch them."

"Why even leave us here?" Reagan says. "It hasn't taken him that long to get there. I don't get it."

"*Insurance*, man. What's not to get? If Roger and the guy somehow got free by the time Fedorov got there, he's got their women as backup. Well, now he doesn't need the insurance."

Out the corner of her eye, Emma sees how Reagan looks over. Watches them.

"So..." he says. "What now?"

"Don't be so fucking stupid," Teddy says. He lowers his voice, almost a whisper, Emma can barely hear him over the crackling of the fire's flames. She hears enough, though. She hears, *tying up loose ends.*

Whatever happens next, when they get where they are going, is Fedorov's prerogative. They won't survive it. Fedorov and Yuri can't take a chance on leaving them alive. They'll end up in a grave somewhere, heavy snow falling onto the ground above them. Perhaps up in the Chugach Mountains, where Tom first came across Roger, where this whole thing started.

Lily is awake. She's rubbing her eyes. "It's time to go," Emma tells her. She doesn't tell her anything else. She can't. She'll find out for herself. Emma doesn't have the heart to say it. That they're defeated. That their situation looks hopeless.

Well, not hopeless. They still have a chance. Emma just doesn't know what it is yet, or when it will come to them. She won't give in yet, though. She can't. She won't go down without a fight.

"Outside," Teddy tells them, indicating with his gun. "Let's go, come on, hurry up."

Lily stands with Elijah. She holds onto him. He's still

sleeping. Emma holds Lily by the elbow. They go to the door of the cabin. She turns to Reagan. He stands with the bag from the sofa looped over his shoulder. He seems the more reasonable of the two. "Just let them go," she says. "Take me. You don't need to take them, too."

Reagan looks at her, his eyes wide. His mouth opens and closes like a fish.

"Don't talk to him," Teddy says. "Shut up and get in the car."

"You know what he's going to do to them," Emma says, still talking to Reagan, tilting her head toward Lily and Elijah. "Do you really want that? Can you live with it?"

Teddy comes round and hits Emma in the back of the head. "I said shut up!" he says. "Outside, now!" He shoots Reagan an angry look.

Outside, Teddy jabs a finger toward the car down the side of the cabin. He grabs Emma high on her arm and pushes her toward it. "Dig it out," he says. "Get the snow off."

"I don't have a shovel," Emma says, defiance in her voice.

Teddy's eyes are dark. "Then use your fuckin' hands."

Emma does not move. Teddy raises the gun like he's going to hit her with it. Reagan brushes past him. "We'll do it together," he says, dragging Emma with him, saving her from Teddy's wrath. "It'll go faster that way."

Teddy holds back. He makes no effort to help. He watches them as they work. Emma does not look back at him, but she can feel his eyes on her. Can feel how much he wants to strike her. How much he wanted it when he had the gun raised above his head.

45

Tom can hear singing. It's deep and it's full of joy, and it is Russian.

The guards to the left start grinning. The door at the top of the stairs is thrown open with a clatter. The singing is louder. Fedorov comes down the stairs, kicking his legs out in front of him. His hands are full. In his left, he carries a bottle of vodka. Under his right arm there is a car battery, and in his right hand, there is what at first glance looks like a small cattle prod.

It's not a cattle prod. It's a picana. Tom is familiar with picanas. He knows exactly what they are, and what they are for. Not as long as cattle prods, they are designed and manufactured for torture, nothing else. Someone, somewhere, makes them, and they know what they are used for – and they keep on making them.

Tom closes his fist tight around the Santa Muerte pendant. She digs into his palm, almost hard enough to pierce the skin.

"My boys, my boys," Fedorov says to his men with his

vodka arm spread wide. "Has our guest been behaving himself, yes?"

"He's just been hanging around," says one of the guards.

Fedorov laughs like this pun is one of the funniest things he's ever heard. He sets the car battery and the picana down on the table next to Tom's knife, takes another drink from the vodka, then puts it down next to everything else. He steps back with his hands on his hips, and looks up at Tom for the first time. He is smiling. The burns on the left side of his face are pulled tight and shining.

"Mr. Rollins," he says. He curls the *R*. "It is so good to be seeing you again, my friend. It has been too long."

"I could go longer," Tom says.

Fedorov throws his head back and laughs like *this* is the funniest thing he's ever heard. He turns to his men, waves them away. "You may go," he says. "Mr. Rollins and I would like to spend some quality time together, alone."

The guards grab their weapons and head out of the basement. They're grinning as they go, shooting Tom looks. They close the door at the top of the stairs.

"I'll save you some time," Tom says. "I don't know where the money is."

Fedorov smiles. He indicates the burns. "You and I, my friend, we are beyond money. I will get the money from Roger, later. Right now, he is working away, like little worker bee."

"You looked in on him yet? I hope you sent him my regards."

"In my excitement, I come straight for you. Down these stairs, like child on Christmas morning, yes? Roger can wait. Tonight is for us, my friend."

Fedorov starts singing again as he moves toward his table, preparing his tools. Tom does not know the song. Fedorov takes off his shirt. There is a tattoo on his back. It's big and black, devoid of color, and covers almost every inch of his flesh. It is St Basil's Cathedral from Red Square in Moscow. There are tattoos on his front, too. There are nautical stars on each of his pecs. He moves the car battery, gets it into position, turning it around. He notices Tom's KA-BAR. His singing stops briefly. He picks it up, turns it over in his hands, studies it.

"How many men you have killed with this knife?" he says.

"I'd like to bury it in at least one more," Tom says, looking Fedorov in the eye.

Fedorov holds the knife out, presses the flat of it to Tom's cheek. "Oh, you are so full of humor today, yes? I am glad of this. It would be so boring if you were not to speak. Tell me of your time in the Army, my friend."

Tom does not answer this.

"Oh, so now you are being quiet?" Fedorov tuts, shakes his head. He takes the knife away, but does not put it back down. "You disappoint me. Just when I was beginning to feel we were getting to know one another. In Russia, I was in the SVR." There is a wicked glint in his eye. "But I was kicked out for being a naughty boy."

Tom wonders, as he did the first time he was told this story, just how naughty someone has to be to get kicked out of the SVR.

"My expulsion, however, it was blessing in disguise, yes? Because then I am free. I find work. I find work so easy, a man with my skills, I am very in demand, and I make such money. Then, my new employers, they tell me they have somewhere they want me to be. And so, I come to America. I am almost real American. Like you, yes? Like everyone in this house. We are all chasing American Dream, yes?"

He presses his right hand to his heart, still holding the knife. He starts reciting the pledge of allegiance. When he's done, "See? I know it well, yes? I know it all. Real American."

He presses the side of the knife to Tom's face again. "Perhaps I cut you up, yes?" He leans in close. He is smiling. There is hunger in his smile. "Perhaps I ruin your handsome face, just as you ruined mine, yes?" He turns his face, allows Tom a good, close-up look.

He takes the knife away. "Perhaps I will," he says. "The night is yet young. I have such plans for us, my friend!" Something catches his eye. He notices the scar in Tom's side. He presses the tip of the knife to it. "You have already tasted a blade, I see. It looks deep. It looks like you are lucky to be alive."

"It's a recent addition," Tom says.

"And you come to Alaska to rest, yes? To recover?"

"I came to Alaska for the snow."

Fedorov chuckles. "You are funny man, Mr. Rollins. I call you Tom. We are friends here. I call you Tom, my friend." He cuts Tom across the chest, sliding the knife slowly. Tom grits his teeth, his body stiffening. He does not cry out. He feels the blood running down his torso.

"This is a nice knife, my friend. So sharp. It cut you like nothing. Like through *butter*." He puts the knife down next to the car battery, then laces his fingers together and pops his knuckles. "But let us not get ahead of ourselves! Let us start small!" He adopts a fighter's stance in front of Tom, as if Tom is in any position to fight back. Fedorov starts throwing punches, softening him up, using his torso as a punching bag.

Tom is beaten around, but he uses the movements to his advantage. He presses the Santa Muerte pendant to the rope, and he starts to saw. The movements are disguised by his swinging. He presses down hard, cutting through the fibers. It is hard work, and he knows it is slow going, but he has no other options.

Fedorov does not hit him for long. When he stops,

though, Tom is still swinging. Is still able to use his movements to cover his work.

Breathing hard, Fedorov grabs the vodka. He takes a long drink from it, then pours some over Tom. It burns in the cut across Tom's chest. Fedorov takes another drink, then pours some over the burns on his face. They glisten. He laughs. Puts the bottle back down and starts hooking up the picana. He's singing again.

His back turned, Tom rubs the pendant against the ropes as hard and fast as he can, stopping only when Fedorov begins to turn. He's holding up the picana. The end of it crackles with electricity. It's ready to go. Fedorov is grinning.

46

Yuri and Alina are driving home, Yuri behind the steering wheel. He is in a much better mood than he was this morning, and this time, he is certain that there is nothing Alina can do to ruin it.

Things are falling into place. Tonight, he is rid of his enemies. Tomorrow, there is a strong likelihood he will have his money back – and, if he doesn't, if Roger proves to be as full of shit as Yuri thinks he is, it doesn't matter. He'll be dead, and Fedorov will have been sure to take his time about it.

Tomorrow night, however, is the beginning of something special. From tomorrow night, he is looking to make a lot more money than half a million dollars. He will soon become the richest man in the state. He will *rule* Alaska.

When he gets home, he will make some phone calls. Councilman Manning and Mayor Pullman will need to be put on alert, ready to play their parts once things are initiated. He'll have to call Moscow, too. Mikhail likes to be kept up to date. He'll tell him everything is proceeding as planned. He'll be glad to hear it. Mikhail has not needed to know about the slight hiccups of Roger Noakes and Tom Rollins. Mikhail would not have been pleased to hear about this, and Yuri is glad he has not told him.

Of course, as ever, there is one thorn in Yuri's side. One dark cloud on his sunny feeling.

Alina is silent beside him. Her face is miserable. She has not said two words to him since they got back in the car, since she was so eager to leave the house behind. She does not have the stomach for what was about to happen back there. She looks out the window with sad eyes. Her eyes are always so sad these days. Yuri shakes his head, determined he will not be dragged down by her. He has no time for her regular melancholy. He remembers when she used to be fun. These days, since this whole thing began with the missing money, and for a time before that, too, she has been a burden.

Yuri thinks he is bored with her. It may be time to get rid of her. To find a replacement. She is still beautiful, of course, and her body remains fantastic (unlike the last one, who became too comfortable in her lifestyle and gorged herself on American foods), and she looks good on his arm, but she's becoming unpredictable, as well as everything else. He did not sign up for mood swings. He will make that very clear to the next one. Perhaps next time he won't go Russian. An American girl, maybe? The risk with American girls, if they're local, is that if they go missing, someone might notice, might try to find them. Non-local, then. For every problem, there is a solution.

"I feel sick," Alina says.

Yuri looks at her. It's true – she does look sick. She looks pale, but then, she is always pale.

She presses a hand to her stomach. Another hand goes to her mouth. She swallows, like she's about to throw up.

The thought crosses Yuri's mind, *The bitch had best not be pregnant.* "Do not be sick," he says.

"It's not that simple," Alina says, taking a deep, sharp breath through her nose. She presses back into the seat, bracing herself. "Pull over," she says.

Yuri does not want to. "Hold it," he says. "Wait until we are home."

"It's too far to go. I won't last that long."

Yuri looks ahead. The road is clear. There is nothing around them, trees lining either side of the road with snow-coated fields beyond. He does not want to stop. Does not want to slow down. He wants to get home. Wants to maintain this feeling of buoyancy, of everything coming together.

As he's thought so much lately, it feels every time things are good, every time they are going the way they should, Alina finds a way to ruin it.

"I'm not stopping," he says, his mood already soured, the mood he swore to himself he would not allow her to darken.

"If you don't stop, I'm going to vomit all over the inside of this car!" There are tears streaming from her eyes.

"Jesus fucking Christ," Yuri says, jerking the steering wheel, pulling the car to the side of the road. The wheels skid. He loses control momentarily, but then they come to a stop. Almost as soon as they have, Alina is out of the vehicle, running from it. She stumbles in the snow on the embankment, falls to her knees, and starts retching.

Yuri remains inside the car. He rolls his eyes. She has left the door open. Cold air is blowing in, rendering the warm air coming from the vents pointless.

She stays there at the side of the road for a long time. He can hear her. She's loud. She's throwing up for a long time, or trying to. Her body is arched, hunched over itself. Yuri checks the time. He's losing patience.

He gets out of the car. Stands by it for a moment, watching her. He had hoped the sound of the car door opening and slamming shut would prompt her to wrap things up. It does not. "Hurry up!" he says.

She retches again.

Yuri goes to her, trudging through the snow, kicking it out of his way, kicking it toward her back. She is on her knees still, though one leg is drawn beneath her, like she's ready to stand. He reaches out, places a hand on her back. It is not to comfort her. It's to shake her, to hurry her along, to see if she is nearly done. If she is not, there is a strong urge to leave her here by the side of the road. Let her find her own way home.

Or not.

As he touches her, though, she rises, spins. In the fleeting moment before what comes next, Yuri sees there is no vomit on the ground, lying atop the snow, sinking into it. It's clear.

Then, pain erupts in his abdomen. He feels himself rise off his feet at the shock of it, then his hands go to where it burns, to where it feels like he is tearing.

"Look at me," Alina says.

He does. Her teeth are bared. She looks feral.

Something slides out of his belly. He looks down. It is a switchblade, coated in his blood. She sinks it into him again.

"You will never touch me again," Alina says. "You will never hurt me again." She stabs him a third time, punctuating her final statement, and then she lets him fall.

The ground is cold beneath him. Yuri curls up into a ball to quell the burning pain in his stomach. It does not work. It gets worse.

He hears the sound of Alina's footsteps growing distant, walking away. He hears the car's doors close, both of them – first the driver's side, then the passenger's. Then he hears her driving away.

Yuri is trembling, shivering. It is so cold. *It's the snow,* he tells himself. *It's just the snow.*

It is his blood leaving him. Leaking out, and soaking into the snow. He can see it. He can see it turning red beneath him. He coughs, and he sees it land beside his mouth. He can taste it. Everything is red. All he sees is red.

And then he sees nothing.

47

Fedorov jams the picana into Tom's side. Tom's body goes into convulsions. He'd already gritted his teeth in anticipation, to avoid biting through his tongue as the electricity courses through him. Fedorov's tongue pokes out the corner of his mouth, on the burned side. He takes the picana away. Tom gasps for breath.

His wrists are bloody. It runs down his arms. The ropes he's bound with have chafed him raw. His strength is fading, but he continues to cut at the ropes with the pendant. It's hard when the picana is applied. His body goes into paralysis. He cannot move. It takes everything he has to work at the ropes in between shocks, while Fedorov stops to catch his breath, or take a drink from his vodka, or simply to allow Tom a brief moment to recover. He's not trying to kill Tom, not yet. He's drawing this out. He's having his fun with it.

"You are a tough one, my friend," Fedorov says, taking a step back, the picana down by his side. "Like leather."

Tom spits.

"How much of this do you think you can take, my friend? Everyone breaks eventually. I look forward to seeing when your breaking point is. I think it may take us through to dawn, yes? I think it may take us all through the night." Fedorov looks pleased at this prospect. "I tell you, we will have good times together, yes?"

Fedorov puts the picana down on the table, and he takes another drink. Tom is still swaying side to side, back and forth. The movement conceals what his hands are doing. He's able to continue cutting at the rope. He can feel the fibers fraying, but he still has a long way to go. Fedorov steps back in front of Tom, his hands empty this time. He places them upon his hips, looks Tom up and down, admiring his handiwork so far. He reaches out, dips the tip of his finger in the blood on Tom's chest. He tastes it.

Tom's shoulders are burning. They were numb earlier, but they have come to life now, with all the movement. With the shocks. They feel like they're about to tear out of the sockets. If he were a weaker man, if he did not have the muscles he has, it's likely they would already have dislocated by now.

"I remember, in Russia," Fedorov says, "there was a man like you. You are reminding me of him, truly you are, yes. I had to talk to him. It was in a basement, just like this. I am getting flashbacks. It is like I am back there." Fedorov looks around. "Well, perhaps not *exactly* like this one. This basement is nicer. It is better lit.

"Anyway, this man, he was from another country. A neighbor country. Perhaps you know the one I am speaking of. Very small, but the people there, they are belligerent. They do not always know their place. This man, he knew some things. He knew things that *I* wanted to know. So I asked him. I asked him nicely. He would not answer me, no matter how nicely I ask. What came next was on him – I just wanted to have a chat! A pleasant chat, as you and I are doing, right now."

Tom says nothing. There is no chat. This conversation is all one-sided.

"So, I get out my tools. I have to get my tools, to make him speak to me, yes? I tie him up, like you are. He is hanging, just like you. I press the rod to him, and he lasted a long time. As long as you have now. He was tough, too. He was like leather, too." Fedorov holds up a finger. "But I never doubted I would break him. Not once. Because I always break them. Always.

"And he did speak to me. He told me everything. By the time he broke, he told me his mother's name, his grandmother's name, the name of the first girl he kissed. He cried and begged for his life. He cried for his mother. He wanted to go home. I tell him of course he can go home. He will be going home very soon. So, knowing all that I want to know, and some extra besides, I kill him. I put him out of his misery. I make it quick for him. This man, he had something I wanted, and he gave it to me. I rewarded him with peace." Fedorov strokes the burns on the corner of his mouth. "Tell me, my friend, what do you think I want from you?"

"You can't tell," Tom says, "but I'm shrugging right now."

"Again, Tom my friend, so funny. You are so funny. In other circumstances, we could have been good friends. You make me laugh. Unfortunately, these are not other circumstances. Everything I want from you, Tom, you are already giving it to me. There is nothing else. This ends with your death, and it will not come quick. It will not be swift, and it will not be merciful. You took my handsome face from me, Tom. My vengeance can only be satisfied with blood. Do you understand?"

"I understand that you like the sound of your own voice."

"Yes, Tom, continue to joke, my friend. It entertains me, and I am sure it makes you feel better. You must keep your spirits up for what is to come. You must be tough for what is to come." He reaches out, presses his hand to Tom's cheek. "I need you to be strong for me, Tom. I need you to hold up. I need you to do this for me, my friend."

"I'll do my best to oblige," Tom says.

Fedorov grins, pats his cheek. "I knew you would not disappoint, my friend."

He steps away now, back to the table. "I am thinking," he says, voice raised, back to Tom, "that soon you will have no jokes. I am thinking soon, you will be taking me very serious." He looks back over his shoulder. "Do you know why that is?"

Tom doesn't answer.

"We have guests coming," Fedorov says, grinning. "They are on their way to us right now, as we speak. Soon, they will arrive, and we can all have good times together, yes?"

Tom feels his stomach sinking. He can only be talking about Emma, Lily, and Elijah. "What are you going to do to them?" he says.

"You will see soon enough, my friend," Fedorov says, turning back to the table. "You will all see soon enough." He reaches for the picana.

Before he can pick it up, Tom hears someone rushing toward the door at the top of the basement steps. It is flung open. Fedorov turns, eyes narrowed. "I am not to be disturbed!"

"Fedorov!" a man shouts from the top of the steps. "You've gotta come, man! You've gotta come!"

Fedorov turns. He has not picked up the picana. "What is it!" He is not happy about this disruption. "I was very clear before I came down here – no one is to come to me!"

The man is doubtful. He looks at Tom, then back at Fedorov.

"Tell me!" Fedorov says. "What can he do?" He jerks a thumb at Tom. "There are no secrets between us."

The man hesitates, then says, "Roger is dead."

Fedorov steps forward. *"What?"*

"He's been stabbed. Joe – Joe was watching the door. He says, he says Alina came, she – she was the last one in the room, and now –" The man trails off, but the implication is clear – Roger is dead, and it looks like Alina has done it.

Fedorov looks back at Tom over his shoulder, and then he runs from the basement. The man at the top of the stairs dives back to get out of his charging way. He throws the door shut behind him.

Tom is alone. He does not waste a second. This is his only chance. There will not be another. He cuts at the ropes. He pulls down on them, straining against the breaking fibers with all the strength he has left.

48

Fedorov shoves aside the man who brought him the news, knocks him back against the wall. Fedorov races up the stairs. The door to the room where Roger was kept is open. Joe, his guard, is inside. He's chewing on his fingernails, looking nervous. He looks unsteady, too, propping himself up with one arm against the wall. The color has drained from his face.

The color has drained from Roger, too. It has drained all over the seat he is slumped in, and onto the ground, into the carpet.

Fedorov speaks through gritted teeth. "What has happened here?" He turns to Joe.

Joe cannot answer. He wilts under Fedorov's burning gaze. He manages to stammer, but nothing makes sense.

"Alina?" Fedorov says.

Joe is able to seize onto the mention of her name. "She-she-she came here," he says. "She – she said, she said Yuri told her to check in on Roger. I didn't, I didn't think anything of it..."

"And you did not think to question why Yuri would send *her*?" Fedorov says.

"No, no, sir, I, I didn't..."

Fedorov glares. Yuri and Alina left a long time ago. They left before he arrived.

Joe looks like he wants the floor to open up and swallow him. "I – I'm sorry," he says.

Fedorov looks back. The man who first came to get him from the basement, Bobby, is cautiously poking his head over the top of the stairs. "How did you become aware of this?" he says to Bobby.

"I, uh, I came to take over for him, to give him a break," Bobby says. "I figured I should look in on Mr. Noakes, see how he was doing..."

Fedorov takes a deep breath. Closes his eyes. When he opens them again, he forces a smile. He places his hands on Joe's shoulders. Joe is crying. His lower lip trembles. He looks like a child. "My friend," Fedorov says, "do not be so concerned. It is not your fault, no?"

Joe looks almost hopeful.

"No, it is not your fault. And this – *this* – it is done." Fedorov snaps Joe's neck.

Before Joe's body has hit the ground, Fedorov has pulled his cell phone from his pocket. He calls Yuri's number, staring at Roger's dead body. There is no answer. He tries again and again. He gets nothing. He tries Alina's number. Again, no answer.

He is breathing hard now, his shoulders heaving. He punches the wall in frustration. Notices Bobby has left the stairs, has fled from his tantrum. Fedorov calls Alina again. She kills the call. Fedorov stares at his screen to be sure. She rejected the call. He tries again. It does not ring. She has turned it off, maybe destroyed it.

Fedorov hits the wall, over and over, until the skin on his knuckles cracks, until he is leaving bloodied fist prints. He roars.

49

The pendant has weakened the fibers of the rope. Tom has wrapped his hands around the ropes, holding them as tight as he is able. He pulls down on them. They snap. He hits the ground. He can't move straight away. His arms and legs are weak. Everything hurts, everything burns. The blood is rushing around his body. The numbness returns to his shoulders, his arms. He can barely move them, cannot raise them.

He sucks breath and looks toward the top of the stairs. Someone will come soon, he knows. Either Fedorov will return, or his men will come to check on him, make sure he's still hanging. Maybe they heard him fall, though it's unlikely the sound has travelled up the stairs and through the door.

Tom pushes through the pain. Forces himself up to his feet. He places the pendant back around his neck, grimacing as he raises his arms to do so. The pendant is coated in his blood. It's not the first time. Tom shakes his arms out. They have filled with pins and needles. He grits his teeth, picks up his KA-BAR. His eyes settle on the picana. He tucks the KA-

BAR into his waistband, though it will not be staying there
long. Too much risk of cutting himself. He picks up the
picana and the car battery. They feel heavier than they
should in his weakened grip. His hands are pale. The blood
has not yet returned to his extremities.

He drags himself across the ground, to the bottom of the
stairs. The men upstairs are not coming yet. He braces
himself. "Hey!" Tom calls to them. His voice is dry and raspy.
He clears his throat, swallows. Calls again. Bangs the side of
the picana against the steps. He listens. He thinks he can hear
footsteps approaching the door. He ducks under the stairs.

The door opens. Someone steps onto the space above
him. It takes him a moment to absorb the scene before him.
"*Shit!*" He starts coming down the stairs.

Tom spins out from under them, jabs the picana into the
man's legs. Out the corner of his eye, he sees a second pair
following. The electric shocks drop the man, send him
tumbling down the stairs. The picana gets caught up in his
legs, and is torn out of Tom's hand. Tom grabs the KA-BAR,
jabs it into the ankle of the second man. He screams, starts
falling after his partner, who is now convulsing at the bottom
of the stairs.

There is no one behind the second man, but his scream is
sure to bring the others running. Tom goes to the fallen two.
The second is clutching his ankle, still screaming. They have
both come armed with their M16s. Tom silences the second
man first, burying the knife into his chest, and then he kills
the first.

His head is spinning from so much exertion so soon after
freeing himself from the ropes. His wrists burn with every
movement. They are still bleeding. Tom grabs the nearest
M16. He falls back, unable to stand anymore, and points the
rifle to the top of the stairs. He can hear the others coming

now, running, their boots pounding the hardwood floors. He pulls the other M16 close, in case the first runs out of ammo.

The door swings open. Tom fires.

50

Teddy is driving. Reagan is in the passenger seat, twisted slightly, the gun covering the prisoners in the back. He holds it limply, though, Emma notices. Without much conviction. He can't look at them, either. He keeps his eyes lowered.

"Almost there," Teddy says. He has been in a better mood since they started driving. The radio is on, and he's been humming along to the music playing.

Emma looks up ahead. They drive along a long road, its surface still covered in snow. It has not been cleared. She thinks it is a driveway. Maybe to a vacation home. Another of Fedorov's safe houses, perhaps?

As they get closer, she sees this house is far larger than the cabin Fedorov held them captive in. If it is another safe house, it is not as inconspicuous as the last one.

Teddy's tone changes suddenly. "You hear that?" he says.

Reagan looks back at him. "Hear what?"

Teddy turns off the radio. He winds the window down a little.

"I don't hear anything," Reagan says.

"*Shh!*" Teddy holds his ear to the open window. Emma feels the cold rush in from outside. All she can hear is the wind. Teddy and Reagan are distracted, though. They're both looking toward the end of the road, to the house that is rising up before them. Emma stares at the gun. It's still pointing at them. Reagan isn't looking, but the barrel is angled toward Elijah, sitting between Emma and Lily. Lily has noticed, too. She pulls Elijah closer to her, not that it makes much of a difference in their cramped confines.

Emma's hands have warmed on the journey, since she was forced to clear the snow from the car. When they first set out, she couldn't move them. They were numb. She rubbed them together, trying to improve the circulation. Lily reached over, put her hands around them, breathed on them.

Now she opens and closes them. Makes sure they are all right. Makes sure they are back to normal. Makes sure that they will *work*.

This could be their opportunity.

This could be their *final* opportunity.

They get closer to the house, and they can all hear what Teddy is talking about, now. It sounds like gunshots. Like automatic fire.

"The hell's going on in there?" Teddy says.

Reagan swallows. He turns more toward the house, like there might be something to see. He's fully distracted, now. He's not paying attention to the gun. His hold on it is limper than before. It has lowered. It's pointing at the floor. It's pointing at Elijah's feet.

Carefully, quietly, Emma undoes her seatbelt. She moves slowly. She raises Elijah's legs, clears his feet from the floor. She looks at Lily. Lily is scared, but she understands. She closes her eyes, and she nods, once. Emma slides down in her seat. She will get one chance at this. She breathes deep, holds it, and braces herself.

She stomps down on Reagan's wrist with her left foot, pins it, and simultaneously kicks him in the side of the head with her right. Reagan's head snaps to the side, bounces off the window with a dull thud. He drops the gun. As Teddy turns, Emma dives forward, wraps her arms around his neck from behind. A choked sound escapes him, and he loses control of the wheel. Emma sticks her fingers into his eyes and pulls his head back, an arm still around his neck. She's trying to run him off the road before they can reach the house.

"Grab the gun!" she says to Lily.

Lily dives into the space between them, scrambles on the floor for the gun. When she finally comes up with it, she doesn't know what to do with it.

Emma reaches through into the front, buries her fingernails into the back of Teddy's hand until he lets go of the steering wheel. She grabs it in his place, yanks it to the side. The car bounces over the embankment, buries itself in the bushes.

Teddy pushes open his door, drops out of it.

"Give me the gun!" Emma reaches for it, and Lily is grateful to press it into her hand.

Teddy is on his knees, reaching for his own gun. Emma pushes her door open, falls outside. She lands on her side, both hands wrapped around the butt of the Glock. Teddy has pulled his own free from his waistband. He turns at the sound of her, raising it. Emma is faster. She fires. The bullet hits Teddy in the shoulder. It throws him back onto his ass. He cries out, but he does not let go of his gun. He raises it again, one-handed. Emma fires twice more. Both bullets bury themselves in Teddy's chest. He falls back, flat.

Emma scurries back to her feet, points the gun inside the car, at Reagan. He hasn't moved. He looks back at her, at the gun. He raises his hands in surrender. "Is...is Teddy dead?" he says. His voice is despondent, defeated.

"He's dead," Emma says.

Reagan sighs. He glances back at Lily. "I'm sorry," he says. "I would never...I would never have hurt your son."

Lily holds Elijah close.

Emma can still hear gunfire coming from the house. Tom is in there still. No doubt the shots have something to do with him. He's either firing them, or they're being fired *at* him – they're so frequent she has to assume he has escaped whatever predicament they had placed him in. He might need her help.

"You," she says to Reagan, holding the gun on him. "Get out of the car; come with me. Show me how to get inside."

Reagan gets out the car and keeps his hands raised.

Emma leans into the open door while Reagan rounds the car. "Take Elijah and hide," she says. "Go into the woods, find cover, try to keep warm. I'll come find you once I've got Tom."

"We can go around to the back door," Reagan says, keeping his distance.

"Lead the way," Emma says. She looks back to Lily. Lily nods. Emma catches up to Reagan, prods him in the back to hurry him up. "Let's fucking go," she says.

51

F edorov hears the gunshots coming from the basement. He hears his men dying.

Tom Rollins has gotten free. There's no other explanation for all this noise.

Fedorov is angry. He wants to charge downstairs, to show his men how this situation should be handled. To wrap things up with Tom sooner than he intended, but to be done with this mess once and for all.

But, as angry as he is, he's distracted, too. He's thinking about Yuri. Is worried about him. Fedorov is back downstairs now, his legs having carried him down the steps without his mind realizing what they were doing. He can see his three surviving men pinned at the top of the stairs that lead into the basement. They fire into it, then duck back around the door frame as the gunfire is returned. One of them isn't so fast. Tom's bullets catch him, drop him. Fedorov rolls his eyes. He has trained his men himself, but up against a man like Tom Rollins, it becomes very clear that they are nothing more than rank amateurs playing at soldiers.

Out of the corner of his eye, at one of the windows, he

sees movement. He goes to it for a better look. It's Emma, and she has Reagan with her, has a gun pointed at his back. They head toward the rear of the house. There is no sign of Teddy, or Lily, or Elijah.

Fedorov remains where he stands, deliberates, torn between his desire to kill Tom, and his worry over Yuri's well-being.

"I do not have the time for this," he says, hissing the words through his teeth. He goes back out into the hallway, grabs the collar of the nearest one of his men at the top of the basement stairs, drags him away. To the other, he says, "Keep him busy. Kill him if you can."

The man left behind gapes, then starts firing into the bowels of the building. Fedorov does not bother telling him that Emma is coming, too. He takes a look at the man he has with him. Bobby. "We are to go now," he says.

"Okay, okay," Bobby says, looking almost grateful to be taken away from where Tom is.

They leave the house. Fedorov is still shirtless, but he does not feel the cold. He directs Bobby to Emma's truck. He tosses the keys, tells him to drive. On the way out, they pass the car that was parked down the side of Fedorov's cabin, which Teddy and Reagan have driven here. He sees Teddy's dead body lying by the side of the road.

"Fucking useless," Fedorov says.

"What was that?" Bobby says.

Fedorov shakes his head. "Just drive."

52

There's still one man left at the top of the stairs, but he's in hiding. Too scared to show himself. Tom knows he's there, though. He waits, poised on one knee, rifle pointed toward the empty doorway. He doesn't hurt as much as he did before. The adrenaline is pumping. It's brought him back to himself.

Tom listens. Now that the gunfire has stopped, the ringing in his ears calms. He can hear the man there, breathing hard. Scared.

"I know you're up there," Tom says. "And I know you're probably looking at all those dead bodies and asking yourself, *Man, how can I stop this guy?* You can't, buddy. But you've still got a chance to walk away from this alive. You hear me? Throw down your gun, walk out that front door, and don't look back."

"Fuck you!" the man shouts back. "You're just a man, and all it takes is one bullet!"

"That's right," Tom says. "One bullet is all it takes. Question is, are you the man who's got that bullet?"

"You're damn right – I got it right here, and it's got your

fuckin' name on it!" He's still breathing hard, but more like he's psyching himself up now. He's about to make a move. About to do something stupid.

Tom gave him a chance.

The last man spins round the door frame, roaring, raising the M16. Tom has anticipated the direction he is coming from the sound of his voice. He squeezes the trigger, puts a bullet through the center of his forehead, cuts his roar dead in his throat. The man falls forward, slumping over the body of one of his dead friends.

Tom doesn't move from his position, not right away. He continues to listen, makes sure there is no one else lying in wait. He can't hear any movement. The house is still. Using the rifle as a crutch, he pushes himself up to his feet and ascends the staircase on careful, silent feet, stepping over bodies as he goes.

He peers into the hallway, then steps out into it. There's no one – just dead bodies. And still nothing to be heard. No sign of Fedorov. Tom sweeps the house. He goes upstairs. There's no one up here, either. Just one dead body – Roger. Tom can see where he has been stabbed.

Tom leaves him, goes back downstairs, rifle still raised, stock pressed into his shoulder. Near the back door, he wheels at a sound, the rifle pointing into Reagan's face. Reagan flinches, his arms raised in surrender. "Please don't shoot," he says.

"Tom?" It's Emma's voice. She's behind Reagan, a gun at his back.

Tom lowers the M16, falls back against the wall, exhaustion catching up to him again. Emma comes to him. She wraps her arms around him, but keeps one eye on Reagan. "You look like shit," she says.

"Right now," Tom says, "I feel like it."

"What happened?" Emma says, taking a step back,

keeping Reagan covered. Reagan isn't trying anything. He keeps his hands raised and his eyes lowered.

"I'll tell you later," Tom says.

Emma nods, does not press it. "I need to get Lily and Elijah," she says. "They're hiding in the trees. Is it definitely safe here?"

"I've swept the house," Tom says. "It's clear. Just...just don't let them go upstairs."

Emma gives him a questioning look, but she does not ask. Much like the explanation of what has happened to him, she assumes he'll answer this later. She heads back outside. Tom watches Reagan.

"Where's your buddy?" he says.

Reagan swallows. "He's dead," he says. "Your girlfriend killed him."

"I'm sure he did something to deserve it."

"Oh, he did a lot of somethings," Reagan says.

"I can believe it," Tom says. They stand in silence for a few minutes, waiting. Reagan does not seem particularly eager to talk.

Emma returns to the house with Lily and Elijah. "Lily saw Fedorov leave," Emma says. "They drove by when she was in the trees."

Lily and Elijah are staring at Tom. Elijah looks scared, hides behind his mother. Tom can only imagine how disheveled and half-crazed he must appear to this child. Tom turns back to Reagan. "Any idea where he might be going?"

Reagan shakes his head. "I don't know," he says, "sorry. Last I heard, he told Teddy and me to come here with the women and the boy. Haven't heard anything from him since."

Tom runs a hand down his face, tired, trying to think. There'll be a way to track Fedorov, to find him, to put an end to this all, but first he needs a glass of water and to find a shirt. Everything else he can push through.

"Looks like he took my fucking truck with him again, too," Emma says.

Reagan looks up at this.

Tom notices. "What?" he says. "*What?*"

Reagan hesitates.

"Reagan, I'm having a hell of a day," Tom says. "Shit, a hell of a week. So if you've got something you might wanna add to the conversation, spit it out now."

"There's a..." Reagan's tongue flickers over his lips. He glances at Emma. "There's a tracker on your truck. It should still be there."

"Great," Tom says, "what're we supposed to do about that from this end?"

Emma looks like she's realized something. "Fedorov's bag," she says. "That's what's in it, right?"

"It has all his electrical equipment in it," Reagan says. "All the stuff he uses for taps, bugs, that kind of thing."

"And you have it?" Tom says.

"It's back at the car," Reagan says.

Tom takes a deep breath. "Let me find a shirt," he says.

53

"**G**o faster," Fedorov says.

Bobby shifts in his seat and presses his foot a little harder on the accelerator. Fedorov can see that he is not comfortable driving at high speed on these snow-encrusted roads, and especially not in a truck that he is unfamiliar with, but Fedorov does not care. He keeps trying to call Yuri. By now, he must have more than a dozen missed calls. He would have noticed. And, more than that, it is not like Yuri not to answer on the *first* call.

He's tried Alina a couple more times, too, but he knew before he dialed that these were futile gestures. Her phone is dead. It doesn't even ring. Fedorov just needs to keep his hands and his mind busy, make it feel like he is doing *something*.

His head snaps to the side. "*Stop!*"

Bobby slams on the brakes. They skid, begin to turn, finally manage to stop. They're in the middle of the road. Bobby holds the steering wheel tight, eyes wide, breathing hard. Fedorov spins in his seat. There is something lying at the side of the road, something he almost didn't see as they sped by. An animal, perhaps, except it did not look like an animal.

Fedorov gets out of the truck without a word. He stands on the road, looking back. He can see other tracks in the snow. It looks like a car has pulled to the side, next to whatever this form is by the road.

He starts walking before he realizes what he is doing. His legs are carrying him forward, while a sense of dread rises in him. His throat is burning. He grits his teeth. The burns on his face begin to twitch of their own accord. His torso is still bare, but he does not feel the cold. As he gets closer, he can see that it is not an animal.

It is a man.

Fedorov breaks into a run, again before his mind registers what he is doing. He drops to his knees beside the body curled into a ball on its side.

It is Yuri.

Fedorov rolls him onto his back and looks him over, sees how pale his face is, sees how the snow around him is soaked a deep red. Blood. He looks just like Roger did, back in the room at the house. Killed in the same way. Fedorov scoops an arm under his shoulders, holds him up. Can see the small puncture wounds in his torso where he has been stabbed.

"Yuri," he says. "Yuri, open your eyes, my friend."

Yuri does not. Yuri cannot.

Fedorov feels his eyes burning. He speaks to Yuri softly in Russian. He presses a hand to the stab wounds. They are dry now, crusted with blood. It barely stains Fedorov's fingers.

Fedorov throws his head back, something bubbling up in his throat. He roars, screams, a strangled cry that sounds like a pained animal. He screams until it dies in his throat, until it is choked out.

Alina did this. The ungrateful bitch has betrayed the man who brought her here from Russia, who gave her a better life, who gave her everything she could ever have dreamed of, and beyond.

Fedorov is shaking. It has nothing to do with the cold. He presses his forehead to Yuri's, his eyes closed.

"I will find her for you, my friend," he says. "I will see that she pays. She *will* pay for this. She *must*."

He puts his other arm under Yuri's legs, into the bends of his knees, and he stands. Yuri is light. Like a feather. Like he doesn't weigh anything at all.

Fedorov carries him back to the truck. Bobby is standing beside the driver's door, watching. He hurries back inside as Fedorov approaches. Fedorov lays Yuri's body down gently in the bed of the truck. He returns to the passenger seat. Sees, out the corner of his eye, how Bobby warily watches him.

"Drive," Fedorov says.

Bobby does. It is a while before he ventures to talk. "Where – where am I going?"

"To the house," Fedorov says, looking straight ahead, a strange calm coming over him now.

"Uh," Bobby says. He hesitates for a while again. "Whose house?"

"Yuri's house!" Fedorov does not have the patience for stupid questions. The answer should have been obvious.

Bobby winces, but he asks another question. "What – what are we going to do?"

Fedorov breathes in. He thinks of Alina. He thinks of Tom Rollins. He thinks of Emma Raven, and Lily Noakes, and little Elijah.

"We will finish what Yuri started," he says. "I will call Moscow, and see how they want us to proceed, though I feel I know already what they will say. And then, I will hunt down everyone responsible for the death of my friend, and I will burn their world to the ground."

54

Emma drives. The car she arrived in, with Teddy and Reagan, was jammed into the bushes. They couldn't get it out. Tom found keys on the bodies of the dead men inside the house. He, Emma, and Reagan have taken one of their cars, parked well back from the house in order for them to stage their earlier ambush on Tom, when he arrived with Roger. He gave another pair of keys to Lily, told her to take Elijah and find somewhere safe to spend the night – a hotel, or a friend's house. Told them, in no uncertain terms, not to go home until they heard from him.

"Where's Roger?" she said.

Tom expected this question. "I... I don't know," he lied. "I'll find him."

In the car, following the tracker, Tom has told Emma the truth about what happened to Roger.

"Jesus," she says. "Why didn't you tell her?"

"That her husband was an asshole?" Tom says. "I think I'm going to have to try and find a way to word it more gently than that." He sighs, still hurting from his time with Fedorov in the basement. "And she's already been through so much –

her and the kid. We need them to be somewhere safe for now, out the way, where we don't have to worry about them. I tell her that her husband's dead, we run the risk of her doing something stupid."

Emma nods. She glances at Reagan in the backseat. His hands and ankles are tied together, but he's not trying anything. He's sitting very still and looking out the window. He's given up.

"Why do you think he did it?" Emma says.

"I don't know," Tom says. "Why did Alina kill him? I have theories, but that's all they are. I can't know anything for sure."

Emma calls to the back, to Reagan. "How well did you know Alina, Reagan?"

He looks up, surprised to be addressed. "Not – not at all," he says. "But I know Yuri could get jealous real easy, so I tried not to ever look at her, and I know a lot of the other guys were the same."

"She have a background in accounting?" Tom says, turning.

"Uh, no, I don't – I don't think so," Reagan says, not really understanding the question.

"What did she do back in Russia?"

"I think she was a waitress, but that's just what I heard."

Tom turns back around. The tracker is in his lap. He directs Emma along the roads. As tired as he is, he needs to find Fedorov, to stop him. To put an end to this once and for all, for Emma's safety and the surviving Noakes'.

"What're you thinking?" Emma says.

"I think Alina stole the money," Tom says.

"Yeah?"

"And I think either she knew Roger would find out she'd done it, or Roger helped her."

"If he helped her, why'd she kill him?"

Tom shrugs. "Same reason Roger betrayed me, I guess. Self-preservation. If she *is* who took the money, she's going to want to keep that quiet."

"Didn't she leave with Yuri?" Emma says. "What does she expect to happen when he finds out?"

The tracker has been stopped for a short while. Tom turns, shows it to Reagan. "Where is this?" he says. "It look familiar?"

Reagan leans in to better see. "Yeah," he says. "That's where Yuri lives."

Tom wonders if Fedorov has had the same thoughts as he – if he's gone to warn Yuri of his beliefs. If so, he dreads to think what Alina may be going through right now. He gives Emma a look, and she returns it. She's having the same thoughts.

The tracker starts moving again. Emma glances over, sees it. "Freaks me out to know that thing was on my truck," she says, "and we don't have any idea for how long."

Tom watches the vehicle move. They're already close to where it was stopped, to Yuri's house.

"Go to the house," Tom says.

"Okay," Emma says. "What're you hoping to find there?"

"Yuri," Tom says. "Stopping Fedorov is one thing, but if we don't cut off the head of the snake, it's just gonna keep coming."

He directs Emma to the house. They go up a steep hill to reach it, but the snow here has been cleared away completely, and the car does not have much trouble on the ascent.

"What's the situation likely to be here?" Tom says to Reagan. "How many guards? What am I walking into?"

"I'm not sure there's anyone left," Reagan says. "Between the cabin and back at the house there, I think you've killed them all."

Tom grunts. "I'll be sure to keep them in my thoughts."

Emma stops at the top of the driveway leading to the house. "How close should I go?" she says.

Tom looks. There are no vehicles out front. No one patrolling. He looks to the windows. Can't see anyone looking out. "Closer," he says, "but take your time." He pulls out the Glock he liberated from one of the men back at the house. The M16 is to his side, between the seat and the door. Emma reaches the front of the house.

"Wait here," Tom tells her. He gets out of the car, slings the M16 over his shoulder, then opens Reagan's door. He cuts the ropes on his ankles and pulls him out, pushes him in front of him, uses him as a shield. They go up to the front door. "Check it," Tom says.

Reagan does. It's not locked. He pushes it wide. Tom forces him in ahead, the Glock pointing over his shoulder. He scans the downstairs. Cocks his head to listen to the rest of the house. There's no one to see, nothing to hear. Tom looks into every room, holding Reagan in front of him.

"Upstairs," Tom says.

Reagan does as he's told. He uses both bound hands to hold onto the handrail on his way up. Tom keeps a hand on his collar, to keep him steady and slow. They reach the top. It's clear. "You spent much time in here?" Tom says.

"Never upstairs," Reagan says.

Again, Tom goes room by room. It doesn't take him long to reach Yuri's bedroom. Yuri is there, lying on the bed. They go to him. His arms are crossed on his chest. His eyes are closed. He's white, drained of blood. Tom can see where he has been stabbed. Same size as the weapon that was used on Roger.

Alina.

"Let's go," Tom says.

They return to Emma and the truck. While Tom reties Reagan's ankles, he tells her what they found.

"So where do we think Fedorov's going now?" Emma says.

Tom gets back into the passenger seat. "Ideas?" he says to Reagan. Emma starts driving, following the route of the tracker once again.

"Uh, well," Reagan says. He hesitates.

Tom turns, looks at him. "Tell me," he says.

"There was a plan...I don't know, I mean, if Yuri's dead... I don't know if he's still going to go through with it."

"What was the plan, Reagan?"

"To, um, to sabotage the pipeline. The Trans-Alaska Pipeline."

Emma looks up. "What?"

"What kind of sabotage?" Tom says.

"I don't know for sure," Reagan says. "But knowing Fedorov, he's probably gonna blow part of it up."

"Blow it *up*?" Emma says, sounding like she's struggling to comprehend what she is hearing. "Is he fucking insane? Does he have any kind of idea of the ecological damage *blowing up* the fucking pipeline will cause?"

"I don't...I don't think he cares," Reagan says. "I don't think any of them do."

"We need to stop him," Emma says.

"We're going to," Tom says.

Emma is thinking. "We're hours away from the nearest part of the pipeline," she says.

"That'll give us a chance to catch up," Tom says. He notices how she has sped up since Reagan has shared his thoughts on Fedorov's prospective destination.

Tom watches the tracker. "He's stopped again," he says.

"Just tell me where to go," Emma says. "I'm gonna cut this motherfucker off before he gets anywhere near the pipeline."

The tracker is still for almost ten minutes, and then it starts moving again. Tom gives Emma appropriate directions. "Where'd he just stop?" he says to Reagan.

"I'm not sure," Reagan says. "He's got places everywhere – stashes for weapons and supplies. If he's going for the pipeline, then maybe he was picking up explosives."

"It doesn't matter why he stopped," Emma says. "Matters that we catch up to him before that tracker stops moving completely."

Tom watches the road, watches how Emma overtakes the other vehicles on it, gets past them and speeds on. "I've got faith in you," he says.

55

F edorov mutters to himself in Russian. He notices how it makes Bobby uncomfortable, the way he shifts in his seat, cuts his eyes to the side, but Fedorov doesn't care. Bobby doesn't say anything. He stays in silence, fearing for his life.

Fedorov remembers carrying Yuri's cold dead body into his home, up to his room. Laying him down on his bed and pressing a soft kiss to his forehead. There was no sign of Alina, nor of the car she had got away in. Fedorov checked the wardrobe in their room. Her clothes, most of them, were gone. She'd fled.

She can wait, for now. Fedorov will deal with her later. He can't imagine she's stayed local. He is going to have to search hard, but this does not concern him. He always finds who he's looking for.

He stood over Yuri's body, his eyes closed, while Bobby waited downstairs. Fedorov pressed a hand to Yuri's chest, patted him goodbye, then placed a call to Moscow. He told Mikhail what has happened.

Mikhail was silent at the news. "That is...a shame," he said eventually.

"I thought you had best know," Fedorov says.

"Yes. Rightly so. Well. It would seem, Fedorov, that you have just been promoted."

Mikhail was all business. This did not surprise Fedorov. He had not expected anything less.

"Is everything in place regarding the pipeline?"

"Everything is ready."

"Then do it," he said. "There is no reason for this unfortunate circumstance to derail our plans completely."

"Yes," Fedorov said. "It will be done."

He left the house with his jaw clenched and his fists balled, Bobby rushing to follow. He directed Bobby down the road, to one of his cabins. Fedorov does not like to sleep in any one place more than one night in a row. He likes to stay on the move. Does not like for anyone to be able to find him with ease. His men – not that there are many of them left now – know the only way to get hold of him is by phone call.

In this 'home' he has stored the explosives for the pipeline sabotage. Has kept them in the cabin closest to where Yuri lives, so when the time came, he would not have to travel far to get his equipment.

He took Bobby into the cabin with him to gather what he needed. Fedorov chose the dynamite. Bobby's eyes widened as he handed it to him – either at the quantity, or the fact it had been pressed into his hands at all. Fedorov did not know which, nor care. He sent Bobby to put it in the back of the truck and to strap it down to prevent it from rolling, while he remained behind and gathered up the cord and detonator. He is going to cause chaos, and destruction, and this comforts him. He is going to make a bigger explosion than necessary, and this is what distracts him from Yuri's death. This is what allows him to push through, to blink away tears when his eyes begin to burn. This will be his temporary vengeance, setting this damn state aflame. Then, once AI Construction Services are at work – earning millions, billions, whatever, as the Bratva wishes – once everything is in place, *then* Fedorov can take his true revenge.

Tom Rollins.

Emma Raven.

Lily Noakes.

Little Elijah.

Alina Sidorova.

For now, they can wait. For now, he has his orders. He must carry them out. It's what Yuri would have wanted. Fedorov will take over operations in this area, as the Bratva says, but he will accept this position only to honor Yuri's memory. Taking his place, doing what Yuri no longer can, will keep Yuri with him always.

They're heading for the pipeline now. They're still a couple of hours out. "You know where you are going, yes?" Fedorov says.

Bobby gives a start at Fedorov's voice, not expecting to be spoken to. "Yes," he says. "I think so."

"I have a very specific area in mind," Fedorov says. He tells him where it is, the random stretch of pipeline unguarded in the wilderness. "Do you know it? No, I did not think so – I do not imagine many people will go there, and that is why I have chosen it. I have scouted it out already – so many times already. I am prepared. If I think you are going the wrong way, I will correct your course."

Bobby nods.

"I must make calls," Fedorov says, pulling out his phone.

"Do you think...?" Bobby says, then stops when he sees Fedorov's phone.

"Yes?" Fedorov says. "Continue. I am listening."

"Do you think he's coming after us?"

"Who?"

"The man from the basement," Bobby says. "The guy who was killing everyone back at the house."

Fedorov grins. "I'd like it if he were," he says. "But he does not know where we are going."

"Okay," Bobby says. It's hard to tell if this calms him or not. There is concern on his face. He's been frowning all the while he's been driving.

"I make calls now," Fedorov says. "Is there anything else?"

Bobby shakes his head.

Fedorov calls Councilman Manning first. The councilman's voice is full of trepidation when he answers. It always is when he knows it's Fedorov on the other end. "Yes?"

"Councilman, my friend," Fedorov says, forcing himself to be as jolly as he usually is. "There has been a slight change of plan."

The councilman stammers. Fedorov does not let him finish.

"Things are moving up, sooner than expected."

"How soon?" Manning says.

"*Very* soon, my friend. I'm on my way there now."

Manning splutters.

"Calm down, councilman. You do not need to say anything. You just need to prepare yourself for what comes next. Are you prepared, Councilman Manning?"

Manning cannot answer.

"I am afraid this call is not over until you respond to me, my friend."

"I – I – I hear you. I understand."

"And you shall be waiting, yes? You shall be on standby?"

Manning sighs. His voice, when it comes, is very small. "Yes."

"Excellent! You shall hear from me soon. Stay by the phone."

He hangs up and calls Mayor Pullman next. The call goes much the same as it did with the councilman, with a couple of exceptions.

"You're fucking insane," Pullman says. He's belligerent, but he knows there's nothing he can do to stop this.

"Now, now, Mr. Mayor," Fedorov says. "It is not nice to call names, no?"

"I don't care about calling you any fucking *names*, you fucking sociopath."

Fedorov chuckles. "Be prepared, Mr. Mayor. You will be hearing from me soon, I am sure."

Pullman grumbles, but there's nothing left for him to say.

Fedorov and Bobby make the rest of the journey in silence. Fedorov starts to feel better, more like himself, but he knows this feeling will be fleeting. He hopes it will carry over, at least until he is through with the pipeline. Then, he knows, the mourning for Yuri will resume. The grief will return. Dealing with Tom Rollins, and all the rest, will provide some relief, but when they are gone? Well, then he will have to deal with his feelings head-on.

This is a new sensation for Fedorov. He is not accustomed to loss. He's usually the one causing the loss.

He doesn't like it.

The time passes, Fedorov lost in his thoughts. The hours pass. It gets so he is not focused on the road, almost misses their turn. "This way," he says, sitting up suddenly and pointing.

Bobby panics, has to swerve across the road, in front of an oncoming car, to make the turn. The car blares its horn. Fedorov laughs. Bobby is breathing hard. He wipes his sleeve across his forehead.

"We are almost there now," Fedorov says. He's still laughing. It looks like the laughter alarms Bobby more than the earlier muttering. "Follow this road along, my friend. We will be there soon."

Fedorov points the way for him. "Pull over here," he says after a while.

Bobby looks around. "I don't see the pipeline."

"It is over this hill," Fedorov says. "The road runs out. We must walk from here."

Bobby pulls over. They get out of the truck and go around the back. Fedorov opens it. "Grab it all and follow me," he says. He starts to turn, but realizes Bobby has not moved. He's staring into the back of the truck. Staring at the dynamite.

"*All* of it?" he says.

Fedorov nods. "All of it."

"Isn't it...isn't it...too much?"

"Why would I bring it if I do not intend to use it?" Fedorov says.

"It's just..." Bobby hesitates, not wanting to upset Fedorov. Fedorov waits for him to continue. Bobby breathes hard, psychs himself up. "This amount of explosives – it could do more damage than it should. It could ignite the oil inside, wreck the whole line."

Fedorov grins. "I did not realize you were an engineer, Bobby," he says. "You have been holding out on me, my friend."

"I'm not, it's just – it's just, it's obvious, right? This is too much."

"If we destroy the whole line, then we destroy the whole line. So what?" Fedorov shrugs. "We will then rebuild the whole line."

Bobby blinks. "It could set all of Alaska on fire."

"*All?* I think you are exaggerating now, Bobby."

"I'm not so sure I am," Bobby says.

"So." Fedorov looks at him. "What are you expecting me to do, Bobby?"

"I just think... I just think that you should pull back a little. You're worked up about Mr. Ivanov, I get that, but I think you need to calm down and think about this before you go through with it."

"I am calm, Bobby. Do I not seem calm to you?"

Bobby holds up his hands. "Fedorov, *please*, this is too much. A little sabotage to get to rebuild the line, fine, but not *destroying* the whole thing. You can't do that."

Fedorov says nothing. He considers what Bobby is saying. "You are from Alaska, Bobby, yes?"

"All my life," Bobby says. "I was born in Juneau. Moved to Valdez about ten years ago. I can probably count on one hand all the times I've left the state."

"This is your home," Fedorov says. "You feel a connection to it. You do not want to see it harmed."

"Well, no, no, of course not." Bobby is relaxing a little. He thinks Fedorov is seeing things his way. Thinks that he is coming around, that he has realized what he was about to do, blinded by his own grief.

Fedorov smiles. He reaches out, pats Bobby on the shoulder. "Alaska is not my home, Bobby," he says. With his other hand, he pulls the Beretta taken from Emma from his waist, shoots Bobby through the face. Dead before he hits the ground.

Fedorov mutters to himself, rolls his eyes. "I must do everything myself, yes? Very well. I will do everything myself." He reaches into the back of the truck, gathers up everything that he needs. Arms full, he leaves Bobby where he lies. He can deal with his body later.

Right now, he has some explosives to set.

56

"It's not moving," Emma says. There is a hint of rising panic in her voice. "What the fuck! He's stopped moving?"

Tom remains calm. "We're not far out," he says. "Don't get worked up. Focus. Just keep going. We're almost there."

They're about ten minutes away from where Fedorov has stopped, by Tom's estimation. He hopes these ten minutes are enough. That what Fedorov is planning to do will take longer.

They take a sudden turn and follow the road down. This road has not had much care. The snow has not been cleared from it. They bounce and jostle, but Emma does not slow. Reagan, his wrists and ankles bound, is thrown around, held in place only by his seatbelt. Tom hears him cry out a couple of times when he bangs his head.

"That's my truck," Emma says, leaning forward.

Tom looks. He sees it. Sees also the man lying in the snow at the back of it. Sees how the snow around his head is red.

57

Fedorov is on his knees in the snow. He has strapped dynamite around the pipe, secured it into place. He is connecting the cable to the detonator when a noise catches his attention. The roar of a car's engine battling through the snow, the crunch of its wheels rolling along. Fedorov listens.

The car comes to a stop around the same area the truck is parked. Where Bobby lies dead. Someone will be getting out; someone will be investigating. Once they see Bobby's body, they will either call the police, or they will follow his footprints through the snow. They will try to stop him.

A thought occurs to Fedorov, a flash in his mind from back at the house, shortly after he found Roger's corpse and then struggled to get in touch with both Yuri and Alina. He remembers seeing Emma through the window, coming down the side of the house, heading for the back, pushing Reagan ahead of her. He came here in her truck. The tracker is still on it.

Do they know about the tracker? If Reagan is still alive, he may have told them about the tracker. They could have been following him here this whole time, as Bobby wondered.

Fedorov could shit himself for forgetting to handle such a key detail, for forgetting to remove the tracker from her truck, but he doesn't. Instead, he smiles. It has brought them to him. The resolution of his grieving process may come sooner than he thought.

He stands, looking toward the hill. No one is coming yet. He still has time to get ready. He bites the burns on his bottom lip, flicks his tongue out and runs it along the gnarled flesh. Turning, he moves. Whoever is coming, whether it is Tom Rollins or someone else, he needs to be prepared for them.

58

Tom follows Fedorov's footprints through the snow, Glock held in both hands. He's left Emma in the car with Reagan. Told her to watch over him, but really he doesn't want her getting anywhere near Fedorov, or a potential explosion.

Tom does not step directly over the hill. He knows that if Fedorov is down there, he will be watching the line of the hill, and that if he steps directly into it he will stand out against the sky like a sore thumb. An easy target. Instead, he drops, crawls up to it, peers down. He can see the pipeline.

There's no one there.

Tom checks the area. The footprints go down to the pipe. There are trees behind it, off to the right. Tom scans the tree-line. He slowly gets up, following the footprints. He moves slowly, his eyes searching. They keep going back to the trees. He can't see Fedorov. No movement. There's nothing to hear, either, no crunch of movement through the snow.

There's dynamite strapped to the pipe. Tom gets closer to it. He can see on the ground, in the snow, where Fedorov has been kneeling, connecting it all together. Can see where the cables end. There is no detonator.

There's a noise in the trees. Tom's head snaps toward the sound, gun raised. Again, he cannot see any movement there. The noise does not persist. It could have been an animal. It could have been Fedorov.

The footprints lead away from the dynamite. Tom follows them again. They're going toward the trees. He ducks under the pipeline, following the trail.

From the side, he's attacked. Fedorov strikes him in the face, laughing as he does so. It feels like a hammer blow, and Tom goes down, seeing stars, realizing how Fedorov has misdirected him. Created a fake trail that leads off into the woods. How he backtracked, and hid himself behind one of the supportive struts of the pipeline. He's been waiting for his moment to strike. He must have heard them arrive, heard the car pulling up to where the truck was parked, where the man's body lay dead at the back of it.

"Mr. Rollins," Fedorov says, reaching down and wrenching the gun from Tom's hand. "What a pleasure for you to come and join me. Unfortunately, we cannot spend as much quality time together as I'd like."

Fedorov is turning the gun he took from Tom. He's going to shoot. Tom kicks it away. It goes off. The bullet buries itself in the snow to his left. Tom kicks again, connecting with the inside of Fedorov's thigh. Fedorov drops to a knee. Tom sits up, punches him, grabs the gun back – but, before he can turn it, Fedorov knocks it from his hand. The gun flies out of reach. As it goes, Fedorov reaches for another tucked into his waist. A Beretta. Tom's Beretta. Tom grabs his wrist, angles it away from his face. Another bullet hits the snow. Tom slams Fedorov's wrist down across his knee, then kicks the gun from his hand.

"No matter," Fedorov says, tackling Tom to the ground

and reaching both hands for his neck. "I always prefer the personal touch." He tries to squeeze. Tom grabs both of his thumbs, tears them back, breaking Fedorov's grip. He gets both legs up, presses his boots to Fedorov's chest, kicks him away.

Fedorov rolls through. He's laughing. "Ah, my friend," he says, standing again, brushing the snow from himself. "You are still so full of fight. I feared I had shocked it out of you."

Tom gets back to his feet, but he's slower than Fedorov. Slower than he usually is, than he'd like to be. Despite what Fedorov says, Tom is not as full of fight as he could be. He's sore still, and tired.

"There's no picana this time," Tom says. "And I'm not tied up." He raises his fists. He has his KA-BAR still, but he keeps it in reserve, doesn't let Fedorov know about it just yet.

Fedorov charges, running through the snow, kicking it up behind him. Tom ducks his first punch, catches him in the ribs with a left jab, then follows up with a right across the burns on his face. Fedorov spits blood, laughs. Tom pushes on, throwing punches. Fedorov laughs through the landing blows, then throws one of his own. Tom catches it under his left arm, holds it tight against his side. Fedorov head-butts him, bloodies his nose. Tom does not let go. He clamps both hands on the back of Fedorov's head, drags him down, drives his knee into the center of his face.

Fedorov pushes him off, steps back, touches the blood leaking from his nose. "Ah, my friend, you are determined today, yes? But I am determined, also. You will die today, Mr. Rollins. And then your body will burn to dust in the fires of this pipeline. Tell me, have you come here alone? Or have you come with your little darling?"

Tom ignores his questions. "Why go through with this?" he says. "Yuri is dead. Destroying the pipeline isn't gonna bring him back."

"But perhaps it will help with my grieving process, yes?" Fedorov grins, showing bloodied teeth. "I answer to more masters than just Yuri, my friend. They want the pipe destroyed, and so I shall destroy it. If they want this land to burn, then it shall burn. Fuck this state. Fuck your country, Tom. Fuck your American Dream. It is not all it is cracked up to be, no?"

"I'm not going to let you destroy it," Tom says. "And I'm not going to let you hurt anyone else."

"Then it would seem we are in agreement, yes?" Fedorov says. "One of us is not walking away from here."

Fedorov charges again, but his lunges are not so clumsy as before. He feints from the right, then lands a blow low in Tom's side, where he knows the scar from his stabbing is. He punches Tom in the chest, then the cheekbone. The blow feels hard enough to almost crack the bone. Tom manages to block his next punch, then land one of his own, but Fedorov seems almost impervious to every shot Tom throws. He counters with another of his own, knocking Tom to the ground.

Tom twists, lands on his front. Feels Fedorov's boot stomp down into his lower back. Fedorov presses down all his weight, steps over him. He turns, kicks Tom across the jaw.

"Tom, my friend," he says, reaching down, grabbing Tom by the back of his collar. "I want you to see this." He drags Tom along the ground.

Tom blinks hard, shakes his head clear. Fedorov pulls him along to where the dynamite's wire lies waiting in the snow. He picks up the end of it with his other hand, and starts walking again, still dragging Tom.

Tom reaches back, pulls out his KA-BAR. He buries it in Fedorov's calf.

Fedorov goes down, cursing in Russian. He backhands Tom, then falls, reaching for the knife. Tom pushes himself up on his arms, but Fedorov, with his other leg, kicks him across the face. Tom sees his blood spray from his mouth across the white snow. He goes down, head spinning again. When he manages to turn, he sees his knife is still in Fedorov's calf. Fedorov leaves it. His hands are busy. Tom looks. He's wiring up the detonator.

Tom scrambles, lunges, lands on top of Fedorov, trying to wrestle the detonator from his grip.

"This is not a safe distance, my friend," Fedorov says. "The explosion will kill us both." He's smiling. Tom does not doubt for a second that he will do it. He's mad enough. "Perhaps you will be my shield, yes? Shall we find out together?" With his free hand, he grabs Tom by the front of the shirt, pulls him close.

His left hand holds the detonator. Tom grabs it with both of his, prevents him from pressing his thumb down on it. Fedorov hits him in the side of the head, but Tom does not let go. He head-butts Fedorov instead, snatches the detonator from his loosened grip, throws it to one side. Fedorov claws at his face. Tom wraps a hand around his fingers, wrenches them back, snaps them. Fedorov cries out. Tom reaches down his leg, pulls the KA-BAR free from his calf. Fedorov cries out again, harder this time. In his fury, he punches Tom, knocks the knife from his hand. He pushes Tom off.

"You piece of shit," he says, getting to his feet, limping toward the detonator. "You son of a bitch!" He reaches down.

Tom catches up to him, stomps down on his wounded calf. Fedorov drops to a knee. Tom grabs the detonator before he can. He wraps the wiring around Fedorov's neck and pulls it tight. Presses his knee into Fedorov's back. Fedorov reaches behind with his unbroken fingers, trying to grab the detonator. Tom keeps it out of his reach, squeezes the wire tighter. He can see how Fedorov's eyes bulge, how his face is reddening.

Fedorov twists loose from Tom's knee, then throws his

head back, his skull connecting with Tom's chest. He does it again, and again, knocking the air from Tom's lungs. He rises, does it again, connects with Tom's face. He stands, tearing the wire from his neck. He gets the detonator. Teeth bared, he makes to press the button.

Tom moves faster than he ever has before. He slams the knife through Fedorov's arm, the blade tearing through the inside of his wrist, through the ligaments and tendons. Fedorov drops the detonator. He turns to Tom. Tom holds his pierced arm. He slams it back into Fedorov's face, the knife protruding through his wrist burying itself into his eye. Fedorov rears back, screaming. Tom slams the flat of his hand into the handle of the knife, driving it deeper. Fedorov falls straight back, lands flat, forearm pinned to his face, the knife through his eye and into his brain.

Tom falls, catches his breath. He keeps one eye on Fedorov, making sure he's really dead. That he doesn't suddenly sit up.

He doesn't.

Tom gets up. He disconnects the detonator, then pulls his knife free from Fedorov's face. He finds his fallen Beretta. He looks toward the pipeline, to the dynamite strapped to it. He'll need to disconnect it, then he'll go back to Emma, and Reagan.

And then, he supposes, they should probably call the police.

59

It's been two weeks since Tom stopped Fedorov at the pipeline.

Tom figured being on the scene of a major incident so soon after his unofficial pardon wouldn't be the best look for him, so he's laid low after the police were called. Checked into a hotel in Valdez and hid there. Emma comes to get him, now. She's known where he was, but she hasn't reached out while she's been talking to the police. She called him for the first time this morning, to tell him she was on her way.

"I hope you've been nice and comfortable," she says, collapsing onto the bed as soon as she enters the room.

"How'd it go?" Tom says, taking a seat by the window.

"Oh, y'know, me, Lily, and Reagan all got our stories straight right after the cops tactlessly told Lily her husband was dead."

"I don't imagine she took it well," Tom says.

Emma looks at him, one brow raised. "Nope," she says. "But, bless her heart, she's a trooper, and she stuck to the script."

"Which was?"

"That her husband had been forced into laundering money for a member of the Russian Mafia operating in the area, and they got dragged into something they wanted no part of when the whole operation started to go south."

"And why'd it go south?"

"Because the Russian Mafia were planning on blowing up the pipeline, and the Americans they had working for them didn't care much for that idea." She puts her hands together, and takes them apart like an explosion. "Civil war. They all ended up killing each other out at that house, and they managed to kill Fedorov before he was able to blow up the pipeline, and then they disappeared into the wild."

"So where'd you and Reagan figure into this?"

Emma pushes herself up on one elbow. "Innocent bystanders," she says. "My friend Reagan and I were just visiting our good friends Roger and Lily Noakes when the heavies came knocking, and we got dragged into it all."

"Reagan walks away free?"

"Well, he did come around in the end, didn't he?" Emma says, pushing herself up to a seated position now. "And he held all the cards, when it came to making our story stick. The risk of jail meant he could have dropped your name at any time, and our tale of American dissidents would have crumbled away."

"All right," Tom says. "Fair enough. Good for Reagan. How were the cops?"

"Oh, man," Emma says, rolling her eyes. "They were *rough*. They were coming at us *hard*, days of this, constant questioning, looking for cracks in our story. Then, something *real* interesting happened."

"And what was that?"

"Councilman Manning and Mayor Pullman turned up at the station."

"I don't know who they are," Tom says.

"Yeah, well, you don't need to know the ins and outs of local politics. All you need to know is that they got the cops to back off."

"That's interesting."

"Oh, it certainly is, but I'm not looking a gift horse in the mouth. That was a week ago, and the cops haven't bugged us since. I've waited to make sure. So." She pats her hands either side of her. "Shall we get you checked out? Lily has invited us to the funeral in a couple of days. We'd better go get you a suit."

Tom stays at Emma's until the funeral. The police do not come back around. They lie together in her bed. Emma places an arm across his chest. It's dark outside. The house is still. "Where'd this come from?" she says, touching the Santa Muerte pendant he has continued to wear since the basement with Fedorov.

"It was a gift," Tom says.

"From who? The Russians?"

He grins. "I've had it a long time. She brings protection. I felt like I needed her."

Emma props herself up, holds the pendant in her palm, leans closer for a better look. "Is there blood on her?"

"It's probably mine," Tom says. "I keep trying to clean her, but I never seem able to get it all off."

When they attend Roger's funeral, it is closed casket. This isn't a surprise. The return of Roger's body has been delayed by the autopsy and the police investigation. Tom and Emma sit at the back. Tom checks the room, and the outside. There are no cops present.

"How do you feel?" Emma whispers, leaning close.

Tom takes a deep breath. "He almost got me killed," he says. "But all I can think about is Elijah. About how he's going to grow up without a father. I think that makes me sad, more than anything else. More than angry."

Emma reaches over, takes his hand, squeezes it.

After Roger's body has been lowered into the ground, they stand near the grave while people give their condolences to Lily and Elijah, and an older couple standing with them who Tom guesses to be Roger's parents. Elijah is sniffling. His eyes are red and his cheeks blotchy. He keeps wiping at his lowered face. Tom cannot look at him for long.

Lily finds them when the crowd begins to thin. She leaves Elijah with his grandparents. "Thank you for coming," she says, embracing them both.

"How're you both holding up?" Emma says.

Lily takes a deep breath. "Some days are better than others," she says. "Today is a hard one. Elijah is struggling. He keeps asking when his daddy is coming home. I don't think..." She chokes up, swallows. Takes a moment to compose herself. "I don't think it's really sunk in for him yet, not fully. Maybe...maybe today."

Emma nods.

"I'm sorry." Tom isn't sure what else he can say.

Lily gives him a sad smile. "You did all you could," she says. "You did more than anyone else would."

Lily's tone and mood change suddenly. She looks around, checking to see who is near, then leans in closer and lowers her voice, becoming conspiratorial. Emma and Tom exchange glances, then lean in with her. "I was sent some money," she says, her eyes still darting to the side, outside of their little grouping. "Do you know anything about it?"

Tom frowns, shakes his head.

"Money?" Emma says. "How much?"

"Fifty grand," Lily says.

"Wow," Emma says. "I don't have fifty grand, let alone fifty grand to spare."

Lily bites her lip. "I don't know who it's from, but it came with a message."

"What was the message?" Tom says.

"It said... You know how sometimes when you transfer money, you can write the reason, and then in the other person's account, it'll say something like, I don't know, like 'Groceries'? Well, this one said, 'For your loss.'"

Tom thinks of Alina. Roger's killer. The one who, he believes, stole Yuri's money. The action that set this whole thing in motion.

"Should I...should I report it?"

"Fuck *that*," Emma says.

"Emma's right," Tom says. "Whoever sent it, whatever their reason, they want you to have it. Use it as you see fit."

Lily straightens back up, breaking the huddle, though her expression remains concerned. She wraps her arms around herself, suddenly cold. "I've been thinking..." she says. "I might...I might leave here. Me and Elijah. My parents live in Florida. I was thinking we might go and join them. After everything that's happened, there are too many bad memories here. With this money, we can go somewhere else, start over."

"Then do it," Emma says. "That money's giving you the opportunity, so do it."

Lily nods. "I'll think about it," she says. She's starting to drift away, back to Elijah and her parents-in-law. She reaches out, takes a hand from Tom and Emma each. "Thank you both," she says, "for everything you did for us." Then she leaves. They watch her walk away, back to Elijah. She leans down to him, wraps her arms around him, holds him tight.

Emma leans into Tom, rests the back of her head on his shoulder. "You didn't send her the money, did you?"

"I don't have fifty grand to spare, either."

"What *do* you do for money?"

"I have savings."

"Savings don't last forever."

"No, they don't, but I'm frugal."

She chuckles. "So who do you think it was?"

"I have an idea," Tom says. "Doesn't mean I'm right, but it's the theory I'm going to go with."

"You gonna share it with me?"

"I'll tell you all about it in the truck."

60

Tom and Emma venture up the Chugach Mountains, to where Emma's cabin used to be. It is her first time seeing the wreckage of it. It has snowed lately, nothing heavy, but enough to cover the worst of the damage.

"Well," she says, hands on her hips. "It sure ain't here anymore."

"I'm glad you can't see the bodies," Tom says, looking round.

"What, you think it would be my first time?"

Tom steps closer to the wreckage, to what remains of the cabin that was his home for the better part of the last six months. He will have to find the bodies, he knows. To bury them. He can't leave them just lying out in the open. The snow will thaw, eventually. "I owe you for this," he says, motioning to the rubble. "For what I did."

"All things considered," she says, stepping up beside him, "I'll let you off." She looks down, then around. "I'm going to rebuild it. The insurance will cover it."

"Will the insurance cover explosives?"

"I'll tell them it was a gas leak."

"It'll pass for one," Tom says. "When you gonna start?"

"Have to wait 'til spring, I reckon."

"I'm willing to help with the rebuild," Tom says. "Like I said, I owe you."

She steps into his arms, wraps hers around his waist, pressing to him like she's cold. "Why do I get the feeling that come spring, you're not gonna be hanging around much longer?"

"Because I like to keep moving," Tom says. "These last six months are the longest I've stayed in any one place for a very long time. But I'm willing to stay here a while longer and help out here, if you want me to."

"I'd never try to hold you back from your road trips, Tom."

"That's not what you said when I first told you what had happened up here."

"Yeah, I know, but a lot has happened since then." She sighs. "And I knew when you first arrived that you'd move on eventually. I can't keep you here just to help build a cabin. I've been ready for this all along."

Tom nods. He kisses her.

"So," Emma says, blowing hair from her face. "Where do you think you'll go next?"

Tom looks over her shoulder, beyond her, into the distance. Thinking. "I don't know," he says. "I haven't decided yet. Haven't given it much thought at all, truth be told." He looks at her now, winks. "But spring isn't here yet. I reckon I've still got a good few weeks to come up with something."

Emma grins. She touches the Santa Muerte pendant hanging out the front of his shirt. "Let's go back home," she says. "I've got some ideas on how we can pass the time while you make your mind up."

They turn and go back to Emma's truck. Tom's hands are buried in his pockets. He stops when he reaches the passenger door, looks back to where the cabin used to stand. He thinks back on sitting in there on cold nights with the fire roaring. Remembers hunting, and foraging. Chopping wood. Standing by the window and watching the snow fall, listening to the wind. He breathes in the cold, clean air, and with it comes a thousand pleasant memories. He thinks of Emma coming up to visit. Thinks of her leaning in the door frame after he has answered her knock, and how she'd smile at him.

"What're you doing?" she says, behind him, getting into the truck.

"Nothing," Tom says, getting in beside her, turning his back on where the cabin was. "Just remembering what it used to look like."

EPILOGUE

Her skin sizzles comfortably under the Greek sun. It is hot and warm and bright on the beach in Corfu. It has been since the day she arrived, more than two months ago now.

Alina rolls onto her front, feels the rays on her back. She smiles. Through her sunglasses, she looks along the length of the beach, at the other people here strolling hand in hand, or playing in the sea. They're all so bronzed. She still has some catching up to do.

She closes her eyes. Soon, she will go up to the bar on the beach, get into the shade and out of the sun. She will drink cocktails, and men – Greeks and tourists alike – will fawn over her. She will entertain their compliments for her own amusement, and then she will return to the beach. Later, before it gets dark, she will return to her apartment and get changed, then go to the restaurant where she works as a waitress. Most of the customers speak English. For the locals, her Greek is passable. They appreciate her efforts, and smile encouragingly. They all laugh together when she gets a word or a phrase wrong. Nikos will be at the restaurant, too. Nikos is helping her with her Greek. He has made himself readily available to her for many *private* lessons.

"Very good, Veronika," he will say, praising how well she is doing. He will reward her with kisses, and she will reward his tutelage in kind.

Veronika Makarova. That is who she is here. That is who she is now. This is her new start. They will never know her as anyone else.

She chose the name herself. She visited a man in Valdez, back when she was still in America, who she'd heard made fake IDs. His name was Steven Kane. She gave him her new name, paid him before she stole the money with the allowance she had saved from Yuri, and he did the rest.

"Passports and papers aren't my usual bag," he said. "I usually just make driver's licenses for high school kids to get drunk with."

"Then this will be a challenge for you," Alina said.

He came through on it.

And now, Veronika Makarova gets to her feet, burying her toes in the warm sand. She walks down to the sea, the small waves lapping at her shins. She stands there for a while, looking out to the horizon, to the clear blue sky. Then, she lowers herself into the water, and she swims.

The End

ABOUT THE AUTHOR

Did you enjoy *Snow Burn?* Please consider leaving a review on Amazon to help other readers discover the book.

Paul Heatley left school at sixteen, and since then has held a variety of jobs including mechanic, carpet fitter, and bookshop assistant, but his passion has always been for writing. He writes mostly in the genres of crime fiction and thriller, and links to his other titles can be found on his website. He lives in the north east of England.

Want to connect with Paul? Visit him at his website.

www.PaulHeatley.com

ALSO BY PAUL HEATLEY

Printed in Great Britain
by Amazon